Saddle to Sunup

The Darling Brothers Book 3

Emmy Sanders

Copyright © 2025 by Emmy Sanders

All rights reserved.

The names, characters, businesses, places, and incidents portrayed in this book are either the product of the author's imagination or used in a fictitious manner. Any similarity to actual persons, living or dead, events, or locales is coincidental and not intended by the author.

No part of this book may be reproduced in any form or by any electrical or mechanical means, including information storage and retrieval systems, without written permission from the author, except for the use of brief quotations in a book review.

No generative artificial intelligence (AI) was used in the writing of this work. The author expressly prohibits any entity from using this publication to train AI technologies to generate text, including, without limitation, technologies capable of generating works in the same style or genre as this publication. The author reserves all rights to license uses of this work for generative AI training and development of machine learning language models.

Beta Reading by Christie and Jen & Maxie of Smut Readers Society

Editing by M.A. Hinkle

Proofreading by Lori Parks and Charity VanHuss

Cover Design by Natasha Snow Designs

A special thank you to RJ Boerstler and Blair Wynters for your help with Remi

ISBN: 9781967130146

Content Warning: This book contains a motor vehicle accident, minor injury, and a brief hospital stay.

This one goes out to Christie, my biggest cheerleader.

"The ace heart marches to the beat of its own drum, and it's a beautiful song."

Contents

Note to Readers   1

Chapter 1   2

Chapter 2   9

Chapter 3   16

Chapter 4   25

Chapter 5   34

Chapter 6   43

Chapter 7   52

Chapter 8   61

Chapter 9   70

Chapter 10   79

Chapter 11   88

Chapter 12   98

Chapter 13   108

Chapter 14	115
Chapter 15	124
Chapter 16	134
Chapter 17	144
Chapter 18	154
Chapter 19	163
Chapter 20	172
Chapter 21	182
Chapter 22	192
Chapter 23	201
Chapter 24	208
Chapter 25	217
Chapter 26	226
Chapter 27	235
Chapter 28	244
Chapter 29	252
Chapter 30	262
Chapter 31	271
Chapter 32	281
Chapter 33	291
Chapter 34	301
Epilogue	309
About the Author	316

Note to Readers

This series includes a character who's Deaf and several characters who use American Sign Language. Please note ASL and English do not share the same grammatical structure. However, for ease of reading, ASL conversations are written using English grammar.

Chapter 1

LAWSON

"This way."

I follow the whisper of a voice to see Oakley huddled behind a tree, the tea towel he wrapped around his head as an eye patch tied bulkily over his light brown hair. The stick he's using as a sword is at his side.

I sneak close, peering around the tree.

"You see them?" he asks, voice hushed, the register a little lower at eleven than it used to be.

It's a strange thing to notice, the passage of time, and my heart beats swiftly with it.

I refocus on the pirates. They're huddled on the shore, their ship a log anchored in the tiny bend of river flowing just outside the woods we're hidden within.

"I see them," I confirm.

"On my count," Oakley says, hunching low. "One... Two... Three!"

We spring from behind the tree, our sticks cutting through the air in front of us, the pirates no match for the strength of our swords. The fight is over quickly, every one of our enemies lying in tatters. Oakley and I stumble forward to catch our breath beneath the shade of a willow tree. The branches sway gently in the breeze, surrounding us in tendrils of green, sunlight peeking through the leaves and scattering pixie dust on the air around our heads.

"Good fight," Oakley says, sounding out of breath.

I hum my agreement, setting my stick on the ground and leaning my head back against the sturdy trunk of the tree. The branches spread out overhead, looking like an earthborn star.

"What is it?" Oakley asks, slipping the tea towel off his head. He blinks several times, his multihued eyes flashing.

Oakley has the most interesting eyes I've ever seen. Each is a blend of brown and blue. Heterochromia, he told me it's called. Sometimes folks will have one brown eye and one blue. Sometimes it's a burst of color ringed by another. In Oakley's case, each eye is marbled, almost. Blue and brown together as if someone dabbed the colors on with a paintbrush.

I shrug, but Oakley flicks my forehead, causing a tiny sting I don't actually mind.

"Tell me," he persists.

"Do you ever think about growing up?"

His brow furrows. "'Course. Everyone's gotta do it."

"We're growing up," I point out. "Right now. And when we do…"

I don't have to say it aloud for Oakley to get it. We both know this game we play is just that, a game. But even so, our own Neverland is my favorite, imagined or real. A place where we can fight pirates and hide away under our safe willow tree, just the two of us, lost boys by choice because being lost together never once has been scary.

But everyone grows up except for Peter Pan. And someday soon, it'll be my last day with Oakley beneath this willow. The last time I'll sit with him as the pixies dance on the air, born from the sunbeams cutting through the tree.

One day, I won't see any of it. Not the pirates. Not our safe little cove. And certainly not the pixies.

One day, I will be grown. And then what of me and Oakley?

"Hey," he says gently, flicking my forehead again.

"Cut it out," I grumble, a halfhearted protest at best.

He gives me a grin, although it tempers after a moment. "Growing up doesn't mean growing apart, Law."

I swallow harshly. "You mean it?"

"'Course. Where would either of us even go? This is our home. And you and me? We ain't ever gonna let something silly like getting older change who we are. We're best friends. We'll always be that."

My eyes sting as I reach into my pocket, rolling the smooth ceramic surface of the thimble I stole from my mother's sewing supplies between my fingertips. Wendy gave Peter a thimble. A kiss, she called it. A youthful promise.

I pull the thimble from my pocket, offering it to Oakley. His head cocks as he plucks it from my palm, a floral design painted onto its surface. I feel as if my heart might beat right out of my chest as I wait for him to say something. Anything.

His blue-and-brown eyes meet mine, a smile in them I recognize.

Without a word, Oakley scrambles upright. I watch as he swings the willow branches out of his way, jogging over to the nearby tree line. He stops before his namesake—an oak tree—and scours the ground.

When he comes back, it's with a wide grin on his face. The sun shines on his hair as the willow branches sway back into place, making me believe, for a moment, he really could fly covered in pixie dust like that. He grabs my hand, and I automatically open my fingers.

Oakley sets an acorn in the well of my palm, small and nearly weightless. Peter gave Wendy an acorn button. This is even better.

I close my fingers around the token of friendship, and Oakley does the same to his thimble. He holds out his pinkie, and there's no question. I curl mine with his.

"I promise, Law. No matter how old we get, nothing is going to change. I'm your best friend, and you're mine. And we'll always be together. 'Kay?"

I nod in a fierce jerk, wanting desperately to believe the words of my friend. But belief is a tricky thing, as ever-changing as time, as elusive as pixies. If you don't hold on to it tight enough, you might just look back to find it gone.

I tighten my pinkie around Oakley's, his promise digging into my palm.

I won't let go. I won't, I won't, I won't.

"The two of us," I say in kind, my own vow. "Forever."

My hands flex, the rough leather of my steering wheel digging against my palms as the memory from so long ago fades into the highway in front of me. My truck's headlights cut through the early morning darkness, dawn not yet having arrived. I've been on the road for over twenty-four hours, only stopping briefly to rest and refuel.

I passed the border into Kansas an hour ago, my hometown of Darling, Montana far in the rearview.

My hands flex again, the acorn no longer curled within my palm but tucked safely away inside the center console beside my seat. I fight the urge to check on it only to lose. Popping the compartment open, I fish out the small acorn, the curve of it familiar and comforting, even as I've often wondered if a person my age should keep such a thing.

It was given to me thirty-two years ago.

Surely a token shouldn't mean the same at forty-three as it did at eleven. But I've never forgotten the promise made that day.

Friendship that would never change. Would never fall victim to the passage of time.

It was a promise broken. And I aim to rectify that.

The cap of the acorn is rough beneath my thumb as I toy with it, taking the turn off the highway that my GPS guides me down. The anger I've been trying my best not to entertain returns, the fire of it hot in my chest.

It's not fair to be mad at Oakley. That's what I keep telling myself. We're *not* eleven anymore. Or eighteen. Or, heck, thirty. We did grow up as we had to, but he left. He left, and now I'm alone.

I'm alone when he promised I never would be.

I can't put the blame on him for my recent divorce. Losing my home of nineteen years in the separation isn't his fault either.

But none of it changes the fact that I *am* mad. Rightfully so or not, I'm damn pissed at my friend for leaving Montana and not coming back.

And he's gonna know it.

My GPS gives another direction I follow, Oakley's house in the countryside looming closer as the dawn sun breaks over the horizon. It's early in the day to arrive unannounced, but Oakley wakes with the birds. Always has. It's part of a cowboy's lifestyle, whether that cowboy is in Montana or Kansas.

And Oakley Beaumont? That man is a cowboy down to the tips of his steel-toed leather boots.

I pull carefully down his drive, my truck rolling over stones and dirt as his house comes into view. My swallow is heavy as I turn off the ignition, the silence that follows stifling. I place the acorn back into its home before shutting the compartment door. My palms feel sweaty now that I'm finally here after my rather impulsive decision to chase down my wayward friend.

I haven't seen him in person in three years. Not since I was forced to say a reluctant goodbye.

Dust kicks up when my boots hit the drive. All is quiet save the typical sounds of the countryside. A few animals nearby making their morning calls. A vehicle passing out on the road. An engine kicking into life. Tractor, as far as I can tell. But Oakley's house is still.

I make my way to the front door, wiping my palms on my jeans as I ascend the couple steps. My heart is racing, anger swirling with the desperate need I have to set eyes on Oakley again. To reassure myself that he's well and whole, despite him telling me on our phone calls that he is. I don't know whether I want to punch him or hug him, but I figure I'll decide once he opens the door.

I square my shoulders before knocking on the white painted wood.

It takes a minute for the bolt to disengage. My breath seizes, a lump in my throat I wish would disappear. But no amount of swallowing has it moving anywhere, and the door is swinging open now.

Oakley goes stock-still upon seeing me standing on his stoop. His eyes, the blue and brown, swing over me, from my face down my body and back up again, as if he's trying to determine whether or not I'm real.

I am. Very.

He looks freshly woken, although I doubt I was the cause. His hair, sun-streaked brown, is rumpled. His stubble is thick. He's still wearing pajama pants, the fabric a lightweight gray. I know for a fact he doesn't sleep with a shirt, but I'm not surprised he threw one on to greet his guest, even if he didn't know his guest was me.

Almost nothing has changed since the last I saw him, even as everything has.

"Law?" he says, my name spoken in a mixture of astonishment and plain disbelief.

My eyes prickle, but I stand tall and say what I came here to. The words I've been reciting in my head ever since I got in my truck to drive across the country and retrieve my friend.

"You're coming home."

Chapter 2

OAKLEY

I stare in shock at Lawson, who shoulders past me without another word. He beelines for the hallway, looking into the bathroom before finding my bedroom at the next doorway.

He disappears out of sight.

"Lawson?" I call, shutting the front door before hastening to catch up to him.

The man is in my closet now, pulling out a suitcase he unceremoniously tosses to the ground.

"What are you doing?" I question.

"I told you," he says, unzipping the large bag. "You're coming home."

For long seconds, all I can do is blink at the man, trying to reconcile him being here in the first place with the fact that he's currently trying to shove the contents of my wardrobe into a suitcase.

"Law."

He grunts, pulling a few shirts off their hangers, his motions agitated. "You gonna help or what?"

"Am I gonna... All right, hold up."

Lawson stops only once I grab his arms, my shirts piled haphazardly in his grip. There's a sheen of moisture in his brown eyes that takes me off guard, but Lawson blinks and it disappears.

"What's going on?" I ask carefully, feeling very much like I'm dealing with a spooked animal right now.

"I told you—"

"Oh, I know what you said. But I told *you* last we talked that I'm staying here. I have a job in this town and a life—"

"A life," he practically spits, sounding incredulous. He tosses the shirts down, and I let him go, taken aback by his uncharacteristic ire. "You *had* a life. And you left it."

"That's not fair. You know why I left."

"For Stevie," he says, crouching down again and shoving my shirts into the suitcase, unfolded. "And where's Stevie now?"

I suck in a breath, and Lawson stills, his gaze meeting mine. There's apology there, but he doesn't back down, even as his voice gentles.

"Y'all broke up months ago, Oak. They're gone, but you're still here. Why haven't you come home?"

My swallow is harsh. "Stop packing my shit, Lawson."

"No."

He goes to my dresser, tugging a drawer open and tossing a handful of my underwear onto the shirts in my bag. Socks follow. When he realizes the bag is full, he grunts and heads for the hall.

"Where are you going?" I ask, following after him.

His eyes sweep the living room before he heads for the kitchen. "Where's Bell?"

"Lawson Darling. I am *not* leaving."

"Like hell you aren't. Bell?"

Lawson goes for the back door as he calls again for Bell, but I block his exit, my hand on the wood. "Are you listening to me? You can't just...show up here and pack up my things and expect me to follow."

My friend spins, toe to toe with me as he sets his jaw. We're the same height, so his eyes meet mine easily, a hurt there I'm not expecting.

"You followed them."

He doesn't need to clarify who. "Stevie was my partner."

"And who am I?" he asks, waiting for me to answer.

I let out a quiet breath. "My best friend."

"That's right, Oakley Beaumont. I am. And I would never leave you like they did."

Lawson tugs open the back door as I stare after him, my chest painfully tight at the unspoken words. *Not like I left him, either.*

"Bell!" he calls, stepping outside.

"Law," I say, tired beyond measure, despite the fact that I just woke up. "What are you expecting to happen here? Bell's not gonna fit in either of our trucks, and I can't leave her behind."

"I brought my trailer."

He...

I backpedal, heading for the front door and tugging it open. There's a goddamn trailer attached to Lawson's truck. *Jesus Christ.*

I hear a soft rhythmic chiming as I recross my house, Bell the Miniature Galloway cow trotting up to Lawson. The man is all smiles as the cow reaches him, looking as happy as a cow can look. Her body is entirely white, her nose, ears, and hooves a stark black in contrast. She reaches Lawson's hip at her adult age of six, small for a cow but not *small* by any means. The bell around her neck jingles as Lawson gives her the pets she's demanding.

"You brought your trailer," I say flatly.

"Like I said," Lawson drawls, "you're coming home."

"Did you ever stop to think this is my home now?"

Lawson looks over at me, his hair, darker than my own, styled back neatly. His facial hair is trimmed neatly, too, and he's wearing a lightweight shirt that wouldn't be out of place if he were teaching instead of here, trying to bodily move me from my house.

"Oakley. You know exactly where your home is, and this isn't it."

"I have a job here," I point out.

"And you'll always have a job waiting for you at the ranch."

He's talking about Darling Ranch, the beef and dairy cattle operation at his childhood home. But whether or not his brother Jackson is willing to hire me back isn't the point.

Lawson steps through the door, Bell at his heels. She meanders into the kitchen as he returns to my bedroom.

"Be good," I warn my cow before following after Lawson. He's shoving my pants into a duffel bag now. "And what about my house?"

"You have a house in Darling."

My eyebrow pops up. "Oh, do I? 'Cause last I knew, I sold that years ago."

Lawson is quiet for a beat before he says, "The newest renters left a couple weeks back. I...asked your parents to hold it. It's ready and waiting for you."

I go still, stunned. "And when the hell were you planning on telling me this?"

"I'm telling you now."

I can't stop the laughter that rolls out of me. "You've got some serious nerve, you know that? Are you even going to say hello? I haven't seen you in three damn years and—"

Lawson's arms come around me tight before I can even finish my sentence. He hugs me so forcefully I swear my ribs creak. I hug him back just as hard.

"Hey," he says, voice choked.

I huff another laugh. "Long time."

"Yeah. It has been."

It's a good minute before Lawson and I part. I look him over. Truly look him over. There's a tension around his eyes he doesn't normally carry, different from the faint lines that have popped up with age. A slight frown causing his mouth to pinch. He looks tired. Worn in a way that has my worry resurfacing.

"What's going on, Law? Is it the divorce?"

He grunts, dismissing that as he goes back to shoving my pants into the duffel. I leave him to it for now. "It's fine. Laura and I have been separated for a while."

"Sure, but—"

"This isn't about me."

I highly doubt that. "Tell me what it's about, then."

He stops packing, looking up to meet my eye. "There's nothing here for you, Oak. And don't try to tell me there is. The only reason you came out here was because of Stevic's job."

"I like it here well enough," I defend.

"Well enough." He scoffs. "That's not *good* enough. What the hell is tethering you here? Give me one thing."

I rack my brain.

"We already covered your job and housing situation," he goes on, as if it's that simple. "I've got a trailer for Bell. We can fit the rest of what you want to bring in our trucks. Name one good reason for you not to come home."

I can't name a single thing. Except it's not that simple. It feels like admitting defeat. My relationship crashed and burned. My reason for moving, as Lawson pointed out, is no longer a reason to stay gone.

But what does moving back to Darling accomplish besides broadcasting my failed attempt at creating a life for myself?

I'm forty-three. I thought I'd be settled down by now, and I was on track for that. Up until Stevie decided this life—our life—wasn't what they wanted. And I can't fault them for that. I wouldn't have wanted them to stay if it meant unhappiness for either of us.

But it still hurts. To know how much I was willing to give, only to learn it wasn't enough in the end.

Lawson makes a soft sound that draws my attention, his words unerringly piercing the heart of me, as they so often do. "We miss you, Oak. I do. Your parents. Wendy."

"Aw, come on, Law. That's not fair."

He smirks, knowing damn well his daughter is my weak point. I love Wendy to death, and leaving her and Lawson to come to Kansas was the hardest thing I've ever had to do.

"Come back to us," Lawson pleads.

Fuck.

I slump down onto the floor, elbows on my knees and head in my hands as I scrub my fingers through my hair. "Damn it, Law."

"You're coming?"

"Doesn't seem like I have much choice, does it? Pretty sure there's no getting you out of this house unless it's with everything I own and my damn cow. You don't play fair."

"Never said I would," he mutters.

I shake my head. Lawson is one of the most levelheaded people I know. But when he gets set on something, there's very little that can be done to change his course.

His hand lands on my calf, squeezing once. "I am sorry about Stevie."

I lift my head. "Are you?"

"I'm sorry they hurt you, Oak. You have to know that."

"But you're not sorry they're gone."

Lawson has never outright said he doesn't like Stevie. But there was always an undercurrent between them I couldn't parse out. Lawson gives everyone the benefit of the doubt, but he was never warm with my partner. And Stevie, well...they certainly didn't care for Lawson, either.

My friend chews his words for a moment. "They weren't good for you."

"That so?" I nearly huff, wondering why he's only saying so now. "Why don't you tell me how you really feel, Law?"

Despite my teasing tone, Lawson answers seriously. "They never treated you the way you deserve."

My heart thumps. "And what do I deserve?"

Warm brown eyes hold mine, and I wait for the blow to my chest I know is coming. It does, a second later, with one concise word.

"Everything."

Chapter 3

LAWSON

Oakley tosses kitchen utensils into a box, looking a thousand miles from here. "You realize I have to leave for work soon, right?"

"You need to go?"

He raises an eyebrow. "I'm not gonna quit over the phone."

"Fair enough."

He shakes his head, closing the box that's now full. "Can't believe I'm doing this. Actually, I can't believe *you*, Mr. Dependable, are encouraging me to do this."

"It's time," I tell him.

He huffs. "So you say."

Oakley steps over Bell to set the box near the front door, his cow curled up in a sun spot like a cat. Her eyes are closed, head tipped toward the rays.

"Wendy will be excited to have her back," I note, stuffing a few throw pillows and blankets into another box Oakley had on hand from his move here. "She's missed Bell."

"She can have her then," he mumbles.

"You don't hate Bell."

"She's a menace."

I look at the cow currently sunning herself. "Mhm."

"We both know I never would have taken her in if it weren't for Wendy."

My daughter raised Bell when she was only a calf for our local 4-H. None of us thought it would be a problem, seeing as the family ranch raises cattle for beef. But when it came time to sell Bell for what would certainly be a similar fate, Wendy was devastated. Oakley swooped in, saving the day and buying—or rather, adopting—the miniature cow.

I guess it was different for my daughter, having hand-reared Bell herself. That was her first and only 4-H.

"Laura won't let Bell stay at her house," I caution, in case Oakley is actually entertaining ideas of Wendy taking her back.

He eyes me, not yet changed out of his sleep pants and tee. He'll need to get dressed soon if he's heading into work. "You said 'her house.'"

"Yeah? I've been moved out for a while."

"I know that. It's just... I think it's the first time I've heard you say it that way."

I hum. Ever since Laura and I split, I've been staying at the ranch, sleeping in the same bedroom I used to when I was young. It feels different now. It *is* different now.

Wendy is still living with my ex-wife. We agreed uprooting our daughter from her home didn't make sense.

But I'm not sure what does make sense these days.

"How's Wendy doing?" Oakley asks, as if reading my head.

"Good," I answer honestly. "I think she's taken the divorce best out of all of us."

He's quiet for a moment, and I realize what I let slip.

"I've been fine," I add quickly.

"Yeah, you keep saying that." Oakley grunts as he steps back over Bell. "Want something to eat? I needa get ready."

"Sure."

Oakley sets to work making breakfast as I pack up his things. I stack his pictures carefully, his family and my own featuring prominently. The two of us with Wendy. Oakley with his parents. I don't see any evidence of Stevie, and I'm glad for it, if only to have proof Oakley isn't still hung up on them.

"Will your boss be mad?" I ask.

He stops scrambling eggs to look at me. "Now you're worried about my current state of employment? You didn't seem all that concerned when you barged in here demanding I move back to Montana."

I shrug.

He huffs out a breath. "She won't be *happy*. But it's the start of summer, so they've got an influx of new hires. It'll be as fine as it could be. Does Jackson know I'm coming back?"

"Not yet."

"Should I call?"

"I'll handle it."

Oakley looks bemused. "Want to pick me out some new bath towels while you're at it? Maybe look over my taxes?"

"If you need me to—"

"Jesus, Lawson, I'm joking. I can handle my life."

I grunt, and Oakley shakes his head, sliding the eggs onto plates with a fork, seeing as he already packed his other utensils. Bread pops from the toaster, and he grabs the slices, along with butter, bringing it all to his kitchen table.

"Ketchup," he mutters, doubling back for my sake. "Take a seat."

I set the stack of picture frames into the box with the blankets, but before I can make it to the table, there's a loud crash. Oakley's plate is no longer on the tabletop but twirling on the ground, Bell sprinting out the open back door as Oakley himself whirls around.

"Belladonna!" he yells, full-naming the cow who's streaking across the yard to the tinkling of her bell. A few pieces of scrambled egg are left in her path of destruction, but most of the food went into her mouth. Oakley turns to me, eyes wide, his hand held toward the door. "See?"

I bite my tongue as Oakley storms to the back of the house, continuing to call after the cow.

"It's not too late to eat you, you know! *Christ*. My eggs, Bell? Really?"

"You're not going to eat her," I say calmly, sliding my plate into Oakley's spot as he picks up the remnants of his own meal. When he opens his mouth like he's about to argue, I give him a stern look and point to his chair. Only one of us is in a hurry, and it's not me. "Sit. Eat your breakfast. I can make myself something else."

He doesn't fight me on it, plopping into the chair with a shake of his head. "How's steak sound tonight?"

"We're not eating the cow."

Oakley grumbles, but he dutifully scarfs down his breakfast. I remake my own as he heads to his bedroom to change for work.

My phone pings as I'm sitting down. My daughter's tone. I check it to find a text waiting for me.

Wendy: Is he coming?

A smile quirks my lips as I type back.

Me: Yeah. Oakley's coming home.

It's early evening when I hear Oakley's truck in the driveway, the man returning from his last day of ranching here in Kansas. I finished packing most of his stuff while he was gone, barring the big pieces like furniture that we'll need to move together.

He kicks his boots on the stoop before opening the door, his eyebrows bouncing up slightly when he sees me taping boxes in his living room. "Oh. You're still here. I'd half wondered if this morning was a fever dream."

"You're perfectly well," I assure him. "Want to head out tonight or wait for the morning?"

"Jesus," he mutters, scrubbing a hand through his hair as he tosses his hat onto a stack of boxes. He looks around, likely seeing all the empty spaces his possessions occupied just earlier today. "Is this really happening?"

"It is."

"Oh, 'it is,' he says."

I ignore his tone. "Why don't you take a shower while I plate up our food? I made pasta salad with some of the chicken in your freezer. Figured we should use it up."

Oakley stares at me.

"What?" I ask.

"Lawson," he says flatly, hands on his hips. "You realize you're parenting me, right?"

"I am not."

"You *are*. First showing up the way you did and...making demands. And now you're telling me when to shower? Wanna wash my back while you're at it?"

"If you need me to."

"If—" Oakley cuts off on a grunt, kicking his boots to the side before all but stomping down the hall. A few seconds later, I hear, "Did you pack up my goddamn sex toys?"

"Nothing to be ashamed about," I call. "Sex is a perfectly healthy activity for a man your age."

"Jesus fucking Christ."

I chuckle to myself as a door slams, the shower turning on just after. I finish with the boxes I'm taping before following the noise and opening the bathroom door. "You never answered my question."

"Fucking hell, Lawson!" Oakley pulls the shower curtain to the side, bubbles from his shampoo trailing down the side of his face as he stares at me, wide-eyed. "You mind?"

"Are we leaving tonight or in the morning?"

He blinks at me, mouth open. "The morning. I'm gonna need a good night's sleep to deal with this shit."

"All right." I go to exit the room when I notice a bruise blooming over Oakley's shoulder, big and blotchy. "What's this?"

His nostrils flare when I touch the purple skin. "Hazard of the job. It's nothing."

"You sure?"

"I'm fine. Now unless you're planning on hopping in, would you shut the damn door? I'm getting cold."

I take a step back and tug the curtain into place. "Dinner in ten."

Oakley mutters something I can't make out as I close the door behind me, heading back through the house. Bell is in the backyard, enjoying the last of the sun, so I set to work plating up our dinner. Oakley emerges from the bathroom before long, stopping in his bedroom to change. His hair is still wet when he joins me, not overgrown enough to fall into his eyes but close.

Seeing food on the table, he drops into a seat, eyeing me as I bring fresh lemonade over. "Thanks, hubby."

"Don't be a smartass," I tell him.

"Yes, Pops."

He laughs when I smack him upside his head, not hard, but hard enough to know I mean it. There's a smile on his face when I sit down opposite him, and he digs quickly into his food.

I watch him for a moment, my chest feeling tight in a way that's different from how it was on my drive here. And in the months preceding. Years, even.

I've missed Oakley so damn much.

"I'm not parenting you," I tell him, my voice coming out rougher than I'd like. He stops shoveling food into his mouth, eyes meeting mine. "You say I came here making demands. Well, that's because I've got a right to. You're my best friend."

He opens his mouth, but I go on before he can speak.

"When you care about someone, you look after them, Oak. And you've been out here, no one looking after you for years now. And don't try to tell me Stevie looked after you. They didn't."

He doesn't say a word.

"I'm not trying to treat you like a child. I just... I love you. So damn much. And I've missed you. So let me look after you a little, all right? It's the least you could do after being such an asshole."

"I was the asshole?" he asks, sounding amused.

"Damn right you were. You couldn't even come home for Christmas?"

He lets out a sigh. "You know Stevie—"

"Yes, I damn well know Stevie tried their level best to alienate you from everybody else in your life who cared. You see that, don't you? Everything was about them. Making concessions for them. What about you, huh?"

His brow furrows. "It wasn't that bad, was it?"

I let out a humorless laugh, my dinner all but forgotten. "Loving someone means protecting every piece of who they are, past, present, and future. It doesn't mean asking them to change and then leaving when they fail to live up to that impossible task. Stevie never saw you for who you are. They didn't even try. So yes, it was that fucking bad."

Oakley doesn't once blink, even as his chest expands with his heavy breath. "You never say 'fuck.' Not unless you're really mad."

"Well, I'm mad."

His breath puffs out. "I can see that. Why the hell didn't you say something sooner, Law? If you thought Stevie was so bad for me, why didn't you say so?"

"You had your sights set on them, and by the time you two were serious, Stevie was already interviewing for new jobs." I toss my hands in the air, frustrated. "Was I supposed to tell you not to go? Would you have listened? If I'd pushed, Stevie would have excised me from your life."

"I wouldn't have let that happen."

"I wasn't about to take the chance," I shoot back. "You fell hard and fast, Oak. You went all in, and I can't blame you for that. It's who you are. But I couldn't risk losing you. I couldn't. And now I have you back, and I'm not letting you go again, you hear?"

Oakley's foot hooks my own beneath the table as I try to corral my breathing. "Law. Look at me."

I bring my eyes back to his, the marbling of blue and brown almost otherworldly. It brings to mind memories of stick swords and chasing pixies under the shade of a willow tree, back when we were old enough to know our worlds were bound to change yet too young to realize just how much.

"You won't ever lose me," he says, each word even and precise. "It's not possible."

"You left me."

It's out before I can stop it, the hurt in those three syllables evident even to my own ears.

Oakley blows out a slow breath. "I didn't leave *you*. I just..."

"You had your priorities," I say woodenly, disentangling our legs. "And I wasn't one of them."

"Lawson."

I disregard Oakley's softly spoken plea, bringing my plate into the kitchen and rinsing the dish before setting it on the counter to be packed. On my way through the living room, I grab one of the blankets not yet boxed up. "I'll be in the guest room."

Oakley doesn't try to stop me, and I'm grateful, not wanting to hear cajoling words or the suggestion that I'm being unreasonable. I know I am.

But I still hurt.

Not for the first time, I wonder why Oakley leaving cut so much deeper than my separation with my wife.

Chapter 4

OAKLEY

The sun slants through my passenger window as I follow Lawson's pickup, trailer included, along the highway out of Kansas.

His words play on repeat in my head.

"You left me."

Wanting a distraction from the heavy ache in my chest, I ring my dad. He picks up quickly, his voice cutting through my truck's Bluetooth.

"Oakley?"

"Hey, Dad. Did, uh... Did Lawson mention I'm moving back?"

He hums, a thoughtful sound. "He did not, but I wondered as much when he asked me and your mom to keep your place free for a while. What'd he do, drive down there to haul you home?"

"Yep. That's exactly what he did."

My dad laughs, calling for my mom, his voice distant as he says, "Oakley's on the way home, Sienna."

My mom's voice is equally as quiet. "That so? Tell him the house is cleaned up and ready. I'll stock the kitchen."

"She doesn't have to do that," I interject.

My dad makes a *psht* sound. "Nonsense. You'll be on the road for twenty hours. You gonna stop at Plum's on your way through with a miniature cow in tow?"

He's got a point. "Well, tell her not to go overboard."

My dad doesn't relay the message. "Bring Lawson by for dinner once you're settled. Y'all still like those dino nuggets? I think they have spicy ones now. Sienna, don't they have spicy dino nuggets at Plum's?"

I sigh.

"Tell him I'll leave the key under the mat," my mom says.

"Your mom says—"

"Yeah, I got it," I tell my dad. "Thanks."

He grunts his acknowledgement. "I'm glad you're coming home, Oakley. We've missed you."

There goes that ache in my chest again. "Yeah. I've missed y'all, too." Lawson signals for an exit, so I do the same. "Dad, I gotta go. I'll see you soon, all right?"

"Drive safe."

I can hear my parents in the background talking about dino nuggets for a moment before the call ends. Forty-three going on four, apparently.

I follow Lawson into the parking lot of a fast-food place. He parks off to the side with the trailer, so I pull up next to him, rolling down my window.

"Get us some food?" he asks. "Coffee, too."

My lips twitch. I suggested we make breakfast before leaving this morning, but Lawson wanted to get on the road as quickly as possible. I can't blame him, considering our plan to drive straight to Montana without rest. Finding somewhere to stay for the night with Bell would be a logistical nightmare better avoided.

He sure didn't make it long without coffee, though.

"Any requests for your Royal Highness?" I ask.

Lawson doesn't comment on my cheekiness. "You know what I like."

Suppose I do.

With a salute, I pull around to the drive-through, ordering enough food and drink to last us a while. Lawson looks amused when I hand his share of the haul over through his open window.

"Some of this for Bell?" he asks.

I stare at him, appalled he'd even joke about such a thing. "Don't you dare think about feeding any of this to my cow, Lawson Darling. She's bad enough as is. Could you imagine if she got a taste for fast food? She'd be like a shark after blood."

He huffs a laugh. "Oh, so *now* she's your cow?"

"Don't start," I warn him. "I can still turn back around, y'know. Then she'll be *your* cow and *your* problem."

"You won't do that," he says, confident he's got me on his hook. And damn if he doesn't. "Come on. Let's get back on the road."

"Yeah, yeah," I mutter, peeking into the trailer to make sure Bell is all right. Of course she is, her tail swishing merrily. She's probably plotting her next attack.

I return to my vehicle, and Lawson pulls back onto the road, me following. I want to be mad at my friend for so easily uprooting me from the life I'd tried to create in Kansas. But apparently, my roots weren't buried down that deep, were they?

Lawson was right. There wasn't a thing tethering me to my temporary home in the end. And now that Montana is on the horizon, the two of us traveling steadily that way, all I feel is a familiar sort of longing for everything I chose to leave behind.

My house. My job at Darling Ranch. My family. Wendy. Lawson.

I traded one life for another, thinking the benefits would outweigh the loss. They didn't, though, did they? Even with Stevie and I at our best, I never felt settled. I kept waiting for it to come, that feeling of home.

But it never did.

Which is probably why I didn't fight harder when Stevie told me it wasn't working. Deep down, I knew it wasn't, either.

And it's why I can't be mad at Lawson for dragging me back to Darling.

It was inevitable. I just wish my failed attempt at love hadn't hurt the one person I never meant to.

Once I have some food in my stomach, I ring Lawson's brother Jackson. Although younger than Lawson by a couple years, Jackson is the head of the family ranch, ever since the responsibility passed from his parents to him. Lawson never wanted it.

"I wondered when I'd hear from you," Jackson says in greeting, his voice piping into the cab.

"I take it you already talked to Law?"

"He called this morning at an ungodly hour. Everybody was pretty worried about him these past few days. He didn't tell anyone but Wendy where he was going."

I cringe. That's not like Lawson at all. "Sorry for the trouble."

"Not your fault. You coming back?"

"Still have room for me?"

"Always," he says, voice a little gruff. Heaven forbid the man show any tenderness to the outside world. He and Lawson are polar opposites in that regard.

"Well, I appreciate it," I tell him truthfully. "I really am sorry for the trouble. When do you want me back?"

"Next week? Take a few days to get settled in again at least. There's no rush."

"All right. Don't suppose you have room on the first shift?"

He chuckles. "There's room. See ya four o'clock on Monday."

With that, Jackson clicks off the call, and I breathe a sigh of relief. It's not that I doubted Lawson's conviction that a spot at the ranch would be waiting for me, but the reassurance after quitting my job without any notice whatsoever has my chest loosening ever so slightly.

I didn't think it would be this easy, returning to my old life. But it's almost like it was waiting for me.

I sit in silence for a few minutes before calling Lawson.

He picks up, the rumble of his vehicle mixing in with mine. "Needa pee already?"

"No," I huff. "Entertain me. I'm bored."

He snorts. "It's gonna be a long trip then."

"Not if you entertain me. Talked to Jackson, by the way."

"Uh-huh. Told you I handled it."

"I know. He said you didn't tell your family where you were going?"

There's a brief pause. "Didn't need to."

"You know they're the worrying type."

"I'm a grown man. They don't need to worry."

I don't think that's how it works when it comes to family, but I keep my mouth shut on the topic, sure Lawson knows as much. Hell, he's a dad himself. He gets it.

"Law... Why haven't you found a place yet?"

There's another beat of silence. "I like the ranch fine."

"You don't. You like your quiet."

Lawson's always been different than his brothers in that regard. Jackson runs the ranch now. Colton is a farrier, just as much a part of the bustle as everyone else. And Remi, the youngest, looks after the horses and petting farm animals.

Lawson, though, ever since he was a child, has been drawn more to stories and literature than the grueling work of the ranch life he was raised in. Him becoming an English teacher was a surprise to no one.

He's not soft. Not exactly. Lawson is blunt. Downright demanding at times. He gives just as good as he gets.

But he's also idealistic in a way most folks aren't. His head is in the clouds, a trait that reminds me of his father, Hank.

Lawson is a dreamer. Always has been.

I think he always will be.

"It's fine," Lawson insists about living at the ranch. "I'll find a place eventually."

I hum.

"What?" he asks, voice even.

"Will you tell me what happened with you and Laura? I thought things were getting better. You were in couples' counseling."

"I told you. We just...drifted apart. It was too big a chasm to repair."

There's gotta be more to it than that. "Did you want to repair it?" I ask, voice quiet, as if that'll make it easier to talk about.

Lawson doesn't answer right away. I give him time to sort through his thoughts, knowing he'll speak up only once he's ready.

"No," he finally says, the word so short I'm startled by it.

"No?"

"I thought I did for a while. But...no. There was no fixing it."

I swallow roughly, my chest tight again. "I'm sorry I wasn't there." When he and Laura were having troubles, when he moved out, when the divorce went through... I wasn't there for any of it.

"Yeah," he says, his voice nearly lost to the road. "I am, too, Oak."

Fuck.

"You gonna forgive me?" I rasp.

"Already have."

"Really? That easily?"

"It's not complicated," he says, when it feels anything but. "I was mad. I told you. Now I'm moving on."

I shake my head, constantly astounded by this man. "God, Law. You're so..."

"What?"

"Forthright," I tell him. "You're so damn honest and open. Except, apparently, when it came to my relationship with Stevie."

"Because that wasn't about you and me. It was about you and them."

"Well I'm giving you permission to be honest about my future partners," I say a touch hotly. "I trust you more than anyone. So don't...keep shit to yourself just because you think I won't want to hear it."

"All right."

"Yeah?"

"Yeah. Full transparency. I promise."

I nod to myself. "Okay, then."

"You needa shave."

"Pardon?" I sputter.

"You look like you just rolled out of a barn. Shave your damn face, Oakley."

I stare at the back of Lawson's trailer, indignant. "Fuck you very much. My facial hair is fine."

"You're gonna give someone beard burn."

"I'll have you know that's half the appeal."

He's quiet for a moment. "Really?"

"Yes, really."

"Huh."

Jesus Christ, straight men. "I take it back. I don't need your honesty."

"Too late."

I mutter a "Fuck," and Lawson laughs. I redirect us quickly. "Tell me about Wendy. Has she finished applying for colleges yet?"

The next hour passes with Lawson catching me up on his daughter and which colleges she'd most like to attend after her final year of high school. I feel another pang of guilt knowing I missed so much of her life while in Kansas, even as we stayed in near-constant contact. I missed a lot. My dad's knee surgery. My mom's retirement from the local flower shop-slash-nursery. The end of Lawson's marriage.

I missed *them*, period.

And I missed my town, even as I tried not to.

Midday, Lawson and I stop for a quick bathroom break before getting back on the road. As the highway passes, I make several calls. First to my neighbor, letting him know to stop by and take whatever food he wants in the next couple days. After that, to one of the guys at the ranch who mentioned he'd be more than happy to resell what little furniture I left behind. Then a cleaner, who'll scrub the place top to bottom. And finally, the realtor who sold me the house in the first place. It'll be back on the market in a week.

It's remarkably easy, tying up all the loose ends from that life. Lawson said moving on doesn't have to be complicated. And I suppose, in some ways, that's true. It's a choice. One a person needs to be ready to make.

I guess I'm ready to return to where I was meant to be.

And the future? Well, I'll figure that out one day at a time.

Chapter 5

LAWSON

It's the early hours of the morning when Oakley and I make it to his house, having driven straight through the night. He lets Bell out of the trailer first, guiding her into the large, fenced backyard before unclipping her lead. The cow takes off, getting her zoomies out.

Oakley and I leave most of his possessions for after we've had some sleep. He doesn't even ask if I'm staying or going, just opens the door and waves me in.

His house is much as I remember before he sold it to his parents and moved. The walls are light blue and yellow, the furniture is old in a way that's charming instead of looking run-down, and barring some of the more personal items Oakley brought with him to Kansas, even the decor is the same. His parents hardly changed a thing when they opened it up as a rental.

Oakley heads for the kitchen first, filling two glasses with water as his eyes roam, same as mine did. He shakes his head a little. "Looks the same."

"It does," I agree, accepting the drink he passes me.

Oakley downs his own before canting his head. "Come on."

I expect Oakley to direct me to the guest room, but he doesn't. He gives my arm a tug as he rounds the corner into the main bedroom, dropping his suitcase inside. I set my own backpack of essentials down, watching as Oakley tosses back the covers. He lies down, fully clothed, and groans.

"Coming?" he asks when I continue to stand there. "We're gonna talk."

"Now?"

"Mhm."

Heaving a sigh, I settle into the space next to him, my eyelids heavy as my head hits the pillow. Oakley's hands are behind his head, his stare on the ceiling, same as mine.

"I'm not going to apologize," I tell him.

His head turns my way. "For what?"

"You know what. Dragging you back here. It needed to be done."

"For whose sake? My own?"

I chew my lip, and Oakley flicks my forehead.

"Stop it," I tell him, swatting his hand. He only huffs a laugh. "Yes, for your sake, Oak. You were being stubborn about staying there because you thought we'd judge you for coming home. We never would."

He hums.

"For your parents' sake, too," I add. "Renting this house was a load of trouble for them. It'll be easier now with you buying it back."

"Is that so?" Oakley says, sounding amused. "Sure does look like they had trouble keeping this place maintained."

I ignore the comment. "Not to mention for Wendy's sake. She missed you. A lot. You said you'd come back at least once a year, and you didn't."

His voice is soft. "I know. And I'm sorry about that."

I nod in a jerk.

"Is that all?" he asks.

It takes considerable effort to turn my head, but I do, meeting Oakley's painted eyes. I can't tell him it felt like losing a limb when he drove off with Stevie. That every year that passed without him coming home, even to visit, scared me more than the simple passage of time ever could. I can't say missing him was the hardest thing I've ever had to endure.

I've always been close with Oakley. Closer than I am with anyone else. But I recognize the way I need him in my life isn't a fair burden to put on a friend.

How would I even explain it? It's selfish, wanting to be his first priority. But once upon a time, when we were kids, Oakley was my entire world, and I was his. I never wanted that to change.

It wasn't supposed to.

"Law," Oakley says, voice quiet. "Full transparency, remember? You promised."

My eyes sting, but I refuse to let the tears fall. "I wanted you back for *me*. For my sake, all right? I've tried so damn hard to be what everyone needed me to be. A good husband. A good father. A good brother and son and friend. And all the while, the person I needed most was across the goddamn country."

Oakley's eyes are wide, but the words are rolling out now, and there's no stopping them.

"I missed you so much it was unbearable, Oak. I know it's not fair to you, but I need you here. You don't get to leave again."

He blinks, a slow thing. "You know, I've always found it funny when folks talk about you as this utterly unflappable presence. People around town, parents of the kids in your classes, your family even. And you are calm and collected, Law. Around just about everybody but me."

"Because it's different with you."

"Why?"

"You're my person."

He lets out a short puff of air. "I'm not leaving again. All right? I'm sorry, Lawson. I didn't... I didn't realize you were so lonely with me gone."

Lonely. The word doesn't do it justice, but I nod anyways, my throat tight.

"Fuck," Oakley mutters. "C'mere."

I let Oakley tug me close, my head on his chest as his arms wrap around my shoulders. The pressure that's been under my ribcage for damn near years unspools with my exhale. Every ounce of it, flowing free, gone as if it was never there at all.

Laura's voice rings in my ears. Her telling me it's not right, how much I depend on Oakley. Saying men our age shouldn't be so close.

But what about Laura's friends? What about the women she'd get together with, sipping mimosas in our kitchen, exchanging hugs and smiles and talking about everything going on in their lives?

Why is it different for me and Oakley just because we're men?

I let my ex's voice drift from my mind, my hand settling on Oakley's ribs as his fingers hold tightly to my back. His chest hitches, but he only holds on tighter.

"I'm sorry." His words are softly spoken, but I hear them perfectly well, the reverberation a rumble in my ear.

"I know."

"I'm forgiven?" he asks.

"Already told you you are."

"Still gonna chew me out some more?"

I huff, even as a smile graces my lips. "Might."

"All right then. Get some sleep."

With the dawn sending the day's first light through the window, I close my eyes. It's all too easy to fall asleep in this house that's always felt like home.

It takes longer to unpack Oakley's possessions than it did to stuff them into boxes. I stay for over a day, helping with the task, having nowhere else I need to be with school out for the summer.

I can't quite temper the smile on my face, seeing Oakley resettle here in Darling. Even if Oakley himself is currently wearing a scowl.

"Of course my parents replaced all the things I took with me," he grumbles, an assortment of spatulas in his hand. He dumps them into a drawer. "I don't need two toasters. Or two dressers. Or a dozen spatulas."

"So make a donation pile," I suggest, folding a throw blanket before draping it along the back of his couch.

He huffs, but my gaze redirects to the back door at the sound of it opening. Bell strolls in, the automatic door closing behind her after a few seconds, the pull ropes both inside and out swaying with the movement.

"And they left the automatic cow door," he mumbles, despite being the person who installed it in the first place. "Don't get into shit, Belladonna. And wipe your feet!"

Bell passes over the long mat in front of the door, her hooves looking relatively clean. She immediately sticks her head into a cardboard box, the only one with food.

Oakley sighs as Bell trots down the hall with a box of crackers. "Could you?"

Nodding, I head after her. I find Bell in the guest room, trying her best to tear into the snack. She blinks her big, black eyes at me as I take the crumpled box. "You know better," I say softly, offering a few crackers in my palm that she hastily snaps up. "Next time, just ask."

Bell cozies down on a rug as I head back to the kitchen, Oakley looking through the cabinets next to the fridge now. He runs a hand through his hair, the stubble on his face looking a touch shorter than it did the other day, as if he shaved it down somewhat. His comment on beard burn comes to mind, and I wonder at it.

Laura never said she liked that, but...we weren't particularly compatible to begin with. Not in so many ways. It wasn't readily apparent at the start of our relationship, not when I was trying my best to be the man she deserved.

Would that feel good, the sensation of rough stubble on my skin? I have no idea, not having ever tried it for myself.

There are so many things I've never tried.

Oakley's jeans are faded, his t-shirt snug enough on his form to see the swell of his work-honed muscles. He's handsome in a rugged way; I've heard it enough from folks around town. But his nose has a small, crooked bend in it, and there's nothing remotely conventional about his eyes.

Handsome doesn't feel like enough to describe him.

Oakley catches me watching and cocks an eyebrow. "What is it?"

"Just wondering," I tell him truthfully. "I invited Wendy over for dinner, by the way. She should be here in..."

I trail off as I hear a vehicle outside, followed by boots stomping up the porch stairs.

"About now," I finish.

Oakley looks amused, but his attention diverts to the front of the house as my daughter comes storming through the door. She walks right up to Oakley, punches him on the shoulder, and then gives him a fierce hug.

Oakley grunts under the force of her attack, his eyes wide. "Jesus, Wendy. Look at you. You're up to my chin now."

"Yeah, well, I grew up a lot while you were off playing *Wizard of Oz*."

"Kansas," I mouth to him.

He squeezes my daughter tighter, his eyes slipping closed. "It's good to see you, Wen."

"You, too," she says, voice cracking. "You're not leaving again."

"Christ," he mutters, eyes opening and finding mine. There's a small smile on his face. "You two are just alike."

Wendy finally steps back, quickly swiping at her face. Oakley shakes his head as he looks her over. She's grown a lot in the years he's been gone. From a gangly just-teenager to the seventeen-year-old she is now. She's looking more like a young woman every day, and it's obvious Oakley is surprised by the change, not having seen the day-to-day evolution as I have. Pictures aren't the same.

"So," Wendy says almost defensively, hands on her hips, "you *are* staying, right?"

"I am," Oakley answers.

"Good. Where's Bell?"

As if hearing her name spoken, Bell comes trotting down the hall. Wendy rushes over, throwing herself against the miniature cow, cooing up a storm as Bell's tail swishes, the bovine's eyes half closed in bliss.

Oakley looks my way. "I think she missed the cow more than me."

"Likely," I tease.

He glances down at his closed fist, confusion on his face for a moment before he slowly cranks up his middle finger. "Ah, there it is."

I grab a pillow from the couch and toss it his way. Oakley laughs as he swipes it out of the air, sending it careening back in my direction.

"What's for dinner?" Wendy asks, ignoring the antics of two forty-some-year-old men who should know better.

Oakley gives Bell a surreptitious look. "Steak?"

"Oh good Lord," I mumble, heading for the fridge. Luckily for everyone, I find a few ribeyes inside, as well as some bell peppers. "Get the grill going. We're doing kabobs."

Oakley doesn't argue, practically bounding out the back door to light the grill. My eyes catch Wendy's. She doesn't need to say a word for me to understand the smile at the corner of her lips.

We're both glad Oakley is back.

We eat outside, Bell grazing in the yard as the three of us sit at the picnic table on Oakley's patio. I'll need to head home soon—to my temporary home at the ranch. But for now, I kick up my feet on the bench seat near Oakley, content to savor this moment I wasn't sure I was going to get again.

The sun is low in the sky. The wind is blowing gently. If I squint, I can almost see pixies flitting on the breeze. Almost.

My best friend is home.
Maybe that's magic enough for me.

Chapter 6

OAKLEY

Darling Ranch looks the same as the day I left.

With a few notable exceptions.

"I assume you're Ashley?"

The blonde who's setting down a basket of biscuits on the long dining table inside the Darlings' ranch house gives me a grin. He holds his hand out my way, the room around us bustling with activity. "That's me. But just Ash is fine."

"Nice to meet you, Ash. I'm Oakley Beaumont."

"Oh, I've heard of you," he says, letting my hand go. "Lawson's friend. I don't know what I was expecting, but I can't say you're it."

I don't have time to inquire further before Jackson trails into the room, his eyes unerringly latching onto Ash. The two exchange a quick smile, the besotted look on Jackson's face the *second* notable difference at the ranch. His gaze finds me quickly.

"Oakley," he says in greeting, plopping down in a seat across the table. "Welcome back. Looks like you're already getting settled?"

"I am," I tell him. "Ira's been catching me up to speed."

The older ranch hand gives a nod as he bites into a buttered biscuit from the gluten-free bowl. That's new, too. When Laura was working here as a cook before Ash came along, there weren't gluten-free options.

"Good," Jackson says, preparing his own plate. "I'll ride along with you today as a refresher. Hazel's been retired, so we'll get you set up with a new horse."

"Something happen to her?" I ask. The mare is younger than the usual retirement age for a workhorse.

Jackson's mouth twists. "Blind in one eye. Noah's taking care of her now. You'll probably see him around a good bit."

"Noah," I say slowly, when it clicks. "Noah King? The other farrier in town?"

"And Colton's boyfriend," Ash puts in, eyes practically twinkling.

I swallow my bite of food wrong, having to clear my throat before I can speak again. "I'm sorry. Colton's dating his long-standing business rival? That Noah King? As in...a man?"

Ash is outright grinning now. "For the record, I totally called it."

"When did this happen?" I ask, huffing a laugh.

Lawson's mother, Marigold, takes a seat near the end of the table, her voice joining the fray. "Oh, not that long ago. They only made it official recently, but those boys were sneaking around for months before that. Welcome back to town, Oakley. It's good to see your face."

I give Marigold a genuine smile she readily returns, her brown eyes reminding me so much of Lawson's. "It's good to be back."

She spoons herself some scrambled eggs. "Guess now I have an answer for why my son is smiling again."

I go still, my pulse a heavy beat in my ears. I catch Ash wince, but I refocus quickly on Marigold. "You're talking about Lawson?"

"Who else?" she says lightly, most everyone on the other side of the table involved in their own conversations, not paying us any mind. "No mother wants to see their child struggling. But you've brought a little light back into his life, and I'm grateful for it."

I have no clue what to say. It's one thing for Lawson to admit how much he missed me while I was gone and entirely another to find out he hasn't even been *smiling*. For how long? Since the divorce? Before then?

Guilt once again rears its head, but he never *said* anything. He kept telling me he was fine. That everything was fine.

Until he showed up on my doorstep and demanded I come home.

It's so like the man to try his best not to pawn his troubles off on others. As if Lawson hurting is his own pain to manage and not anyone else's.

Doesn't he get it?

He's not alone.

"Oh, I know that face," Marigold says, a happy lilt to her words. "Sure am glad you're back, Oakley."

I grunt, trying to decide how early is too early to haul Lawson out of bed and have words. Seeing some of the ranchers push back from the table makes me realize the breakfast hour is nearly up. It'll have to wait.

I finish up my own meal and am slipping on my hat when I spot Remi come through the dining room door. The youngest Darling brother sees me, a smile jumping to his face as he signs a quick, *'Hey, you're back.'*

'I am,' I sign in return, the motions feeling rusty considering my past few years of minimal ASL use. *'Good to see you.'*

Remi returns the sentiment, grabbing a biscuit off the table and sidestepping a few of the ranchers as he sends me an off-balance, *'Catch you soon.'*

I nod, heading with the remaining ranchers out onto the back deck. Everyone is setting off toward their objectives for the morning, the sun casting only the barest hint of light over the horizon. A haze is blanketing the land, dew from last night still hanging on the grass, moisture visible even in the air. The clouds overhead are tinged pink, like cotton candy, and the dairy cows call their morning hellos, picking themselves up off the ground to head toward the big red milking barn.

This is ranch life. The beautiful. The nitty gritty. The earthy welcome of it all.

Boots thump gently on the deck boards, Jackson coming to stand beside me. "Gorgeous, isn't it."

It's not so much a question as a statement, but I nod nonetheless. It sure is.

Jackson gives my shoulder a clap. "You leave again, and I'm setting my dad after you. He knows his way around a castration."

I blink in shock as Jackson jogs down the handful of deck stairs to the grass below.

He stops, looking back at me. "Coming?"

With a laugh I can feel straight down to my heart, I follow Jackson toward the horse barn.

Yeah. It's damn good to be back.

The day passes swiftly, albeit with a good dose of grime and grit. Jackson keeps with me through it all, but not much of the process has changed since I was last here, so it's easy to get back into the saddle, literally and metaphorically.

By the time two o'clock hits, I'm worn out in the best way. Jackson sends me off with a hearty slap to my back, and I ride my new companion, Clover, back to the stables. He's sweet, if not a little green. But I don't mind the horse being young, not when he's so quick to listen.

After dismounting, I lead him through the barn doors, several of the other first-shift ranchers getting their own horses settled. The process doesn't take all that long, removing Clover's gear, giving him a wash and a brush, and rewarding his good behavior with a couple carrots. He munches those up quickly, setting in on the hay in his stall next. Remi will come through to feed the horses their grain later, once they've cooled down.

I give Clover a long pat down the side of his neck, his coat shining a rich chestnut brown. "Thanks for the good first day," I tell the horse. It makes all the difference, having a riding companion you're well suited to. No one wants to be struggling with the reins while there are cattle to be dealt with.

The horse doesn't answer, but his gentle huffing breath sounds a lot like contentment.

With a final pat, I leave Clover to his hay and head out of the stall. I give a few goodbyes to the other ranchers, making my way across the grounds slowly, taking everything in again.

I can see Snickerdoodle the pony off in the petting farm, a few chickens passing near her feet. The goats are running around inside the fenced-off space, their bleats audible, even from here. I stop still when I spot Lawson on the back deck of the ranch house, reclined leisurely in a chair.

He waves, and I get moving again, heading his way.

"Good first day back?" he calls.

I pull off my hat, running a hand through my hair as I send the brimmed leather toward Lawson like a frisbee. He catches it, huffing as he sets it aside. "Just fine," I tell him, dropping down in the chair next to his, the shade on the deck welcome.

"Only fine?" Lawson asks dubiously. His ankles are crossed, the whiskey-brown of his eyes watching me closely.

"It was great," I say honestly. "Except for the part where I found out you've been struggling, Lawson, and not allowing anyone to help."

He looks taken aback. "I've been fine."

"Oh, now *you've* been fine. It sure doesn't sound like it."

His expression closes off slightly, a mulishness taking place that he gets from his mother. And his father. "I don't know who's been talking, but it's nothing anyone needs to worry about."

I scoff. "What were you just saying to me? That when you care about someone, when you love them, you look after them. Isn't that right?"

He doesn't say a thing.

"You don't count in that?" I ask. "Why the fuck not?"

Again, no response.

"You've got so many people in your corner, Law. Why've you been shutting them out?"

"Because none of them could've helped me anyway."

I huff. "Why the hell not?"

"They weren't you," he says forcefully, the words practically spat out. "None of them were you."

"Jesus, Lawson. Sometimes I just wanna strangle you."

He looks indignant, his face scrunched up in a way that almost has me laughing. Almost. "Why?"

"I was a phone call away!" I tell him. "Always. And you never *said* anything. Only ever, 'I'm fine.' You weren't fine. And maybe I should've pushed harder, but I didn't know it was so fucking bad. *Goddamn* it, Law. Why didn't you ask me for help?"

"Because you were gone. You weren't here. And I didn't know how to ask for something I shouldn't need in the first place."

"A friend?" I question.

"A lifeline."

My heart thumps painfully in the silence that follows those tersely spoken words.

Lawson drops his face into his hands, scrubbing harshly before he turns to me. "I had a lot to figure out after the separation, all right? Things about myself. About what I wanted. It wasn't anything my family could've helped me with. I needed time. And I needed..."

He doesn't say *you*, but it sits in the air regardless.

I unglue my tongue from the roof of my mouth. "I would have dropped everything and driven back here if I knew you needed it."

"I didn't want you to know," he says, that stubbornness reappearing. "You were dealing with plenty."

With Stevie.

I blow out a heavy breath, looking at the dairy cows in the field in front of us. Their tails are swooshing, the sun above high in the sky. "Why did you and Laura split, Law?"

I don't need to see my friend to know he's chewing his words. He must realize I'm not letting it drop this time because, finally, he says, "I wasn't in love with her anymore. I'm not sure I ever was."

I look over at him slowly. At the wrinkle in his brow as he stares ahead. The pain in his eyes, and the set to his squared jaw that tells me he's trying hard not to overshare his emotions. It's not something he's ever been particularly good at. And I realize if I'd been here, I would have known something was wrong. I would have seen it on his face, as I can see it now.

Nineteen years, he was married to Laura. He was with her for twenty-two.

"God, Law. I'm sorry."

He meets my gaze. "What for? You didn't know. I didn't even know."

I shake my head. "Not that. I'm sorry for not realizing how badly you've been hurting."

He swallows hard. "It's getting better."

"Is it?"

"Yeah."

I nod, the breeze ruffling my hair and making a wind chime nearby sing a few notes. "All those things you were trying to figure out. Did you?"

He lets loose a breath. "Working on it."

I hold out my hand, and, after a moment, Lawson accepts it. He doesn't seem to mind the dirt on my palm. "I'm here now," I tell him hoarsely. "I'm here. So whatever you need from me, I'll give it, all right?"

He nods, not saying a word. The chime sings again, sounding like the tinkling of bells.

I clear my throat as I let him go. "By the way, my parents want us over for dinner. Tomorrow night work?"

"That works."

"'Kay."

Lawson and I sit out on the back deck of the ranch house for some time, both of us watching the cattle and the breeze. Ash drops off some iced tea after a while, offering a wink before he heads back inside. Off to the west, the mountains rise toward the sky, their peaks nearly disappearing amongst the clouds.

Beautiful mountain. That's what Beaumont means.

Maybe I was always meant for Montana.

Maybe I was meant for a lot of things I was too scared to claim for my own.

Chapter 7

LAWSON

"Lawson, sweetie, help me with the whipped cream?"

"Mom," Oakley starts, a warning in his tone.

"No, it's fine," I assure him. "I'm happy to help."

Sienna graces me with a wide smile. "See, I knew I always liked you. Here."

Oakley shakes his head as his mother sets me up with the portable mixer. She places a carton of heavy cream down, pulls the countertop canister of sugar over, and pats my shoulder.

We're in the elder Beaumonts' house, the two-story farmhouse-style home as familiar to me as any other I've lived in. The lavender wallpaper in the entry. The mosaic of colors in the kitchen tiles that reminds me of a vegetable garden at the height of summer. The nick in the banister at the foot of the stairs.

That one's Oakley's fault. He took a piece out of it when we were seven and thought riding an old-fashioned wooden sled down the stairs would be a good idea. It wasn't.

I swear his parents left the nick just to use as fodder against the both of us.

Oakley brings plates and utensils outside at the behest of Sienna as I pour the heavy cream into the chilled bowl. The clang of the beaters against ceramic drowns out most else for the minute it takes to whip the cream, a spoonful of sugar added near the end. All set, I put the mixer aside and bring the whipped cream out back.

The table is already set up, dinner laid out and Robert, Oakley's dad, cranking up the umbrella. It offers some shade as we take our seats, bees and the occasional hummingbird flitting around the plentiful gardens Sienna has always kept. She thanks me as I set the bowl of whipped cream beside what looks like a peach pie.

"Dig in," Robert says with a grin.

Oakley passes me the platter of dinosaur-shaped chicken nuggets with an eyebrow raised, a hefty dose of *can you believe this?* in his expression. I keep my amusement to myself as I take a few of the nuggets, glad to see hamburgers are waiting, as well.

"So, Lawson," Sienna starts, pouring herself a glass of lemonade. "Tell us what you've been up to these past many years."

Oakley makes a disapproving sound. "Hey, now. I damn well know you had Lawson and Wendy over plenty while I was gone, so the guilt trip ain't gonna work. Try again."

Sienna chuckles, unperturbed by her son's halfhearted ire. "How'd you get him back?" she asks instead.

I glance Oakley's way. He's already into his burger. "You want to tell the story or should I?"

He rolls his eyes, waving a hand to give me the go-ahead.

I refocus on Sienna and Robert, both giving me their rapt attention. "I showed up and told him he was coming home."

"That easy?" Robert asks, an eyebrow raised.

Oakley gets most of his looks from his father. The same perpetually ruffled, light brown hair, same sharp cheekbones and heavy scruff. Robert's eyes are pure blue, however. Sienna carries the brown and a far shorter stature.

"I wasn't taking no for an answer," I tell the elder Mr. Beaumont.

His laugh has Oakley doing his best to look put-out.

"Well, we're all glad you're home," Sienna says to her son. "We can get the deed to your house transferred over anytime."

"I'm buying it back," Oakley says. "You're not just giving it to me."

"Sure," Sienna agrees. "Now tell us how our favorite grand-cow is doing."

Oakley catches his parents up to speed on Belladonna and her thieving ways, threatening more than once to remove her access to the indoors. He'll never do it. He may grumble and complain about the cow, but she's family to him. Just like Wendy.

We end our dinner with peach pie, a few birds singing as the trees cast long shadows over the yard. Even with the lingering scent of the grill on the air, the smell of flowers is strong here, the gardens perfuming the patio where we're sitting.

Being that it's summer, no one is in any hurry to get a move on. It's late by the time Oakley and I leave his parents' house, the man himself the only one with work in the morning. Since I picked him up, I drop him back off, my mind tumbling over the conversation we had the other day.

Maybe Oakley can sense it, because he doesn't say goodbye. "Come on. Have a drink with me."

Nodding, I follow him into the house. Oakley unlocks the back door, giving Bell access before he heads into the kitchen, pouring a finger each of Darling whiskey into two glasses.

"Christ," I mutter.

He merely chuckles. "I won't get you drunk."

"So you say."

We take seats on the couch, bootless feet propped on the coffee table and the silence stretching for a moment. Emotion clogs my throat as I realize just how much I've missed this. Sitting with Oakley. Talking to him like this, in person, where I can see his face and he can see mine. There's no one else in my life I've ever felt as comfortable being open with. Oakley said I'm forthright, and with him, that's true.

It's not as easy with everybody else. Not when it comes to the personal thoughts inside my head.

"You wanna start or should I pry it out of you?" Oakley asks.

I take a small sip of my whiskey. "I think... I'd like to get fucked."

Oakley coughs, jackknifing forward as he thumps his chest. "Jesus."

"By a man," I clarify.

"Yeah, I figured as much," he ekes out, voice tight. "That was *not* what I was expecting."

I give him a minute to get his breathing under control. "Oak... I want you to be the one to do it."

He jumps up, setting his glass on the coffee table as he rounds the surface, using it like a shield between him and me. His eyes are wide, incredulity written across every line of his face and body. "*What?*"

"You're pan," I point out. "You've fucked plenty of people, guys included."

"Not my best friend," he says, running his hand roughly through his hair.

I scoot to the edge of the couch, trying to figure out how to make him understand. "There's no one I trust more than you. I want to try it. It's something I have to do. I want it to be you, Oak. But if you don't want to, I'll find someone else."

"Jesus," he says again, spinning away.

"You said you're here for whatever I need from you," I remind him.

"I didn't think you'd ask for *sex*. My God, Law. Don't you think that would make things awkward between us?"

"No."

He turns back to face me, eyebrows high. "No?"

"No," I repeat. "We jerked off together once."

"When we were, like, fifteen. To porn. We certainly didn't touch. We barely even looked at each other."

"But it didn't get awkward, did it?"

Oakley huffs a big breath, shaking his head as he examines me. "Where the fuck is this coming from? How long have you been thinking about this?"

"A while," I admit as he sits down across from me. "Since before the split."

He waves his hand in a *go on* gesture.

I finish my whiskey, setting the glass down beside Oakley's. "Laura and I weren't all that sexually compatible. It's not something I realized at first, not until long after Wendy was born when things started to fizzle. I...was having trouble staying engaged in those activities."

"You never said anything."

"Yeah, well, who wants to admit they have no interest in their spouse? I felt terrible. Like maybe something in me was broken."

Oakley's expression softens. "Law. You're not broken."

"You don't know that."

"I do, actually. If you're wanting sex but are lacking the physical response, there are things you can do to help with that. If you're just not interested in it, that's another matter entirely. Neither makes you broken."

I ease out a breath, looking over at the wall where three portraits of cows sit above a cupboard filled with games. The pictures were added after Oakley left, chosen by his mom. Each of the cows is wearing a flower crown. One is even white, like Bell.

"We tried different things," I tell Oakley. "To spice up our sex life. Most of it didn't make a difference. Lingerie and toys. Porn, even. The only thing that I got remotely excited about was..."

His voice is gentle. "What?"

"When Laura would peg me."

I finally bring my gaze back to Oakley. He's doing his best not to react, but I can see his surprise. I know how he feels, not having expected I would like it as much as I do.

"So now you want to be fucked by a guy," he fills in. "Why not a woman?"

I shrug, even though it's a question I've been mulling over since Laura and I called it quits. "Because I'm not sure what I am," I finally admit. "And I needa find out."

Oakley falls back against his chair, puffing out a breath. "Jesus Christ, Law. I don't think anyone in the history of ever would be as nonchalant about this as you."

"I've had a lot of time to set my mind on it."

"And now there's no changing course, is there?" He shakes his head a little. "You realize I can't be the one to fuck you, right?"

"Why not? Do you see me as a brother?"

He huffs what might be a laugh. "No. I see you as a friend."

"Sometimes friends fuck."

His eyebrow lifts. "And sometimes it ends badly."

"It won't end badly," I say, sure of it.

"Lawson Darling. Did you bring me back here to settle your sexuality crisis?"

I refrain from rolling my eyes. "No. I brought you back because you're my closest friend, and you being gone made no damn sense. Do we needa go over this again?"

Oakley groans. "Lord grant me strength."

"Maybe it won't be what I think," I say seriously, my chest tight. "Maybe I won't like it with a man. But I won't regret trying. I know there are guys out there who'd be happy to be my first experience. But I'd feel safer, Oakley, if it's you."

He sobers quickly, his expression a mixture of emotions far too complex for me to fully unravel. "It's a bad idea."

"Why?"

"It could get messy."

"Isn't that kinda the point?"

Oakley stills before amusement steals over his eyes. He keeps his lips pressed in a firm line, trying not to betray himself. "Lawson, you better use a fucking condom."

"You can make sure of it if it's you."

"Do not threaten me with irresponsibility," he says, pointing a finger my way. "You're too damn by the book not to practice safe sex, anyway. *Good grief,* I cannot believe this is a conversation we're having."

I chuckle, and Oakley shakes his head, leaning forward to swipe his drink off the coffee table. He downs the whiskey, holding the empty glass in his hands as he stares at me.

"In all seriousness," he says slowly, "I'm really glad you're telling me this, Lawson. I'm glad you know you can trust me. I just... I can't have sex with you."

I pull in a short breath, nodding, even as the disappointment at his words is sharp in my chest. I knew there was a chance he'd say no. That he'd think it was too weird. Or that I might not be his type in the first place.

I just wanted it to be him. The idea of some stranger fucking me isn't nearly as appealing as it being the man I know better than I know myself some days.

"If you change your mind..." I say, letting the sentence hang.

Oakley nods, his face set in a frown. He clears his throat. "You can crash here tonight if you want."

"I'm fine," I tell him, that tiny pour of whiskey not enough to affect me. I stand, feeling all sorts of turned around and unspun, like a bundle of yarn halfway to being a shirt.

"Law," Oakley says, voice soft.

"I'm fine."

"Jesus," he mutters. The next second, Oakley is skirting the coffee table, his arms coming around me tight. My face presses to the bend of his neck, and I cling back, wishing I had more answers than questions.

It shouldn't be so hard, figuring myself out, should it? I've had forty-three years to try, and I'm still not certain of something as fundamental to my being as my sexuality. My parents were always open with us, always encouraging us to be proud of whoever it is we are. Every single one of my brothers is queer. Even Colton figured it out, his bisexuality.

It's never been something I was scared of or unwilling to accept. But my brothers' experiences aren't my own.

And I don't know how to explain something I don't even have words for.

"It'll be all right," Oakley says, his voice passing near my ear, gentle and sure. "You'll figure it out, Law."

I wanted to figure it out with you.

I don't say it. It's too much.

I won't guilt Oakley into sex. Not ever. Especially not after what I experienced with Laura.

"Yeah," I answer, even though I feel as unsure as ever. "Night, Oak."

He lets me go, a softly spoken, "Good night, Law," accompanying me to the door. I stick my feet in my boots, check to make sure I have my keys and wallet, and head outside.

No matter how hard I try, I can't find a single pixie dancing under the light of the moon.

Chapter 8

OAKLEY

I've officially been ruined.

Absolutely and utterly fucking wrecked.

Lawson is sitting at the dining table, having joined the twenty-some Darling Ranch workers and family members here for lunch, something he's only able to do during the summertime when he's not at the school. He's eating. Simply eating.

But I can't stop staring at him.

His words haven't left my head. Not in the week-plus since he asked me to fuck him. Words. Images. Scenarios I've tried desperately not to entertain in the past many decades of our friendship. They're all seeping past my defenses now because of a single conversation.

There's always been a lack of boundaries between me and Lawson. And it's never bothered me, nor have I ever read into it. Lawson was never interested in me in *that* way. Nor interested in anyone, really. Not until college when he started dating a little. Then he met Laura, and that was it.

Anything that *might have been* stayed in a box I knew better than to ever open. Not if I wanted to keep my friendship with Lawson intact. The box was easily forgotten, as fictitious as Neverland, a childish whimsy I never let see the light of day.

But he's cracked it open.

And I cannot, for the life of me, get it to shut again.

Lawson brings his water glass to his mouth, his Adam's apple bobbing as he drinks. I imagine my lips there, pressed to soft skin and coarse stubble, his throat working as he writhes beneath me, struggling to maintain his composure. What would it be like to push him to the brink? Would he beg? Moan? Gasp for more?

I quickly avert my gaze, looking down at my plate as my pulse rushes. I know better than to wonder about—*want*—things too dangerous to chase after.

Lawson doesn't want *me*. He wants dick. There's a big fucking difference.

But *goddamn it all*, he asked for *my* dick.

I'm so fucked.

I banish thoughts of Lawson to the far recesses of my mind as I finish lunch, avoiding his eye and hastening out the door as soon as I can do so. The sun is out, although morning rain dampened the earth, and the air is still muggy with it. I plop my hat on my head, heading toward the stables, determination lengthening my strides.

There's only a couple hours left in my day, but I resaddle Clover and head out to the far fields with a few of the other ranchers. We're shifting the cattle this week, moving them to fresh, grazable land. Calves are prevalent in the herds, most having been born during the spring calving season. Just like their adult counterparts, the calves are a mix of black and black-and-white. The solid black is a mark of the Angus breed kept here, whereas the white comes from the Holstein line. The cross-bred cattle can be either coloration, identifiable if you know what to look for. Although most folks probably just see *cow*.

The ground is soft underneath Clover's hooves, but it doesn't hamper the horse. Me and Colleen, another rancher who's been here for years, are at the back end of a herd, guiding the lot to a new pasture, when I notice a plastic bag looped around the neck of a calf.

I give a whistle to alert Colleen. She nods, noting the situation and changing course to guide him my way. As soon as the little bugger is close enough, I send a rope flying, lassoing him around the neck. The calf panics for all of a second, but then he's bound tight, and I quickly drop down off Clover to meet him.

"It's all right," I assure the calf in a low, soft tone. I make quick work of tearing the bag off from around his neck before letting him loose. He gets to his feet and sprints away, catching up to the rest of the herd, a couple of the others giving him a cursory sniff as he passes.

"Muddy suits you," Colleen calls, a grin on her face.

I look down at my dampened, dirty knees as I rise to my feet. "That why you sent him my way?"

Colleen laughs, which confirms my suspicions.

Getting back in the saddle, I cant my head toward the last of the lingering herd. "C'mon. Let's get this lot settled. My day's about done."

She doesn't argue, and we herd the rest of the cattle through the open gates to the pasture next to this one. Colleen stays out in the fields when I head in, her shift having started later than my own. Truth be told, I don't much mind the muck that's a part of this lifestyle. There's no way around getting dirty at times, and I wouldn't trade being outdoors through any weather for the alternative of being stuck inside with only a window to remind me of what I'm missing.

It's one way Lawson and I have always differed. Our sexuality is another. Or so I thought.

But now Lawson is questioning. And he turned to me, his closest friend, to help him figure it out.

I stand by my decision, even if the saddened expression on Lawson's face when I said no won't leave my mind. Nor the image of him flat on his back, mouth parted and words falling from his lips, a possibility I never dared to imagine could be real.

It's a bad idea. The absolute worst.

And I wish, *God,* I wish he'd never spoken the words in the first place. Because to Lawson, no matter our history and our inevitable future, it'd only be sex. An answer to a question. A means to an end.

I don't think it could ever be that for me.

Some things we hide away for fear of understanding them. I hid that box away for a reason. And I never thought much about it in the years after it was buried.

To have that box unearthed in front of me, lid cracked open and possibilities spilling out...

What was it J. M. Barrie said through the voice of Peter Pan? *"You can have anything in life if you will sacrifice everything else for it."*

I could have Lawson, it would seem.

If I'm willing to sacrifice my heart.

My jeans dry as I return Clover to the stables, the horse and I having found a nice groove together. He nips at my pockets as I brush his coat, which makes me wonder who's in the habit of feeding him treats. Seeing no need to deny the horse, I grab a date from the tack room before I go. Clover is more than happy to accept the small, dried fruit.

As I'm turning around, I spot Lawson standing at the door to the barn. He doesn't say anything with others nearby, simply waits for me to meet him, the two of us walking back across the land toward the ranch house where I'm parked.

"You've been quiet," he accuses.

I puff out a breath. "Had a lot to think about."

"Because of me," he says matter-of-factly.

I don't bother denying it. "You threw me for a loop, Law."

He's quiet for a moment, eyes ahead as we walk. My gaze drifts over him, from the broadness of his body and the seriousness of his brow to his naturally pouty lips. I curse the direction my mind wanders down. Wondering how those lips might feel against me. Picturing the man naked—a sight I've seen before—but the image of him falling apart at my fingertips brand new and searing enough to have my mouth running dry.

This was never a problem. Not before.

"Your answer is still no?" he asks, voice even.

My throat clicks when I swallow. "It is."

"All right."

Fuck.

I want to go back to a week and a half ago when bedding Lawson wasn't an option. I want to shake him and ask why this is so fucking easy for him to even contemplate. But I know it's not. He's thought about this long and hard. The man is dealing with a complete upheaval of his identity. That's not an easy thing, and I *know* he's been struggling with it.

But why did he have to uproot the earth at my feet, too? I was fine. I was *fine* being Lawson's friend. I never needed more.

Except now the fucking box is open. And I fear wishing it buried again isn't an option.

I come to a slow halt, my hand on Lawson's arm stopping him as well. "Why do you want it to be me, Law? I don't think you're even attracted to me, are you?"

It's never seemed like it, at least, not even in my living room when Lawson was asking me to fuck him.

Something flits over his expression. Frustration, almost. Resignation. "I don't know."

"You don't know?"

"I... I don't think it works like that for me."

My gears turn swiftly. "Were you attracted to Laura?"

He winces, the tiniest flicker at the corner of his mouth. "I don't think so."

Aw, fuck.

I work on pulling in a breath, and Lawson goes on.

"I thought I was, but... I think it was affection at most. I didn't realize there was a difference until one of our counseling sessions. We were supposed to think about the last time we'd looked at one another and felt lust, and I just... I never had. It didn't even occur to me the way I thought about her was unusual until that moment."

"Because you two still had sex. You were intimate."

"Yeah."

My chest aches fiercely, but I refrain from rubbing it. "Law... Have you ever looked at a guy and wanted to have sex?"

"I don't know. That's what I'm trying to figure out."

"No, I mean..." A cow in the dairy field next to us moos, and I realize this maybe isn't the best place to be having this conversation, out in the open as we are. "Can we head inside? There's something I wanna ask."

Lawson nods, curiosity in his expression, and we continue on toward the ranch house. Instead of getting in my truck to go home as I'd planned, I follow Lawson inside, both of us taking off our boots. He leads me up to his bedroom where we'll have some measure of privacy, closing the door behind us before going to his dresser.

He pulls a pair of jeans out that he tosses my way. "Here."

Catching them, I switch out my muddy pair for the clean ones. Lawson waits all the while, looking pensively out the window.

I set the dirtied jeans aside, neatly folded. "Can we sit?"

He nods, heading to a chair in the corner. Another sits angled toward it, a small bookcase nearby. Once settled, I try to think how best to approach this. Lawson waits, ever patient, the sun slanting through the window lighting him in gold.

"Law... Do you think you might be ace?"

"What?"

His tone and expression give nothing away, and I realize maybe he's never even considered it. Being that he didn't question his sexuality until recently, it's a distinct possibility.

"Asexual. Like...you're not interested in people in a sexual way."

"I've had sex," he says slowly.

"Sure. But being ace doesn't necessarily mean you don't *enjoy* sex. Like... Okay, when I look at someone I'm interested in, the littlest thing can turn me on. Their lips. The way they move their hands. Their ear."

Lawson's eyebrow pops up. "Their ear?"

"Yeah, like..." I swallow harshly, pulling my gaze from Lawson's own ear. "Thinking about what I want to whisper into it. That turns me on. Or looking at them might remind me of the last time we were naked together, which makes me want to get them naked again. Do you ever experience anything like that? An urge to have that person right then right there?"

Lawson thinks about it long and hard, which seems to me to answer the question. But I don't interrupt his thought process. Finally, he says, "I don't know. Do you see now why I'm probably broken?"

"You're not broken," I say firmly, flicking the man's forehead. "Cut that shit out. Tell me this. What do you like about sex?"

He huffs out a breath, rubbing his temple, his gaze on some distant place in the room. "I like...the release of it. For a while, I liked knowing I was making Laura feel good because it felt like I was being a proper husband. Like I was accomplishing what I was supposed to. But that lessened over the years."

"Law," I say, a catch in my throat I can't quite disguise. "It shouldn't ever feel like a chore."

He swallows harshly. "No, I suppose not. But it took me a while to see that."

God.

"But I want to have sex," he goes on. "For *me*. I want to know what it could feel like after those times where it felt almost right. I don't need lust to be sure of that much."

I nod slowly, my chest drawn tight. "What do you see when you look at me?"

Lawson's eyes run over my face, the same as they always have. Warm in a way that's never changed, not in all the years we've known each other. "I see the person I trust most in this world."

It's all I can do not to make a sound.

"You think I'm asexual?" he asks.

I let out a slow breath. "I think it's a possibility. It's a wide spectrum, but if you've never felt desire for another person before, then it might fit."

"Or maybe I just haven't found the right person."

I'm proud of myself for keeping my face stoic. It's astounding how much can change in such a short period of time. How feelings long ago snuffed out can burn wildly with only the slightest air and provocation, only for the press of suffocation to bear down like a fate now worse than death.

I never loved Lawson Darling as more than a friend because I never let myself.

He's been my person for nearly forty-three years. And I've been his.

But that doesn't make me the *right* person. Not where he's concerned.

And no matter what else, I have to remember that.

Chapter 9

LAWSON

I think about what Oakley said long into the night. About whether or not I might be asexual and what that means for me if true. I even do a good bit of researching on my phone before frustration leads me to giving up, more confused than ever.

Sleep is fitful.

I'm not surprised when one of my brothers finds me late morning, my mood surely broadcast across my face. I *am* surprised, however, by the brother.

"Hey," Colton says, plopping down beside me on the deck. The day is sunny, and I have my laptop with me, trying to get a bit of lesson planning done before the start of the school year.

"Morning, Colt."

He's quiet for a minute, his foot bouncing. I'm guessing he didn't think of what he'd say when he cornered me, only that he should. Brotherly duty and all.

I appreciate it, even if I don't quite know what to say either.

Finally, he breaks the silence. "So. Oakley's back. That's nice."

"Yeah," I agree, although it's not the first time we've talked about the man. As soon as I got back from my brief visit to Kansas, Remi all but chewed me out in front of the family for leaving so abruptly without a word. He forgave me quickly, even though I'm fairly positive there was nothing to forgive.

The only person who needed to know was Wendy. And she was all in favor of me dragging Oakley home.

Colton bobs his head in a nod. "And you seem...happier?"

"Suppose so."

Although certainly no closer to understanding myself.

Colton looks off toward the mountains for a moment before letting out a groan. "I don't know how to do this."

"And...what is this?"

"Me trying to, I dunno, be supportive or whatever. You're happier, but something's still wrong. And don't try to tell me it's nothing. I thought it was the divorce, but you barely flinched once those papers were filed. And now you're smiling again, but there's something in your eyes I don't understand. I've never claimed to be the best at this stuff, but I'm here for you. And I wanna help, okay? We all do."

"I'm grateful for that," I say, my voice coming out hoarse. "I am, Colt. But I think some journeys we need to take alone."

His face scrunches up. "Yeah, I call bullshit on that. Every journey is better with a friend."

I grunt, and he turns to face me more fully, voice firm.

"I think you're scared of whatever it is you're feeling because you don't understand it, and you've always prided yourself on understanding everything before any of the rest of us. It's not a weakness to ask for help, Law. One of us might understand what you're going through. If you're making yourself suffer as punishment for what happened with Laura, well, then stop it. I think you've suffered enough, don't you?"

His words cause my breath to catch in my throat, an emotion that feels suspiciously like guilt curling in my chest.

Have I been punishing myself for a two-decade-long fuck-up? I want to deny it, but I let myself sit in a sad place for a long time, didn't I? I didn't *want* to feel better. Not unless it was Oakley doing the cheering up, but he wasn't here to do it.

And I didn't even tell him the half of it, did I? I could have, and he would have shown up for me, just like he said. I know he would have.

But I kept silent, stuck in what might have been grief over a failed marriage. Except losing Laura wasn't what hurt the most. It was finding out I don't know myself nearly as well as I thought I did. And wondering if I made the wrong choice so long ago.

But my choices brought me Wendy. And even if I regret so very much, I'll never regret that.

"I'm not sad about my divorce," I speak aloud, and Colton stills. "I'm torn up over all the years things should have been different. I can't get that time back. And... I'm scared maybe I won't make the right choice for my future."

My brother appraises me for a long moment. "Noah and I were at each other's throats for over fifteen years. You know why? A mistake someone else made. Life is messy, Law. It's never a perfect road. All you can do is travel down the one that feels right for you. Looking in the rearview won't accomplish a thing except forcing you to lose sight of what's in front of you."

"Shit," I mutter, shocked at my brother's insightful advice.

Colton chuckles, tipping his hat back as he holds my gaze. The sharp blue of his eyes is a feature each of my brothers possesses. I've always been the odd man out in that regard. "You've got a lot of life left to live, Law, God willing. But being afraid of it won't make it what you want it to be."

"You're saying making mistakes is better than not making any choices at all."

"I am. Mistakes can be fun sometimes."

Colton bounces his eyebrows, and I huff a laugh.

"But it'll work out for you," he goes on. "I know it."

"How so?" I ask, wanting badly to believe him.

His smile quirks at the corner. "Well, you've already started chasing your happiness, haven't you? Even brought a little bit of it home with you."

My gaze searches the fields for Oakley, although I don't see him at the moment. My brother chuckles, standing.

"Yep. Knew it. You're gonna be okay, Law."

"Thanks, Colt. I appreciate it. I really do."

He inclines his head. "Mhm. Now stop being a dumbass and come talk to us when you need it. We're family. We'll always have your back."

I nod, my throat tight, and Colton walks off down the deck. He bypasses the stairs altogether and jumps to the grass below, whistling a tune that reminds me of Ash and hearts of gold.

My gaze returns to the far fields, the mountains set behind them. Small flecks of black dot the countryside, the cattle so far away I can barely see them, even if I squint. Oakley is somewhere out there, tending to the herd, a cowboy by trade and at the very heart of him. He's always been a caretaker. Looking after animals, me, my daughter, even that cow he claims to hate.

I count myself lucky to have him in my life.

And I'm not letting him get away again.

Oakley is in the kitchen when I enter his house, the man's hair wet, even though it's far past the usual time he showers after work. I have an idea what caused the delay when I notice all his extra furniture and possessions gone from where they were piled near the dining table.

"Got everything donated?" I ask.

He nods as I join him in the kitchen, a pot on the stove perfuming the air with the savory aroma of tomatoes and herbs. "I'm officially down to three spatulas, which is still more than plenty. Wendy coming tonight?"

I shake my head, leaning against the counter as Oakley dumps spaghetti into a boiling pot of water. "She's at a friend's."

"A boy's?"

I raise an eyebrow at his implication. "Number one, you really think I'd give permission for my seventeen-year-old daughter to stay with a boyfriend, if she had one, unchaperoned for the night? Number two, your question is placing a lot of assumptions on a not-yet-woman who's given you no indication her preference is for boys. Number three, if my daughter is determined to do something untoward with a person of any gender, she'll find a way."

"Untoward?" Oakley whispers.

"But to answer your question, not a boy. Her friend Chloe. And the two *will* be chaperoned for the night. Stir your sauce, Oakley."

"Jesus," he mutters, spinning to stir the tomato sauce. He looks at me with a curious expression. "You think Wendy might be sexually active?"

I fight my cringe. "I think she could well be, even though she claims she's not. We've had every talk under the sun, and I trust my daughter to be safe, even if I don't trust her to tell me each and every possible bad decision she's made in her life."

Oakley huffs a laugh. "You're something else, Law."

"I'm pragmatic."

"Oh, I don't disagree." He shakes his head. "And here you were trying to make me believe you might skip safe sex yourself. I see through you, you know."

"I know," I say plainly. "You always have."

There goes that curious expression again. Oakley clears his throat, turning the burner off under the sauce. "You still set on that?"

"Finding a man? Yes."

He nods in a jerk, grabbing two plates from the cupboard. "Will you date or just..."

His voice peters out, but I understand the direction of his thoughts.

"I don't know. I'm not sure dating someone would be a good idea right now, not when I don't even know if that's something I want with a man. I think being upfront and honest and finding someone just for the night would be best. It should tell me what I need to know."

"Whether or not fucking a guy is something you enjoy," he fills in.

"Being fucked by one, but yeah."

He grunts, moving the pot of spaghetti over to the sink before dumping the contents into a strainer. "You've never had casual sex."

It's a statement, but Oakley knows the truth of it.

"No. There's only ever been Laura."

The look in his eye is one of sadness when he glances my way, and I'm not sure what for. For the end of my relationship? Because I told him sex with Laura never felt like what it maybe should have?

I'm not sure if sex with a man will feel different, but I want to know. I've accepted the fact that I'm not like most when it comes to picking out partners. That, like Oakley said, looking at a person doesn't bring about desire, at least not in the way Oakley described it for himself.

But I don't know if that makes me ace or just confused. Maybe both. At the very least, I think it's entirely possible I'm not straight, as I thought.

Maybe there's someone out there who will fit with me in a way that feels right instead of like everything I've heard it's supposed to be. *Supposed to be* isn't a one-size-fits-all. I learned that the hard way with Laura, trying my best to be what she needed, convincing myself it was right because no one ever told me I might want a person differently. And that'd be okay.

Not until Oakley.

He's moving the spaghetti noodles into a ceramic bowl now, his arms on display below the hems of his short sleeves. He's fit, not overly bulky with muscle but a far cry more defined than I am, thanks to my sitting in front of a desk most days. I look at the back of his ear, trying to find a hint of what Oakley mentioned. Attraction that's linked to sexual desire.

Maybe I'm just not hardwired that way. Because I've never looked at a man, woman, or any person and thought about what we could be in bed.

When I look at Oakley, I see comfort. Warmth. Someone I want to be near.

And yes, if Oakley were willing, I'd very much like him to fuck me so I could find out what it's like. If he could make me feel even half of what Laura did when she pegged me, it wouldn't be bad. Maybe it wouldn't be that mythical *right*, but I'm not sure that even exists for me.

But Oakley isn't an option. And I can respect his decision.

Which leaves me to find a one-night stand, not the easiest thing in Darling. But there are cities nearby and plenty of options out there, I'm sure.

Oakley sets the last of the dinner items on the table, and I join him, steam wafting up from the meal. I'm surprised Bell hasn't made her way inside to investigate, but maybe she already stole away with some food before I arrived.

"Wendy and I are going riding this weekend," I tell Oakley. "Wanna come?"

"At the ranch?" he asks.

I nod, dishing spaghetti onto my plate, followed by a ladle of sauce and a sprinkle of parmesan cheese. Oakley shreds his own parmesan, swearing by it over the ready-made grated stuff. I can't argue with his results.

"Yeah, I'll come along," he answers. "When, uh...do you think you're gonna find someone?"

I assume he means a guy.

"Not sure," I admit. "Would you help me?"

Oakley coughs around his bite of food. "Help you find a fuck buddy?"

"I guess."

He groans slightly. "I don't know, Law…"

"You don't have to," I tell him seriously. "I'm just asking. I think… I'd like to do it soon. I've waited long enough for answers. It's time I go and find them."

Oakley watches me closely, the blue and brown of his eyes like the earth and sky in one. "All right."

"All right, you'll help? Or just all right?"

"I'll help," he says, twirling spaghetti onto his fork. He shakes his head, letting out a sigh that sounds almost like laughter. "Lord, what am I getting myself into?"

I don't have an answer for him, hardly knowing myself.

But I do know it won't be a mistake, sex with a man. Because one way or another, it'll give me a piece of the puzzle I haven't yet solved.

Chapter 10

OAKLEY

Lawson has a gentle smile on his face as we ride along the trails at the back end of his family's property. He seems at peace.

My head, on the other hand, is a chaotic swirl of emotions I don't know how to begin setting to rights.

Lawson is going to find someone to fuck him. Tonight, if he can. And for some inexplicable reason I still can't identify, I agreed to help.

The man's voice floats over in a murmur. "'All the world is made of faith, and trust, and pixie dust.'"

I turn my gaze Lawson's way. He's squinting against the gentle dappling of light coming through the trees, motes of dust curling in the air in front of him, his hand waving through the specks.

My heart beats wildly at the sight, the memory of a much younger Lawson doing the same an ache in my chest. Lawson has always had a sort of unshakable faith in the world. Not a religious kind. More that he believes people to be good on the whole, and he lives his life trying to prove it. Trust, on the other hand, is a trickier thing.

But he trusts me. Even still. Even after the bumps we've traveled over and all the life we've lived, he trusts me to help him figure out something he doesn't trust a single other soul with.

Faith, trust, and pixie dust. All a person needs to fly.

"Oakley?"

Wendy's voice comes from the front of our little group, and I reorient my gaze, as well as my thoughts, her way. "Yeah?"

"Why didn't you and Stevie work out?"

My chest pangs at her question, but the sensation quickly sloughs off. "Just weren't meant to be, I guess."

"Didn't you love them?"

Well, shit.

I meet Lawson's eye, the man's amused expression telling me I'm on my own with this one. Heaving a breath, I explain as best as I can to a seventeen-year-old who hasn't yet experienced the complexities of romance. "Yeah, I loved them for a long while. But not all love is the same. I thought... I dunno. I guess I thought our love was stable, but that's not always enough in the end."

Lawson grunts.

"What?" I ask, curious about that grunt.

His head shake is a slow thing. "Stable won't ever be enough for you, Oak."

"No?"

"No," he says. "You need fireworks."

My head rocks back at his casually confident assessment. "Not everyone needs fireworks when it comes to a romantic partnership."

"I'm not talking about everyone," he replies, swaying gently in the saddle. "I'm talking about *you*. You're too passionate to settle for stable, and you shouldn't have to. You need someone who's going to light the fuse you have ready and waiting. Someone who's going to make you burn."

Jesus fucking Christ.

"I think burning is an indication of a medical problem," I reply hoarsely.

Lawson chuffs, the sound amused.

Wendy looks pensive.

"What is it, Wen?" I ask.

Her gaze skips to her dad before she faces forward again. "Just wondering."

"About burning? If something burns, go see a doctor."

She shakes her head, and Lawson chuckles.

"Speaking of," I say slowly, "you know you can always talk to us about...stuff, right? Like...if there's ever anything you're unsure of or need advice about?"

Wendy looks over her shoulder again, her eyes moving from me to her dad slowly. "Is he talking about sex?"

Lawson snorts. "I think so."

She glances my way. "My parents already gave me the sex talk. You know, while you were gone."

"Ouch," I deadpan. "Aiming right for the heart, huh?"

Her lips twist into a proud smirk.

Christ, when did Wendy Darling go and grow up?

The three of us ride all the way to the base of the mountains before stopping for lunch. It's a warm day, but the shade from the trees keeps us cool enough as we enjoy the sandwiches Lawson made before we left. Plus some leftover blueberry crisp Ash baked the other day.

Wendy talks a bit about her friends from school and her worry over what will happen once they all graduate. Whether or not they'll stay close.

I don't say it, but the truth is there are a lot of friends we lose throughout our lifetime. Not every person we meet is meant to stick with us. Some friendships only last a season in the grand scheme of time.

But the people who stick? Well, there's a reason for it.

I'd know. Mine is sitting right next to me.

We get back in the saddle after lunch, riding leisurely through the woods along a different trail for a change of scenery. Lawson takes up the helm this time, Wendy beside me. It's startling to see how much she's changed in three years. From a gangly teen to, well, still a teen. But so much more mature than she was when I left.

She looks a lot like Laura. Always has. Her hair is a wavy brown. Her facial features are more petite than Lawson's, with a small chin and eyes more hazel than his whiskey. The stubborn pride in those eyes, however, is certainly a Darling trait.

When we arrive back at the stables, it's late afternoon. We take care of the horses, brushing them down, making sure they have plenty of water, and leaving them in the shade of the barn. Wendy gives both me and her dad a hug before getting in her car to head home. To Laura's.

Lawson watches her go with an expression that causes my gut to pinch.

He stays at the ranch to wash up as I head home, although the plan is for him to join me once he's done. My pulse doesn't settle, not in all the time it takes to arrive home and shower off the day. Not even as I wait for Lawson to show.

I don't know how I'm supposed to be calm when I'm about to help my best friend of over four decades get laid for the first time since his divorce. For all the ways in which we've been close, I've never done *this*. I never had to. Lawson was never promiscuous, never wanted my help finding someone at a college party or even before then, back in high school. When I was testing out the waters, he was content to float at the surface, never dipping his toes in.

But now he wants to dive into the same pool I've been swimming in since my late teens, and I'm supposed to just...ignore that for myself? I'm supposed to ignore the fact that Lawson asked to get intimate with *me*, even though I'm more than certain it would be a catastrophic error on my part to accept his proposal, tempted as I am by the possibility that was never in reach before.

Fuck. I don't know how to do this. How to brush aside what every fiber of my being is telling me it wants. That *want* doesn't give a shit about the repercussions. It's base and instinctual and thinks if I get just one taste—*one taste*—I'll be able to go on my way afterwards, same as before. Yet I know that's not the truth. I'll be changed.

Lawson might think we can weather that sort of shift in our friendship, and maybe he's right that it wouldn't tear us apart. But it would tear *me* apart, at least a little.

Could I accept that damage for him?

The knock on my door is expected, but it ratchets my pulse back up nonetheless. Lawson lets himself in, kicking off his boots, wearing a nice pair of jeans and a button-down as if he's going on a first date.

Jesus. The man is too fucking pure.

"Drink?" I ask him.

He shakes his head. "No, I might have a long drive."

Right. If we find him a guy to hook up with, Lawson will go meet him.

I think I might be sick.

I grab myself a glass of water before joining him at the couch. He has his phone out, the hookup app I told him about downloading.

"I got myself ready," he says off-hand. "I wasn't sure if guys would want to take the time to do that in this sort of situation."

"You..." I have to take a breath and start again. "You prepped yourself?"

"Well, yeah. Laura wasn't a fan of that, so I'd do it myself."

Oh good God.

I've never been a violent person, but I have the sudden and desperate urge to find Laura and shake the woman. Compatible sexually or not, she couldn't see to her husband's own comfort?

"Any man that can't finger you before he dicks you down isn't worth your time, Lawson."

He looks mildly surprised by that statement, eyes holding mine. "Truly?"

"Maybe some people have different opinions about it," I allow. "And sure, some folks may prefer to do the prep themselves. But if your partner isn't willing to make sure it's a comfortable experience for you, find someone who is."

He blinks, clearly thinking that over. "I just figured, being a quick thing and all..."

"A hookup doesn't mean it has to be quick. It sure doesn't have to hurt. You have a right to demand some respect from someone who's about to stick their dick in your body."

"Jesus," he mutters, flushing slightly. "All right."

"Yeah?"

"Yeah," he says, sounding more sure. "So how do I do this?"

Letting out a breath, I help Lawson create an account, and we start perusing men near Darling. I let Lawson take the lead, not sure what he might be looking for. Turns out, I'm not sure he knows either. There's not a single physical type he stops to look at. Instead, he reads the information for each, not deciding based solely on appearances. It's slow going, and I can tell his frustration is mounting.

"How do I choose?" he asks after a good half hour.

"However you'd like," I answer honestly. "You can see who's willing to top."

He nods, worrying at his lip.

"You're not drawn to any of them?" I check, wanting to make sure.

He shakes his head. "Never am."

"But you're sure you want to—"

"Yes, I'm sure," he says, pinning me with a look. "I'm doing this, Oakley. I need to know."

"All right," I mutter, my throat tight as I help him sort through some of the options. "What about this guy? He's not too far away, and he's a top. Online, too."

Lawson hems. "I dunno. I don't get the best vibe from him."

I look over the guy's info again, trying to figure out what's throwing Lawson off. I guess he does sound like a bit of a douche, handsome or not. "Okay, what about this one?" I ask instead. "He seems polite."

Lawson nods slowly. "That could work."

"Yeah? Want to try messaging him?"

"What do I say?"

"That you're looking for someone to fuck you tonight and is he interested?"

"That direct?" Lawson asks, the sweet summer child.

"Yes, that direct."

Chest rising once before falling, Lawson starts a message. My own chest constricts painfully as I watch him assemble words, my gut rolling in a way I try my best to ignore. It's just sex. Just Lawson having sex with a man so he can understand himself better. It doesn't have to be me. He asked me first, but it can be any guy.

It *should* be any other guy.

Fuck. *Fuck, fuck, fuck.*

"Okay," he says, firing off the invite. The man is online, and chat bubbles pop up immediately.

I can't fucking breathe.

I stand up, walking into the kitchen with my empty water glass, just to give myself something to do. Lawson makes a thoughtful sound, and then he's typing again.

Bad idea. It would be a bad, bad idea.

"He's free," Lawson says, sounding relieved.

"'Kay."

"I'm going to meet him at his place."

Breathe, goddamn it. "Text me the address? Just in case."

"Sure."

My phone pings, but I don't check it.

Lawson stands, heading toward the front door. My ears start to ring as he says, "Okay, well... I guess I'll let you know how it goes?"

I nod numbly.

Would it be the worst thing? To fuck him just once? Surely I can remain detached. Surely. And even if not...

Lawson reaches for his boots, and my breath stutters.

Fuck, I can't...

"Stay," I say, my voice coming out much too loud.

Lawson pauses. "Stay?"

I swallow roughly, skirting around the kitchen countertop. "I... I'll do it."

Oh, fuck.

"You'll—"

"I'll fuck you," I confirm. "Call it off. Don't go. Just... Stay."

I never said I was a rational man when it comes to Lawson Darling. I've been his in some form or another my entire life.

Friends seems like an inadequate word for a person you'd travel into literal Hell for.

I just pray the flames don't consume me whole.

Chapter 11

LAWSON

Oakley is staring at me like he's not sure what he just agreed to.

"But you said..."

"I know what I said," he replies, walking a step closer, his hands out like he's trying to calm me. Or maybe he's trying to calm himself. "I changed my mind."

"Why?"

"Does it matter?"

Oakley's eyes travel over my face as I assess him in turn, his breath coming a little short. He looks...upset. Not angry. But ruffled.

"I don't want you to do something you're gonna regret, Oak."

He swipes his hair back, the shake of his head unsettling the strands immediately. "I won't regret it. Can you just...call it off? With the other guy. Please."

I pull out my phone, willing to do that at the very least. I don't know why Oakley is so bothered by the prospect all of a sudden, but I type out a quick apology to cancel and send the message off.

"Done," I tell him, slipping my phone away. "Now can you tell me what has you so rattled?"

He looks like he'd rather do anything else, but he inhales shakily and nods. "I never said I didn't *want* to have sex with you, Law."

I still, those words not what I was expecting. "You do want to?"

He groans. "It's not like I ever thought much about it before, all right? You're my friend. Sex with you wasn't on my mind. But...*fuck*. The idea isn't unappealing, and the thing is I *know* I'd treat you right. Those other guys... I just... You're safer with me."

I don't argue that. It's why I wanted it to be Oakley in the first place.

"So if you're dead set on trying this," he goes on, steeling himself, "then I'll do it."

"You're not worried about it making things messy between us? You were before."

He tosses his hands in the air. "It might. But we've made it this far, haven't we? There's nothing that would stop me from being your friend. I'm sure of it."

"So...if I walked into your bedroom right now and dropped my pants?"

His groan this time is loud, his hands on his knees before he stands upright again. "Fuck, I never expected to hear that outta your mouth. Then I'd get you ready, Law. And, yes, I'd stick my dick in you."

"Respectfully," I clarify after his speech earlier.

His lips twitch into a smile, transforming his expression into the amused one I'm so used to seeing on him. "You're giving me shit right now, really?"

I shrug. "You're sure about this?"

"I'm sure about you," he counters. "So yes."

Not about to look a gift horse in the mouth, I nod and head toward Oakley's room. I can hear his exhale as I turn the corner into the hall, but he doesn't immediately follow. I give him time as I step into his familiar bedroom, the walls a light blue, some sun slanting in through the window but the angle such that it's dimmer in here than most of the rest of the house.

Dropping my pants feels natural. How many times have I changed around Oakley, after all? My underwear and socks quickly follow, and I shuffle all the articles of clothing off to the side of the room, where they'll be out of the way. I unbutton my shirt next, my hands calm, my mind feeling the same as I drop the material on the pile.

Naked, I kneel in front of Oakley's bed, spread my knees wide, and lean my chest against his mattress.

Footsteps approach from behind me before Oakley inhales a sharp breath, a thump following like maybe his hand catching the wooden doorframe. A series of quiet curses leaves his lips, and I can't help but wonder what he's seeing.

A naked man waiting at the side of his bed? Someone to enjoy a brief moment of pleasure with? His friend?

I keep my head rested on my arms, my heart thumping as I wait for him to either come closer or decide this isn't what he wants after all. He steps further into the room, a drawer opening off to my right. The rustle of clothing follows, and I realize he's getting undressed.

A frisson of excitement and anticipation rolls through me, and I let out a slow breath.

Oakley kneels behind me, settling between my legs, his proximity impossible to miss. For a moment, I feel charged, the air between us thick like those storms that hit in the fall. When static causes your hair to stand on end and you can practically hear the impending thunder.

Oakley lets out a breath that floats over my shoulder like wind, his voice coming husky. "Do you wanna be touched?"

"Isn't that a given?"

His laugh is a short thing. "What I mean is... Can I touch you in places other than your dick and asshole?"

"Do what you want with me, Oak."

"Jesus."

A warm hand skates down between my shoulder blades, pressure gentle along my spine. I shiver at the feel of callused fingertips dragging over my skin, Oakley's touch rougher than the one I experienced before him. Those fingertips travel upwards again, mapping one shoulder and then the next.

This time, when they travel downwards, they don't stop at the base of my spine. Two hands glide over my ass cheeks, down the backs of my thighs, up again. Around my hips, to my lower abdomen, pausing at the base of my cock.

"You're not hard," Oakley observes, one hand ringing me as the other skates down the front of my thigh.

"I'll get hard when you touch me," I assure him.

As if testing that theory, Oakley works the base of my dick. An exhale puffs from my lungs, my body reacting as his hand slides over me, the dry touch gentle. The tightening in my groin is a familiar pressure, but the sensation of Oakley's hand is entirely new. He strokes me more firmly as I harden, his thumb rolling over the top of my dick in a caress that has me grunting.

"Feel good?" he checks.

"Horrible," I deadpan.

Oakley squeezes my dick lightly in reprimand, his touch sliding back over my hip again, fingers trailing down between my ass cheeks. "You'll be honest if anything feels wrong?"

"I will," I promise. "But it doesn't."

That seems to reassure him because I hear the pop of a lube cap. Wet fingers brush over my hole, and I ease back against them, my eyes slipping shut. Apart from my own fingers, it's been *so* long since I've had this. Two years since the last time I had sex? Longer? I can't even remember, and the anticipation now is lightning in my veins, no longer a low rumble of thunder.

"Oak," I plead, not wanting teasing right now.

He curses again, a finger pressing inside of me.

I roll my face into the cradle of my arms, muffling my moan against Oakley's comforter. *This.* This has always been my favorite part about sex. Having something inside of me. Laura only ever used the strap-on, nothing else. And even that wasn't often. Oakley's finger is so much warmer, so much more *real*.

Oakley's hand soothes down my side, almost like he's petting the flank of a horse, his finger easing out and back in again. "All right?"

"Oak. Stop treating me like a damn virgin and rub my prostate already."

"Fucking Christ," he mutters, a mix of humor and...something else in his voice. He slides his finger in again with intent, and my toes curl against air.

"*Fuck.*"

"You're swearing," he says, sounding awed.

"Yeah, well, feels good. Again."

Oakley's breath puffs from him, his hand gripping my hip as he sets a pace with his finger that has electricity licking over every inch of my skin. The intentional rub of that digit inside of me, the way Oakley knows how to glide along those sensitive nerves I've only been able to coax to life with my own fingers prior to now. It's so much better having someone else do it. He was right about the merits of that.

Oakley's finger slips out, a beat passing before there's more pressure and then two. The stretch is blissful, an ache that's like a damn tension release for every muscle in my body.

"Jesus," Oakley murmurs, a sort of wonder in his voice as he slips those fingers in deep. "You really do like this, huh."

"Told you," I manage, gripping the comforter to hold back my groan, every other piece of me languid and relaxed, even as it feels like sparks are setting off across my skin. Like the hop, skip, and jump of a pixie's feet.

The scraping of stubble over my shoulder blade nearly has me jumping, the sensation far more vivid and real than my imagination. Oakley does it again, a kiss almost but not, his short beard hairs bristling a path along the top of my back. He leans over me, his fingers still working inside my ass, something else entirely settling against my ass cheek.

"Feel that?" he rumbles.

My breath leaves me on a pant.

"You still want that inside of you?"

"I do," I tell him. More than anything.

Oakley's fingers leave me again, what must be three entering me this time. He fucks me with them rougher than before, my gut tightening as he does it again and again, his hand at the base of those fingers a pressure against the outside of my hole every time he sinks deep. I get caught up in the feel of it, more arousing than it has any right to be.

Oakley's hand is wandering again, the one not finger-fucking me slipping around to my stomach, the span of his grip wide. My cock is rock-hard now, rubbing against the comforter at the side of the bed.

"Oak," I say hoarsely, my throat dry. "Respectfully... Get your dick inside of me already. I'm dying here."

He huffs a short breath. "Bossy and to the point. Don't know why I expected anything less."

His fingers slip out of me, the man himself retreating. There's the unmistakable crinkle of a condom wrapper, and part of me is desperately curious to sneak a peek. Apart from that single instance when we were teens, I haven't seen Oakley's cock hard. Only soft. But I don't crane my head around to look, wanting to respect Oakley's wishes to keep this as uncomplicated as possible. Surely it'll be easier for him with me facing away.

His hand settles on my hip again, touch roaming over the side of my ass as his knees press against the insides of my calves. I resituate myself an inch, getting more comfortable, that heady anticipation back in full force as Oakley gets ready to fill my ass.

Just the thought of it has my body in flames.

The blunt head of his dick presses against me, his hand holding steady to my hip now. "Bear down."

At the gentle suggestion, I do, canting my hips back to meet him. The first inch of his cock has me hiccupping a breath. My lungs don't seem to want to cooperate, the glide smooth as he inches inside of me in increments but the newness of it absolutely astounding in its impact.

When Oakley pauses, as if gauging my reaction, I don't let him slow. I reach back, finding first his arm and then a hipbone, and I tug with all my might. Muscles flex beneath my fingertips as Oakley follows my draw, sinking forward until his hips meet my ass, the fullness sudden and profound. He leans over me again, his hands planting on the comforter, his chest lining my back and his cock kicking inside of me as if excited.

So real. So, so different.

"Okay?" he asks.

I nod, and Oakley's stubble presses to my shoulder again, a panting breath leaving him before he draws his hips back and fucks me just like I asked him to.

A tear slips out of my eye, hidden away by the comforter. My muscles feel like jelly as Oakley rolls his hips time and again, the drag of his cock inside of me too fucking good to even put words to. He doesn't say a single word himself, tension radiating from him in a way that doesn't feel negative but rather like a spring coiled tight, ready to unload. His own breath catches as his hips slap my ass, that outside pressure there again, like a reminder he's as deep as he can go, but he's still going to damn well try to get deeper.

Every single thing about this moment is crystal clear. The bristling of his chest hair and that rough stubble against my skin. His hand fisted against the mattress just in my line of sight, the muscles in his forearm straining. The breath I can feel along the back of my neck and the oh-so-real cock tunneling inside of me, warm and hard and feeling as if it were made just for me. To bring me pleasure. A key for a lock, the click of it like clarity after a lifelong storm.

"Law, I—"

"Yeah," I assure him, understanding instantly the worry in his voice. "It's real fucking good. Don't stop what you're doing."

"There you go again," he says, his words panted out around his breaths. "Swearing."

"Fuck," I say again, knowing he'll appreciate it.

His answering chuckle is raspy, his head settling beside my own in a way that feels more intimate than anything else we're doing. I can hear every hitch of his breath and the grunting moans he's trying hard to keep quiet. But not quiet enough. They're masculine, familiar even, although new in this context.

I don't know how to tell him—*if* I should tell him—it's the sexiest thing I think I've ever heard.

His cock is filling me to the brim, stretching me, every inch of me touched, every nerve ending sparking and a desperation eating at the edges of my mind I've never felt before. It's not the urge to finish but the fear I might never have this again.

Oakley doesn't slow, his body fitting to mine in a way that feels utterly right, for once *right* and so fucking blissful I want to weep with it. I'm fighting a losing battle. I know I am. There's no cajoling needed for my body to ride the razor's edge. I'm there already, and I'm going to fall whether or not I want to. Even if I don't want to.

I slip my hand down between me and the bed, aiming for my cock, but Oakley beats me to it, his warm fist wrapping around me, slick still from lube.

"If you needa come, you tell me," he demands, stroking me in time to the thrust of his hips. "You let me take care of you."

I don't have a single argument against that, and when Oakley changes the angle of his hips, I cry out, realizing he was holding back before. The new glide has him driving against my prostate with ruthless intent, and there's not a thing I can do but clamp down on his dick as every single muscle in my body tenses to the point of pleasured pain.

I've had orgasms before. Of course I have. By my own hand or with my ex-wife.

But not a one of them robbed me of breath the way this one does. It doesn't end, Oakley's cock making it go on and on, my body shaking with it, my knees losing purchase on the ground. Oakley's grip keeps me steady, his arm around my waist, his other hand jerking me off against his comforter until I'm fairly certain I can't keep coming and survive.

He gentles his grip when I let out a weak protest, the man himself jolting against me as he fills the condom. His stubble bristles my shoulder again, his breath hot on my skin, his stuttered inhalation barely reaching my ears over the pounding of my pulse.

We stay that way, neither of us moving except for the heaving of our chests, Oakley's hand still loosely cradling my cock and his body surrounding mine like a cocoon.

His voice comes after long minutes, rough and questioning. "Okay?"

My lips press tightly together, my eyes stinging even as I try my best to blink away the impending tears.

Am I?

"No."

Chapter 12

Oakley

I freeze the moment the word leaves Lawson's mouth. *No.*

"Law..."

"Don't move," he says before I can do just that. "I just..." He pulls in a breath, the wobble in his voice ratcheting my alarm. "I... I don't think I'm bi, Oak."

The vise that tightens around my chest is instantaneous, remorse following like a slap to my entire being. The cloud I'd been floating on disperses into nothingness, and I'm left falling from a great height. I shift backwards, readying myself to apologize, to ask if he's okay, if I hurt him, if he needs space, if there's anything I can do.

But Lawson grabs my hip, much as he did earlier, keeping me as close as he can. "Oak. Please."

God.

My cock slips from Lawson's body, but I don't try another retreat. "Are you all right? Fuck, Law. I'm so—"

My *sorry* never makes it past my lips, Lawson's own words interrupting me. "I'm...gay."

I still, wondering if I heard him right. "What?"

"I'm not bisexual," he says, a hitch in his voice, even as he sounds more certain than before. "Not straight, either."

"Are... I mean, are you sure?"

His chuckle is hollow, the shake of it like a small tremor. "I'm pretty damn sure, Oak. I don't even know how to explain it. I just..." There's a pause, achingly long, before he says, "Imagine you've been given the same ice cream all your life. You're told it's ice cream, and you have no reason to doubt that's the truth. But then, one day, someone gives you a kind you've never had before. It's full-fat and tastes completely different, and you realize all this time you've been eating frozen yogurt. And this, *this*, is ice cream. The real deal. You're sure of it."

Lawson lets out a heaving breath, his back warm where I'm pressed against him. I don't interrupt, even as my mind reels.

"I didn't know," he continues, a sort of pain in his voice I wish I could erase. "I didn't know because...I never wanted a guy like this. I had Laura, and I thought I found what everyone talked about when they spoke of romance and a perfect match. But it wasn't right. Not for me. It wasn't...*this*."

Lawson turns his face enough for me to get a glimpse of his eyes, tears lining the brown.

"Fuck," he says with feeling. "I'm gay, Oak."

I press my face to the back of Lawson's neck, my arms snaking underneath his chest so I can hold him in a hug, trembling as it is. Every piece of me, trembling. "Law."

"I know," he says, his voice hitching again. "Believe me, I know."

Over twenty years. So much time he spent with Laura. In her bed. Making a life with her out of a sense of loyalty, even if it never fulfilled Lawson's own needs. He stuck with it because he never knew anything else. Until he did. Until he realized he wasn't happy. Until he couldn't keep with it any longer.

"I didn't know," he says again. "Because I don't think attraction works for me the way it works for most folks."

I nod against him, inhaling a slow, slow breath, neither of us having moved an inch from our spots kneeling on the floor.

"But I know what that was," he goes on roughly. "That was ice cream."

Despite it all, I huff a pained laugh, my chest so tight it feels as if it might snap. "God, Law. I'm *so* sorry. But I'm glad, at least, that you figured it out."

"Thanks to you."

My swallow is heavy. "It was never like that with Laura?"

"No," he says without hesitation. "It wasn't. Not even close."

I nod again, loath to let go of the man but knowing we can't stay like this forever. "Should we get cleaned up? Or do you need another minute?"

He sighs, his back bowing beneath me. "Let's clean up."

It takes some effort to disentangle and stand, my knees protesting the rough surface they were on while I fucked Lawson. I try not to think about that right now. Instead, I swipe off the condom and hold a hand Lawson's way, helping him to stand with his own wince and grunt. Heading to the bathroom, I toss the condom and turn the shower on, not surprised when Lawson walks right in, naked as the day he was born.

I *am* surprised when his hand snakes out from behind the curtain before I can exit the room, halting my momentum. "Where are you going?"

"Uh. Figured I'd let you shower first."

He makes a sound of impatience, giving me a firm tug. Feeling a bit like I'm dreaming, I step in beside my friend, his body already wet. There's cum on his stomach that he drags a hand over, his cock hanging softly and the man himself utterly unperturbed by sharing a shower. As if that's something we do. As if *any* of this is normal.

My heart pounds heavily as I watch him soap off. There's a realness to Lawson's body I appreciate, time having softened his edges some, a lack of vanity or self-consciousness leaving him unbothered by my gaze yet entirely unaware of the effect he has on me. His eyes flit to mine for a second before sliding down to a new set of bruises on the side of my abdomen.

He winces slightly. "What happened there?"

"The usual. Bumped up a bit during a round-up."

His fingers skate over the spot, and my stomach muscles jump. It's such a soft touch, so instinctual, not sexual, not suggestive, just...Lawson.

I clear the tightness from my throat, although my voice still comes out hoarse. "Are you all right?"

He nods, his touch flitting away. Lawson finishes rinsing under the showerhead before stepping aside in a clear invitation for me to take his place. "Feeling foolish, mostly. That I didn't know this about myself. How couldn't I have known, Oak?"

"Like you said, you'd only tried frozen yogurt."

His expression is grudgingly amused. It shifts, however, to a sort of melancholy that makes my chest ache.

Lawson steps out of the shower ahead of me, grabbing a towel from the bar. I hastily finish rinsing off before following after him. He's quiet all the way back to my room, the towel wrapped around his waist as he sits at the edge of my bed, only a couple feet away from the mess I'll need to clean up later.

I sit beside him, damp hair dripping down my neck. "Do you wanna talk about it?"

"We just did."

It's all I can do not to flick the man's forehead.

"Sure," I say slowly. "But maybe it'd help to air whatever you're feeling? To work through it all. With me or...even a professional."

He's silent for a beat. "You think me figuring out I'm gay after having been married to a woman most of my life is going to lead to an emotional fallout."

Christ, this man.

"Maybe?" I admit. "I don't know. This can't be easy for you."

"It's not, and it is," he says, leaning forward, his elbows on his knees. I have the urge to card my fingers through his hair but hold myself back. "I don't like realizing I should have listened harder to that *not right* feeling when it came to intimacy with Laura. But... It's hard to describe. I didn't hate it at the time, at least not in the beginning. It just wasn't...much of anything. And I thought that meant it was a *me* problem. Like maybe sex for me wasn't a big deal."

He blows out a breath, lost in thought for a moment.

"But knowing what I do now...that sex can feel like that? Natural and *right*? Damn it, Oakley. It's like this door is opened up I never even saw before. I'm *relieved*. Because I finally have answers to some of those questions I've been asking myself for so very long. Thank you for giving me that."

I nod, all I can do.

Lawson lets out another breath, shifting back to rest his elbows on the bed. It's a battle not to trace his skin with my gaze. Not to let my eyes wander down to the towel wrapped so precariously around his hips. "Maybe I should talk to someone," he says at last. "But... I don't want to think about any of it right now." His head rolls in my direction, gaze intent in a way that has my pulse jumping. "Can I try something?"

"I... Sure?"

Lawson leans toward me, tugging the end of my towel loose. My heart races, my mouth running dry as Lawson stares down at my dick. It twitches to life, and he sucks in a shallow breath, his fingers skating over the length of it before wrapping around me in a loose fist.

Ah, fuck. Fuck, fuck, fuck.

"Law?" I ask, my voice garbled.

He pumps me once, twice, seemingly transfixed by the motion of his hand on my dick. "Maybe it's selfish to ask," he finally says, thumb rolling over my crown. "But *fuck*, Oak. Make me feel that again?"

I squeeze my eyes shut, all of my baser instincts battling with the rationale I'm trying so desperately to hold on to. It was supposed to be one time. *One time.*

But how can I possibly tell this man no? How can I walk away when he's asking me to make him feel good?

Lawson lets go of my dick, scooting back onto the bed and lying down. He holds my eye as he drags his towel off his hips, gifting me with a view of his soft cock before he's rolling onto his stomach, his ass offered in clear invitation. I damn near swallow my tongue.

My hand moves as if it has a mind of its own, skating along Lawson's backside, over warm skin that's not quite rough but not perfectly smooth, either. Lawson cants his hips up, an anticipatory catch in his breath as he spreads his legs wider.

"You're not too sore?" I ask, my words coming out as if dragged across hot coals.

"Not at all."

I ease out a breath, knowing there's no way I'm going to refuse this man. Shifting, I grab the lube resting beside my pillow and oil up my fingers. My heart feels as if it might just run off.

Lawson draws his leg upwards as I settle behind him, opening himself up for me. The first touch of my fingers has him sighing in relief. I run dry knuckles featherlight across his skin, waking up nerve endings before I trail oil-wet fingers over and around his hole. One slips inside of him easily, the man still relaxed from earlier and eager, apparently, for more.

"You like this?" I ask, knowing he never had another's hand inside him before today.

"I do. You don't mind it?"

"I like it quite a lot," I tell him truthfully, adding another finger and working him open. "Knowing I'm making someone feel good? I could keep at it all day."

"Really," Lawson says, sounding almost contemplative. "Well, I won't stop you."

I huff a laugh, leaning down to scrape my stubble across Lawson's ass cheek. He jolts beneath me before sagging again.

"I think I get it now," he says somewhat breathily.

"What's that?"

"The, uh...beard burn thing."

A smile quirks my lips. "Mhm."

"Another finger?"

I oblige, slipping three in, the accommodation of Lawson's body captivating to see. His cock is plumping now, the base of it visible at this angle. It's strangely heady to know that, for Lawson, arousal is more a choice than anything. And he chose me.

"Oak. Your cock."

"Demanding, aren't you?" I mutter, playing with his prostate for a moment just to see him sink into the bedding.

"You can... spend an hour fucking me if you... feel like taking your time. But enough... of the teasing."

I slip away from Lawson to grab a condom, the man watching me pass by. His eyes home in on my dick, and *Christ*. That look in his eye. Like he's desperate for it.

The mattress depresses as I climb back on, settling between his legs. I roll on the condom, my cock rock-hard, lube wetting the surface as I run a fist over myself to spread the moisture. I sink lower and line up, a single second stretching into a lifetime as I catch Lawson's eye. He doesn't hold my gaze, instead turning his face into the comforter, but the noise he lets out as I press inside of him is one I'm not sure I'll ever forget.

"This better?" I ask him, sinking deep, meeting his ass with my hips and holding there.

My friend of forty-three years huffs a breath and says, "You want a gold star? Earn it."

Jesus goddamn Christ.

"You might regret saying that."

"I don't think I will," he murmurs, shifting his hips enough to grind back on me. "C'mon. Fuck me."

"All right, princess. Hold on to something."

"Princess?" he asks, looking back at me. His cheeks are red, and my heart stutters at the sight.

"Yeah," I say roughly. "You want me to pamper you, isn't that right? You wanna feel good? Grab that pillow right there and settle in. I'm just getting started."

Lawson blinks owl-round eyes at me, his mouth parted, the *want* clear on his face. Ever so slowly, he reaches up to grab a pillow from the top of the bed. The moment he's comfortable, arms wrapped around it and cheek resting on top, I pull my hips back and thrust in deep.

We groan in tandem, and I don't hold back. I fuck into him hard for long minutes, my body bowed over his, Lawson panting against the pillow as I find spots on his skin to abrade. His shoulders, his neck, the tender spot behind his ear. I drag my lips everywhere I can over warm skin and muscle, the urge to latch on to this man and never let go hard to resist.

When Lawson gets close, I ease him back down, fucking him slowly, grinding against him with my hand holding tight to his thigh. I half expect him to demand I make him come already, but he doesn't. He lies there, blissed out, looking so damn content I can feel myself slipping.

It'll be a long way to fall if I do.

So I don't.

I remind myself of what this is and pick up the pace again. Every time Lawson sounds a hair's breadth away from orgasm, I slow back down. Sweat starts to gleam on his skin. My own, too. I run my hand and lips over his body wherever I can reach, holding his leg wide open. Leaving pink patches over the sun-tanned skin of his shoulders. Looping my arm under his chest for better purchase and *grinding, grinding, grinding* until he starts clamping down on my dick.

I don't want it to end. And it takes me a while to realize why that is.

Because there wasn't supposed to be a second time. And there may not ever be a third.

It takes near an hour for Lawson to break. "Oak," he croaks out, the pleading in his voice unmistakable.

"Needa come, princess?"

In answer, he grabs my hand off his leg and shoves it down between him and the bed. I take the blatant hint and wrap my fingers around his cock. It doesn't take any time at all after being edged for so long. Lawson starts clamping down on my dick, I stroke him once, twice, and he flies.

I tuck my face against Lawson's shoulder as I join him in the clouds. His cries of pleasure burrow somewhere deep inside of me, the ecstasy in the sound, the relief and aching joy, a confirmation to those suspicions I boxed up and buried so long ago.

The sun is low in the sky now, slanting through the window in streaks of dimly lit gold. It brings to mind summers long past and two kids chasing pixie dust under the shade of a willow.

Except this, right here, isn't pretend. It's not make-believe.

No, my feelings for my friend are starkly, painfully real.

Chapter 13

LAWSON

The Silkies in the petting farm wander around my feet, their feathered heads bobbing as they pick up seed scattered on the ground. They remind me of dandelion fluff. Like one good wind could scatter them all away.

"Law?"

Looking up, I find my brother Remi approaching from the direction of the small petting farm barn. He lifts his hands once he has my attention, the processor for his CI absent from behind his ear. *'You doing all right?'*

'Why does everyone keep asking me that?' I sign back, my arms feeling heavy.

Remi lifts an eyebrow. *'Probably because half the time we see you lately, you're staring off into space. Something on your mind?'*

I let loose a breath as Remi joins me on the small bench I'm sitting on. Snickerdoodle the pony comes trotting over, and a couple of the chickens scatter, disgruntled clucks accompanying their retreat. Snickerdoodle drops her head right in Remi's lap, and he dutifully supplies her with affection.

'Can I ask you something?'

'Of course,' Remi replies before going back to petting the pony.

I don't know the best way to approach this, so I just jump in. *'Are you familiar with asexuality?'*

One of Remi's eyebrows subtly lifts again, but I can tell he's trying to hold back his surprise. *'I think I have a pretty good understanding of the nuances, yeah.'*

It doesn't surprise me considering Remi is the youngest of us at twenty-nine now. When I was a kid, folks didn't talk about this stuff. My parents were always open with us, always encouraging and inclusive. But even they didn't mention the possibility of being ace. Heck, I don't think half the terms I read about were even in use a few decades back.

It's different now. Our language is evolving, as well as our understanding of a good many things, and maybe I should have done a better job myself of staying on top of that. If not for my own benefit and knowledge, then for Wendy's sake.

But the simple truth is I never considered I might be ace. It hadn't occurred to me because, until recently, I didn't even know the way I felt about people wasn't the *typical* experience. Although—should I even call it that? Who's to say what's typical when we're all so dang different to begin with?

Blowing out a breath, I face my brother. *'Can you help me understand it? What it means to be ace?'*

'Of course,' Remi answers, a thoughtful expression on his face. His hands move the same way, softly. Thoughtfully. *'It's a varied spectrum, but generally, someone who's ace experiences a lack of sexual attraction in one way or another.'*

'But that doesn't mean they don't have sex?' I ask, Oakley having said as much.

'That's true.' Remi pauses, his hand smoothing over Snickerdoodle's neck before he goes on. *'Most people, regardless of their sexuality, fall into one of three categories at any given time. Or they fit somewhere in between. They might be sex-averse, meaning they don't like sex or the idea of sex, and they may even find it repulsive. They might be sex-neutral, meaning they don't have strong feelings about sex any which way and may partake in it. Or they might be sex-favorable, meaning they like the idea of sex, enjoy it for themselves, and may seek to participate in it. I think the biggest misconception when it comes to ace folks is that they're all sex-averse.'*

'And that's not true.'

Remi pinches his fingers in a *no*. *'Definitely not. Someone who's allosexual experiences sexual attraction toward others. That doesn't mean they're going to sleep with every person that turns them on. There are so many other factors that weigh on those choices, same as with ace folks.'*

'I think what I'm not getting is... How do you know if you're ace?'

His smile is soft. *'I think that's the tricky part for a lot of people. And why there's so much gray area. Some would say sexual attraction means physical response, right? So your body reacts to a person. You get turned on, hard, wet, tingly, whatever.'*

Remi laughs at the grimace on my face, smacking my shoulder before going on.

'Others would say sexual attraction is less quantifiable than that, but rather knowing you want intimacy with that person in that way.'

I lift my hands, pausing, and Remi waits patiently, his fingers carding through Snickerdoodle's long mane of tangled hair. The pony's eyes are closed, her head still resting on Remi's lap.

Finally, I sign, *'You're saying desire can be as much mental as it is physical.'*

'For some people, I think the answer would be yes. So, on one end of the ace spectrum, you have people who never experience that. No active desire for others. There's demisexuality, in which people only experience that desire after a connection has been formed. There's aegosexuality, where folks do experience sexual attraction yet don't want to actually have sex with the person. And there's a whole gray area of gray-ace individuals whose experiences aren't always easily defined. Maybe they do feel sexual attraction with a limited number of people or in certain circumstances, but they still identify more strongly with the ace side of things than the allo. Not to mention ace-flux folks whose sexuality is more fluid, or any number of other labels.'

'That's...a lot,' I manage a little stiltedly.

Remi huffs a laugh. *'It is. Do you think you might be ace? I assume you're not asking about this for a friend.'*

I scrub a hand over my face, not even knowing where to start. *'I honestly don't know,'* I tell my brother. *'It occurred to me recently that I don't view people the same way I assumed everyone does. There's no...spark like that. Not for anyone. But I do like sex. Always have in theory. With Laura, it was just...'*

I cut off, realizing how much I'd been about to divulge. But Remi's considerate expression and his nod of encouragement have me going on.

'It was mechanical. Not...passionate.'

'Have you had sex since her?' he asks, motions fluid if not purposefully calm.

I nod.

'And was it different? Better for you?'

'It was,' I admit, memories of Oakley and me in his bed surfacing. How instinctual sex with him was. How damn *good*. *'It was what I always suspected it could be, Remi.'* Blowing out a breath, I look my baby brother in the eye and share the news I'm still coming to terms with myself. *'Turns out I'm gay.'*

There's a beat where my brother doesn't respond, simply stares at me as my words sink in. And then his expression crumples, the same pity I saw on Oakley's face overtaking his.

"Law," he says, voice clogged with emotion as he tugs me in. His arms are like steel bands around me, and despite my best efforts, my throat catches. "I'm so sorry."

Not for being gay, I know that. He's telling me he's sorry for *before*. And I am, too. I wish I'd known sooner, not that I can change the past. But I spent a long damn time married to someone who was only a friend. And by the end, we weren't even that.

I never loved Laura the way she loved me. And maybe that's not my fault; maybe partly it is. But I *am* sorry for how long we spent trying to fix something that started out broke, only to lose what little love we had left for one another.

I'd never undo Wendy, not even if I could go back. But maybe Laura and I could have split before things became so tense. Back before we were making concessions neither of us should have had to.

Remi rubs my back, my brother comforting me in a way I'm not sure I was ready to accept before now. He only pulls away when Snickerdoodle reinserts her head between us, the pony upset about being ignored. Remi's eyes stay locked on mine.

'I'm okay,' I tell him, which is mostly true. I know Oakley is concerned about the repercussions of a revelation like that on my emotional state, but the truth is I've had about as much sadness as I can handle. I don't want to be sad anymore. I want to move past it. And I'm determined to do so. But Remi, too, looks concerned, so I go on. *'It was a surprise, but I'm grateful to know. To have figured it out. I think it took so long because...'*

'Because you're ace?'

'Might be.'

He nods, his hand squeezing my arm, his other on Snickerdoodle's head before he asks, *'Do you want my thoughts?'*

'Couldn't hurt. I'm having a hell of a time trying to make sense of it all.'

His smile is understanding. *'You mentioned a person's physical appearance doesn't draw you in. So let's assume, for a minute, you do fall on the ace spectrum. I think the question to ask yourself is... Has there ever been someone you've wanted to have sex with because it's them, not because they're an easy or convenient choice to get off with?'*

He gives me a moment to think that over before he lifts his hands again.

'If the answer is yes, that might be sexual attraction for you. There's no one right answer when it comes to figuring out your sexuality, Law. It's whatever feels right for you.'

I give my brother a slow nod. I suppose that's the question, isn't it?

Is Oakley an easy choice?

Or do I want him?

Not just a man but *him* specifically?

A few of the Silkies cluck as Snickerdoodle's tail swishes their way, the chickens avoiding her rear end as they scavenge for feed. It's early enough in the day that no visitors are here, the petting farm empty apart from me, Remi, and the animals.

Oakley asked why I'm still living here when I like my quiet. Moments like this sure don't hurt. When the ranch is barely awake, and I can sit in peace with my thoughts or even one of my family members. Maybe I never wanted to be a rancher myself, but I don't hate this place. Far from it.

Is it where I want to be indefinitely? No.

But where else am I supposed to go? I don't want to build a home for one.

'Thanks, Remi,' I finally sign. *'You've given me a lot to think about. In a good way.'*

My brother nods, one hand on Snickerdoodle as he answers, *'Anytime.'*

Remi goes back to his work eventually, but I sit for a while longer amongst the chickens. A minute later, the goats come racing out of the barn, Remi having set the lot loose. They make a ruckus, one jumping up onto the bench next to me, another trying to engage a now-disgruntled Snickerdoodle who doesn't want a thing to do with the dancing goat.

I look west, toward the ranch house and the mountains beyond it.

Part of me wonders if I should try dating again. Now that I know the potential is there with men, do I want to find someone for myself? Someone I could start over with. Or, maybe more appropriately, move forward with.

Do I want a partner in life? A romantic relationship?

I'm almost afraid to hope for it.

For now, I have my best friend. I think that's more than enough.

Chapter 14

OAKLEY

I wander the garden supply section of the local flower shop where my mom used to work, not seeing much of anything. My mind is otherwise occupied.

Which is why it takes me a second to realize the voice I'm hearing is directed at me.

"That you, Oakley? I heard you were back in town."

Turning, I find Virginia giving me a curious smile from behind an armful of plants. In addition to being a well-loved bartender here in Darling, Virginia and I grew up next to one another. We were never particularly close, considering I'm a good seven years older, but her face will always be a familiar one to me. "Hey, Virginia. How's it going?"

"Just fine," she answers, shifting the hanging basket in her hands to her side. "You doing all right? You look a little lost."

"Oh, no, I'm good. I remember where everything's at. Thank you, though."

She raises an eyebrow. "I wasn't talking about the store."

Christ, am I that transparent?

Seeing as I'm not about to tell Virginia about my double-romp with my best friend, a man who thought he was straight until recently, I deflect. "Those for your place?"

She twirls the basket of petunias in her hand. "Sure are. The flowers I bought earlier in the summer died. Truth be told, I don't expect these ones to last long, either. Not all of us can have a green thumb like your mom."

I huff a small laugh. "And your parents? They doing all right?"

"They're fine. You're deflecting."

Well, shit.

Virginia snorts, her hazel eyes bright. "You don't gotta tell me, Oakley. I won't pry. Sure bet Lawson is glad to have you back, though."

My swallow is rough.

Virginia doesn't wait for a response before going on. "See ya around?"

I nod. "I'll stop by The Barrel soon. It's been a while."

"First drink's on me. Have a good one, Oakley."

Virginia heads off to pay for her plants, and I wander over to the nursery. Rows and rows of flora are set atop tables or hanging from beams overhead. Small transplant pots are full of brightly colored flowers, herbs, anything and everything a person could want to fill their garden with. Hanging baskets like the one Virginia grabbed are mixed with collections of annuals or holding indoor plants like spider ivy or pothos. The air is humid, the smell of potting soil and fertilizer heavy.

Picking a small pot of rosemary, one of thyme, and one of basil, I head back into the main part of the store where I saw windowsill planters. I bring my collection to the checkout, making it outside after a good fifteen-minute conversation with Ms. Newton, one of my mom's friends from the many years they worked together.

The sun is scorching today, my truck's AC barely managing to keep up with the heat on the short drive home. Once inside, I unlock the back door, not surprised to hear Bell wandering in a minute later, her hooves clomping down the hall.

"I swear to God, Belladonna, you find your way up onto the counter to eat these herbs, and I'm making rosemary steak tonight."

My cow sticks her wet nose against the back of my knee. I jolt, glaring at her deceptively cute face.

"That was rude," I tell her.

One black ear twitches as Bell sniffs the air before heading off, finding a spot to lie down in the living room. Luckily, she doesn't try the couch, knowing it's not allowed. I have to draw the line somewhere.

As my miniature cow dozes, I set about moving my tiny herb collection from their pots into the narrow planter that's a near perfect fit for the windowsill above the sink. Dirt gets spread across the countertop as I work, just as much of it beneath my fingernails. The AC in the house is on, but I'm still sweating despite my shorts and the ceiling fan running overhead. Montana doesn't get as hot as some places, but it's plenty hot for me this time of year.

As I'm setting the planter onto the windowsill, the green giving the space a nice pop of color, there's a knock followed by my front door opening. My lips twitch into a smile. I don't even have to look over to know it's Lawson. The man has never had any compunction about barging into my space at any and all hours.

"You hoping for dinner?" I ask, hearing boots hit the mat. "'Cause if so, you're in for a wait. I haven't even started it yet."

Lawson doesn't say anything, just pads into the kitchen. When I hear a zipper, I turn.

And then I'm fairly certain I die just a little.

Lawson shoves his jeans and underwear down to his feet, sets a condom on the countertop, braces his elbows against the surface, and looks over at me expectantly.

"The fuck?" I croak, my heart beating like a drum.

"Please?" is all he says.

My breath whooshes from me, my dirt-covered hands suspended midair, my brain not at all caught up to what's happening. But Lawson bends a little lower, his back arching, and *holy fucking shit.*

"Is... Are..."

No, my mouth doesn't want to work either.

Lawson's eyes search mine, the man utterly unabashed about dropping his pants in proposition inside my kitchen. "Please, Oak? I just need..." He makes a frustrated sound. "I just *need.*"

"My hands," I say, a weak protest.

Lawson, seeing that as a problem easily solved, unbends enough to grab me by the waistband and tug me closer. He unzips my shorts, and, not finding a single complaint on my tongue, guides his hand inside to pull out my cock. My briefs fall with my shorts to the floor as Lawson strokes me, only needing to do so three times before I'm fully hard. I brace a hand on the counter for support, everything in me pinging and ecstatic as Lawson, my best goddamn friend, rolls a condom down my cock.

Twisting back around, he says, "I know you don't mind stretching me, but I already did it. Couldn't wait."

My breath comes out in a pant.

Lawson settles back over the counter, the lube on his asshole, now that I'm looking for it, visible. His cock isn't yet hard. "Please, Oak?"

Stepping close, I shake my head, not sure whether this situation should be as arousing as it is but finding I simply don't have the wherewithal to question it. I wrap dirt-covered fingers over Lawson's hip, the man letting out a sigh that sounds like relief.

"Line me up," I manage, my voice hoarse.

Lawson reaches back, holding my cock steady, the head notching against him and slipping inside the moment I press forward. He lets go, pushing back to meet me, and *fucking hell*, I've forgotten how to breathe.

"So much for...romance, huh?" I ask, my lungs resuming function, every part of me caught in the staticky buzz of pleasure as I inch back and press forward again, Lawson's body wrapping me in willing heat.

"You can dine me afterwards."

I bark a laugh, dirt leaving a trail along Lawson's side as I ruck his shirt higher, nails gliding gently over his skin. He shivers, and I fight the instinctive urge to cover every inch of him with my touch. "Sure thing, princess."

He huffs but doesn't protest the nickname. Shifting my hand back to the countertop, I splay my fingers wide, hold Lawson's hip tight, and move. He grunts at the first slam of my cock inside his body, but then he's leaning more of his weight forward, his head bowing, the angle giving me better access. There's a tiny part of my mind telling me this is a bad idea—*again*—but it doesn't hold court for long.

My thumb rests at the top of Lawson's ass cheek as I fuck him hard, my eyes caught on the way I'm sinking inside his body again and again. The man's ass bounces every time we connect, and *fuck* if that isn't a heady sight. All of it. Lawson splayed out against my goddamn kitchen countertop. Dirty fingerprints and smudges evidence of my touch on his skin. The man's head dropped forward like he can hardly hold it up, his groans as he takes the fucking he asked for telling me how much he loves this.

Lawson's hand slides outwards, dragging through dirt on the countertop before he catches himself. "Fuck."

"Got you swearing already," I note, mighty proud of that fact.

"Would you..." He cuts off, panting heavily, a bead of sweat dripping down the small of his back.

"Tell me," I urge, slipping my hand up his chest, holding tight as the smack of my hips on his ass echoes in the room. My gut tightens, and I close my eyes for a moment, needing to draw myself back from the edge.

"Would you kiss my neck?"

The request has me stilling for only a second before I drag Lawson upwards, slotting his back to my chest, the two of us a sweaty mess as we fit together from knee to shoulder.

"Like this?" I ask before dragging my lips across the nape of his neck.

He rolls in another shiver, his ass clenching around me as my stubble abrades his skin. "Again."

My eyes slip closed once more, but I don't consider denying him. I drag my lips along the side of his neck, over salty sweat, up below his ear. The closed-mouth kiss I press there has him drawing in a breath.

I grind against him, shallow thrusts at this angle, each one slow and achingly sweet, like molasses. When I open my mouth to flick my tongue against Lawson's skin, the man moans.

"I think you like that," I say, rolling my thumb over his nipple beneath his shirt.

He stutters a breath.

"And that," I add.

"Think I do," he answers, leaning his head to the side in a way that feels like a glaring invitation.

I drag my stubble back down his neck, fit my lips to the bend of his shoulder, and suck.

"Jesus," Lawson mutters, his hand slipping again where it's braced against the edge of the counter. I can see his cock from over his shoulder, hard now and starting to leak. He doesn't reach for it, instead getting a fistful of my hair and tugging in clear demand.

It goes straight to my own cock, and I rut into him harder, scratching my stubble across his neck and the tops of his shoulders almost ruthlessly, kissing him the only way I may ever have the chance to. His skin is hot and salty on my tongue, the man himself bowing forward again as if he needs the support. I press him back over the counter, his hand and mine streaking through the dirt on its surface. Lawson's sound of encouragement is all I need to pull back and slam forward again.

I let my hips take over, the tight clasp surrounding my cock second to the feel of this man at my fingertips. There's a moment of stark disconnect where I remember this is Lawson. *Lawson.* My best friend of decades.

Not my lover.

Not my boyfriend.

Not anything but a man who drove over here with the express purpose of getting dicked.

I have to remember that. I *have* to.

But right now, none of it stays in my mind. There's only this man in front of me, his vocalizations hurried in a way I know means he's close. I'm not sure I have the stamina to edge him for an hour today. As it turns out, I don't have to.

"Oak."

Lawson's request is clear. I bring my hand to his cock, wrap my fingers around him tight, and stroke. He clamps down on me immediately, his breath catching in his lungs. I don't think he needs the push, but I still lean close and run my lips up to his ear again.

"Show me how good I fucked you, princess."

The man is coming before his next breath. I jerk him through the compressions around my dick, my hips stuttering, my own lungs seizing tight as I fall apart inside this person I know better than anyone. It's not easy to catch my breath. To regain my equilibrium as I rest against Lawson, his cum surely covering the drawers in front of us. I unwrap my hand from around his softening shaft, blinking my eyes open to find dirt everywhere.

At least I had enough presence of mind to keep my hand from the top of his dick.

Lawson doesn't seem to be in any hurry to move, but he doesn't stop me as I slip from his body, my fingers leaving trails down his back. I give his shirt a tug, covering him somewhat, amused by the smudged handprints on his skin.

"You, uh...might need a shower."

He pants out a breath. "What's all the dirt for?"

I snort a laugh, taking care of the condom and nearly tripping over my shorts on the ground in the process. "You didn't notice it before?"

"Noticed. Just didn't care."

"I brought home a few herbs," I tell him, lips twitching as Lawson finally lifts himself to standing. The man has dirt on his cheek and the imprint of what I think is my thumb at the crux of his neck.

Lawson clocks the herbs on the windowsill and nods. "You'll cook dinner while I shower?"

"Excuse you," I huff. "You're not going to help me clean up first?"

"It's your mess," he says plainly.

I point at his cum on my wooden drawers. "And that?"

"I stand by my position. You made the mess."

With that, Lawson snags his clothes off the ground and walks toward the hall, butt-ass naked from the waist down. "Dinner?"

"I live to serve," I call wryly, shaking my head, laughter bubbling up from my throat.

Bell catches my gaze from the living room, blinking her black eyes once.

"You have no room to judge," I tell her. "You're a cow."

Her head flops with a thump onto the rug.

"Jesus," I mutter to myself, grabbing a towel to clean up the cum and dirt spread everywhere.

I'm not sure how I got roped into giving my friend an orgasm, followed by a meal, but I can't quite find it in me to mind.

Or regret a single damn thing.

Chapter 15

LAWSON

"You think she'll be safe?" Laura asks, worrying at her lip as Wendy bounds down the porch steps toward my truck, her bag for the weekend in tow.

"She will be."

"Kids do stupid shit," my ex counters.

"They do," I agree. "But Wendy has a smart head on her shoulders. She'll be fine."

"Dad," Wendy calls, clearly excited and wanting to go.

"Oakley and I will be there to keep watch," I remind Laura. "Plus another half dozen adults."

She nods, rubbing both temples for only a second before dropping her hands. It's a habit that means she's stressed. Probably about a million things other than Wendy attending a summer camp, but this is the stress right in front of her, so it's what she's focusing on.

"I still don't know why Oakley volunteered to go," she mutters.

"Because he loves Wendy," I point out. "And nature."

And I might have suckered him into it so I wouldn't be alone during the trip, not that I admit that to my ex-wife.

She shakes her head a little, disapproval clear on her face. She's never tried to stop Oakley from being close with Wendy. Not once. But she doesn't understand it.

I think, mostly, she doesn't understand me and him.

"We'll be back Sunday evening," I tell her, heading down the stairs.

"Lawson. Don't do anything stupid."

"Me?" I ask, turning back around to face her. "What would I possibly do?"

"With Oakley there, who knows."

"He's not a bad influence," I say a touch hotly. "He's just..."

Fun.

I don't say the word, not wanting Laura to take it as me saying she's not. Luckily, she simply gives me a wave, dismissing me, before calling out to Wendy. "Be safe! Love you."

"Love you, too," Wendy calls back, urging me on with her own wave forward.

I meet her at the truck, getting in the driver's seat while Wendy buckles herself in. "Got your sunscreen?" I check.

"Yep."

"Bug spray?"

"Yes."

"Underwear?"

"Obviously," she says in annoyance. "Come on. Let's go."

Chuckling, I pull out of the driveway and get us on the road. My bag is already packed and sitting in the back seat, camping gear taking up a portion of the bed. We drive straightaway to Oakley's house, finding the front door open and the man himself preparing the last of his things.

"Hey," he calls out, giving Wendy a wide smile as she exits the truck ahead of me. "Ready for some camping?"

"You got the marshmallows?" she asks.

Oakley puffs out an indignant breath. "Please. You gotta ask?"

Wendy grabs the box Oakley nudges her way, full of what looks like fireside snacks. Oakley locks his front door, a grin on his face as he meets my gaze.

"Been a long time since we've gone camping," he notes.

The last time was a good five years back, a trip just the two of us took where Oakley proceeded to ply me with so much whiskey I ended up sleeping in the buff. I woke with a good few mosquito bites on my ass.

"No whiskey this time," I say sternly, raising an eyebrow. "There'll be kids."

He huffs. "I'm well aware this is a PG trip. Here."

I catch the rolled-up sleeping bag Oakley tosses me, carrying it down to the truck as Oakley follows with his hiking bag over his shoulder. We stuff all of it in the bed beneath the cover that will keep it dry.

Wendy climbs into the back seat this time, giving Oakley the passenger spot with more leg room. "Who's looking after Bell?"

"My parents," Oakley answers, buckling in. "And you know my mom will spoil her rotten. She's in good hands."

Wendy appears happy with that, settling into her seat with her phone already out in front of her.

"We ready?" I ask my companions.

Oakley shoots me a wicked grin. "Ready."

It takes forty-five minutes to drive to the campsite geared toward middle- and high-school-aged groups. Several of Wendy's classmates are already here, and she makes an impatient sound as I look for a parking spot. The moment the truck stops, she's out the door.

"Kids," Oakley mutters. "Guess we're the pack mules, then, huh?"

I don't argue it, only grab Wendy's bag from the back and shove it at Oakley's chest. He huffs a laugh, taking it with him out the door, the two of us grabbing what we can of our supplies. Arms full, I check in with the group leader who's been running this summer camping trip for years.

"Liv," I greet.

"Lawson," she says in turn, giving Oakley a nod. "Good to see you outside the classroom. And hey there, Oakley. I hear you've returned to us?"

"Sure have," he says, smile in place. "Still running these kids ragged?"

"Whenever I can," Liv says gamely. As our high school's PE teacher, it's in Liv's job description to keep the kids active. "We're in campsite B this year. Remember where it is?"

"I do," I confirm. "All right if we get our tent pitched?"

I ignore Oakley's snort.

"Sure thing," Liv says, marking something on her clipboard as another set of students joins the group. "I'll be following with the kids as soon as the stragglers arrive. Head on back."

With that, I catch Wendy's eye, getting a quick nod in return before she goes back to talking with her friend Chloe. Oakley keeps pace with me as we walk through the short wooded trail toward campsite B. Another of the adult chaperones, a parent named Dan, gives us a wave from where he's readying the boys' cabin. There are two side by side, one for the girls and one for the boys. Usually, a parent or two stays in each, and the rest of us chaperones sleep in tents.

I don't mind that. It's quieter, at least.

"Don't you think it's odd that we're still so stuck on gender?" I ask Oakley.

He drops one of the bags in his possession to the ground, an eyebrow raised. "I'm gonna need more info."

"The cabins," I explain, waving a hand that way. "For all the strides we've made, we still split kids up into boys and girls. Our society has such a deeply ingrained gender dichotomy, we don't even think about it half the time. And what about the folks who fall between or outside of it? It's isolating."

Oakley nods slowly. "I don't disagree with you. Stevie struggled with that often. Which bathroom to use. How and when to safely present themself. Not everyone in the world is understanding. Or kind."

I let out a quiet breath. "Sorry. I didn't mean to..."

"Bring up my ex?" Oakley asks, an amused lilt to his voice. "You didn't. I did. And it's fine, Law. I can talk about them, you know."

I eye my friend as I unroll our tent. "Does it still hurt?"

He takes a moment to answer that, and my chest feels tight as I wait. I busy myself with the tent prep as Oakley kicks rocks and sticks away from the patch of grass we've chosen. Finally, he says, "Not really. It did for a while, but now... Now it's like the memory of a bruise. Not really there at all."

I nod. Thinking about Stevie isn't something I particularly enjoy.

"You're still pissed at them," Oakley observes.

"Yes," I admit.

He stops what he's doing, hands loosely on his hips as he gives me his full attention. "Why, Law?"

"Because..." *God*, how do I even explain it to him? "Because they hurt you to begin with. In big ways and in small ones. And that's not something I can ever forgive."

Oakley's blue-and-brown eyes hold mine, the expression on his face one I have a hard time putting a name to. "You forgave me."

"It's not the same thing. And of course I did. You're you."

"God, Lawson. I have never in my life met someone as loyal as you. If I asked you to help me bury a body, I'm fairly sure you'd do it."

"I'd ask some questions first," I tell him.

The look he gives me is full of mirth. "Of course you would. We gonna pitch this tent or what?"

Nodding, I toss Oakley some of the metal supports, and we get to work. Not ten minutes later, our campsite adjacent to our group's cabins is ready to go, sleeping bags and backpacks inside our tent. We make a return trip to the truck to grab the rest of our supplies, including the snacks Oakley brought. By the time we're back at campsite B, the kids have arrived.

Liv directs them with ease, everyone stashing their things inside the cabins, picking out bunks, putting on sunscreen or bug spray as necessary. Oakley and I help another of the parents with their own tent, the woods here shaded enough we're not sweating too badly by the time we're done.

"Ten bucks says we find some kids sneaking away for *you know what* before the weekend is over," Oakley whispers.

I swat his chest. "I'm not taking that bet. Behave."

He chuckles.

Once everyone is ready, we head as a group to the mess hall for dinner, the campground offering meals for outings like this. The food is...edible.

The energy in the room is excited, all the kids part of the to-be-senior class, every face one I recognize whether from teaching them myself or seeing them in the school halls. I give Oakley a nudge when one student in particular stands on top of his seat to act something out for his friends, the returned laughter raucous.

"Oh, boy," Oakley murmurs. "Do we need to keep an eye on that one?"

"Might."

"Think he'll cause trouble?"

I shrug. Koda isn't a bad kid at heart, but he feeds off attention from his friends. If they push him enough, he may find himself in a situation he shouldn't be in. It's happened before, both at camp and at school.

Oakley subtly rubs the knuckles of his fist into his open palm, and I bark a laugh before clearing my throat.

"We do not physically reprimand the kids," I say quietly, smacking his thigh, although I know he'd never do that.

His smirk is all playful.

When dinner is done, we return to our campsite. The first night is about settling in. Tomorrow and Sunday, the kids will have plenty of time to play in the lake or explore via hiking around the camp's trails. But tonight, Liv lets them do their own thing, chatting and playing yard games and sitting in groups around the fire pits starting to burn.

I check on Wendy every once in a while. Can't help it. But I don't bother her, knowing embarrassment comes easy for them at this age.

Oakley takes a seat near me, the two of us in front of one of the fire pits. There are sturdy logs surrounding the area. Not the most comfortable to sit on, but they get the job done.

He knocks his knee into mine, the ingredients for s'mores near his foot. "Want a marshmallow, Teach?"

"Roast one for me?" I ask. "You know how I like 'em."

His lips twitch as he reaches for a stick.

"What?"

"Nothing," he answers, tone light. "Not. A. Thing."

"Oak..."

"No, really. It's nothing. Whatever your Royal Highness wants, he gets."

My body flashes hot, the teasing smile on Oakley's face not helping one bit. He didn't outright call me *princess*, but he might as well have. It doesn't feel like he's mocking me. Oakley would never be cruel like that.

But even so, I don't know how to process the comment that so ardently reminds me now of sex.

If he were anyone else, I'd assume he was flirting with me.

"Well," I say, voice a little rougher than I'd like, "you burn my marshmallow, and it's the dungeon for you."

Oakley sputters a cough that turns into a laugh. His voice is whisper-soft when he speaks, cognizant of the kids around. "Jesus, Lawson. You got some sorta kinky playroom I'm unaware of?"

"What? 'Course not. I didn't mean it like *that*."

Oakley continues to laugh at my put-out expression. *Christ*, this man.

Despite myself, I smile as I shove his shoulder. "Get my mallow going."

He tosses me a salute. "Yessir."

As the marshmallows heat, Oakley passes the s'mores supplies around. A few of the kids start roasting their own marshmallows, others eating chocolate plain. Liv offers Oakley a thanks he looks pleased by.

Oakley likes to help others. It's a quality I've always admired about my friend.

Not many people are as goodhearted as him.

Oakley pulls my marshmallows off the fire once the outsides are perfectly browned—*not* burnt—and the insides are gooey all the way through. They're exactly how I like them, and I tell him as much, earning a beaming grin that has me feeling a surge of fondness for this man I've known all my life.

It wasn't the same these past few years he was gone. But now... Now everything feels as it should.

Liv herds the kids indoors at eleven, much to their verbal complaining. But they comply, heading to their cabins or the nearby bathrooms to get ready for bed. The adults take care of the messes left out by the fires before putting the flames out.

Oakley and I wait until all of the kids are inside their cabins and everyone has been accounted for before using the cement-walled bathrooms and retiring to our tent. He lets out a big sigh as he drops onto his stomach atop the sleeping-bag-padded ground, the man looking like a wet noodle in the dark.

"All right?" I check.

"Mm. Just tired. I'm usually sound asleep by now."

I give the side of his ass a slap, an action that has his head whipping my way. "Buck up, cowboy. These kids will be up at dawn and not down again until midnight."

"'Scuse you, I can handle it."

"Can you?"

"I got this. If anything, I'm surprised you're not complaining about the late hour."

"I'm complaining on the inside," I assure him.

That has him chuckling as he rolls onto his back. With a grunt, he curls upright to tug off his shirt, the clear window at the top of our tent giving me just enough moonlight to see him by. It's warm enough he doesn't cover himself with his sleeping bag, and neither do I. I lie beside him in the dark, watching the gentle ebb and flow of his chest, his hands resting on his stomach.

Part of me aches to bridge the distance between us. To rest within the curve of Oakley's arms, where everything is familiar and quiet. I don't ask it of him, knowing I've asked far too much lately.

But boy do I ache.

Chapter 16

OAKLEY

I wake well before dawn, a habit hardwired into me through years, *decades*, of ranching. Which means the dark isn't a surprise.

The man at my front, however, *is*.

At some point in the night, Lawson and I found our way toward one another. I don't know if he moved, if I did, or if it was a mutual effort, but my arm is slung over a still-asleep Lawson, my body curled around his big spoon to little spoon style.

I pull in a shallow breath, eyes closing for a moment as I collect my wits. Slowly, I lift my arm and roll to my back, giving the man some space. Without missing a beat, he turns with me, shifting to his other side and attaching to mine, a hand settling just beneath my chest on my ribcage.

Fuck.

He's still dead to the world, his breaths coming evenly, his hand warm and his proximity the most vicious sort of pleasure. It's not that Lawson and I are never close. We hug plenty, have cuddled before when one or both of us were upset. Hell, I've been inside the man, a recent development I'm still half convinced was a dream.

But for all the years we've known one another, slept at each other's houses, gone camping even, I've never once woken up to *this*.

Is it so wrong to want to pretend it could mean something? At least for a little while?

The first glimpse of sun is lighting the sky a gentle pink through the tiny tent window when Lawson stirs. He inhales deeply, his face rubbing against my chest before his fingers tighten in surprise, the man himself stilling.

He draws back, looking sleep-hazy and impossibly beautiful, his low voice a rumble. "Sorry."

"It's fine," I assure him, missing his touch the moment he leans away and chastising myself for it. "Get enough sleep?"

"It'll do."

A door opens nearby, the gentle slam of wood against wood preceding soft chatter. Looks like the campsite is waking.

Lawson stretches with a groan, and I busy myself with finding new clothes for the day. He barely glances at me as I hastily kick off my shorts and underwear, replacing them just as swiftly.

I understand now why it never seemed like Lawson was interested in anybody prior to his relationship with Laura. He *wasn't*. At least, not in a physical sense.

I, on the other hand, have a damn hard time looking away from Lawson as he swaps out his own clothes. Every inch of the man is one I want to touch, perilous as that journey would be for my heart. And my sanity.

I'm already in too deep. I know I am.

I tug on a shirt as Lawson zips up his bag. He looks over at me. "Ready?"

Nodding, I open up our tent, and Lawson and I head out. After breakfast at the camp's mess hall, the group of kids splits into two groups: those who want to hike and those who want to swim. Lawson and I are paired with the swimming group, so we change into our trunks and put on sunscreen before heading with the kids out to the lake. There's a massive floating trampoline not far from shore, a slide off one end and a ladder up another.

The teens waste no time getting into the water, apart from a few who stay on shore, looking as if they're readying to sunbathe. Wendy is among those already climbing onto the trampoline, her friend Chloe with her.

I eye Lawson, who's kicking out of his sandals. "Race you?"

"Where?" he asks slowly, when it clicks. "You're not getting on *that*, are you?"

I bounce my eyebrows before taking off. Lawson curses behind me, the sound of his feet squeaking through sand following me as I laugh. The water slows me down, chilling me in an instant, but I power through, heading straightaway for the floating trampoline up ahead. I let out the tiniest squeak when the water gets deep enough to cover my crotch. *Fuck,* that is *cold.* Soon enough, my shoulders join the rest of my body under the surface.

Once I reach the ladder, I heft myself up, stopping only long enough to find Lawson in the water behind me. "Beat you."

"You're a child," he mutters, even as a smile lifts the corner of his lips.

Sending him a wink, I finish climbing up onto the float, plot my path, and take off running. A couple of the kids laugh as I pass, but I don't worry about whether or not I'm winning cool points. I get a good bounce going at the end of the trampoline, forward flip through the air, and land in the water with a splash.

When I surface, there's some clapping. Wendy shakes her head, an amused smile on her face. Lawson is swimming toward me.

"How'd I do?" I ask him.

"You realize you're forty-three years old, right?"

"Uh-huh. Pretty good for an old guy, don'tcha think?"

"Jesus," Lawson mumbles, slowing his forward paddle as he reaches me. "You're not *old*. Because if you are, that means I am, and, frankly, I'm not ready."

"You're pretty spry still," I assure him, my mind flashing to Lawson kneeling on my bedroom floor. Him bending over my kitchen countertop. *Christ.* His leg bent up on my bed as I railed him for damn near an hour. I clear my throat, my arms keeping me afloat in the deep water. "We can get old together, how about that?"

I realize how my words sound the second they leave my mouth, but Lawson gets an almost wistful look on his face. "You said something like that to me before. When we were kids. You said growing old wouldn't mean we'd grow apart."

"I meant it," I say, voice hoarse.

He nods, brushing wet hair off his face, a few droplets of water staying on his eyelashes like dewdrops. "I know you did. It's why I had to bring you home. So you could keep that promise."

I swallow, the motion causing my chin to dip below the surface. "Are you still angry at me for leaving?"

He makes a short sound. "I told you I wasn't."

"I know. It's just..."

After a beat of silence, Lawson swims closer to me, his expression ever so soft. For how rough he is at first glance—all dark hair and equally dark if not neatly trimmed stubble, strong features, and height to boot—Lawson has always had a softness about him that's made me feel undeniably protective. Even when we were young. Even still.

"It was the right choice for you then," Lawson says quietly, the nearby kids paying us no mind as they call to one another and splash in the water. "But now, Oak? Now, this is right. You being here. You know it as well as I do. I'm not angry at your past choices. I'm immensely grateful for your current ones."

I have to look away for a moment, Lawson's words hitting deep in a way he's singularly capable of. "You're really happy to have me back, huh?"

"Of course I am. The sex doesn't hurt, either."

I sputter. "*Jesus*, Lawson."

"What?"

The man's eyes are twinkling, telling me he knows *exactly* what. "You're such a shit underneath all your professionalism, you know that? You remind me of Colton that way."

Lawson's face screws up. "I do not."

"You do. You're more like your brothers than you realize."

He grunts, and I huff a laugh at his disgruntled expression.

"They're good guys," I note.

He doesn't deny it. "Told Remi I'm gay."

The shock of that statement has me paddling closer to shore, in need of a damn footing. Lawson stays with me, the two of us standing once our feet can touch the bottom. The kids are behaving, but I still keep half an eye on them, as does Lawson. An adult on shore is doing the same.

"How are you feeling about that?" I ask, voice low.

"Telling Remi or being gay?"

"Either? Both?"

He shrugs one shoulder. "Telling Remi was fine. I didn't really plan it. It just happened."

I don't have to ask, but I do. "He took it well?"

"Of course. The rest of my family will, too. Once I tell them."

I nod. "And...your sexuality?"

Lawson is silent for a moment, his eyes on the kids as he takes time to consider his emotions. It's something I've always found endearing about the man. The fact that he stops and assesses instead of just blurting out the first thought in his head. He doesn't shy away from what he's feeling, even if, at times, he doesn't fully understand it.

"I've been mulling it over a lot. How I could've spent so much of my life not knowing. But then I realize there *were* signs, I just didn't understand them at the time. I always felt like...like I was chasing something indistinct. It was just out of reach, you know? But one time with you, Oak, and it *clicked*. It was so clear to me, so strong I could practically hold it in the palm of my hand. It wasn't a murky sense of *maybe*, but *this, this right here is what it should be*. And now, if I think about going back to what I had before or trying with some other woman, I just... I can't even imagine it. It feels wrong on every level, like a betrayal, to contemplate it."

"Then don't," I tell him firmly, squeezing his sun-warmed shoulder. "You don't need to put yourself through painful hypotheticals, Law. If you know, you know. Simple as that."

"It doesn't feel simple at all. Attraction... It's so complicated, isn't it? There are so many ways to want a person. Or not."

"There are," I say softly, shifting my hand up to Lawson's neck before I can stop myself. He doesn't shy away from my touch—he never has. It makes it difficult to let go, but I do, my hand dropping back to my side. "It feels right, though? The thought of yourself with a man?"

He nods, a slow thing. "It does."

I don't want to say the words, not in the least. But I push them past my lips regardless. "Think you'll try dating then?"

Lawson's brow furrows, but he doesn't have a chance to answer me before there's a commotion that sounds far from playful coming from the direction of the float. We head that way immediately, Lawson's voice ringing out. "Everything okay here?"

Chloe sends an impolite gesture Koda's way. The teen is in the water with his buddies, laughing. "You're a dick," she snaps.

"Language," Lawson cautions, using his teacher voice that, weirdly, does things to me. "Someone care to share what's going on?"

Lawson and I stop at the edge of the float. Only one boy is on top of it, the rest in the water swimming toward shore now, not having stayed to chat. Wendy's cheeks are red, her friend Chloe rubbing her arm as a few of the other girls hover nearby.

"Just boys being stupid," Chloe says. "Sorry, Gavin."

The teen named Gavin shrugs.

"Wendy?" Lawson asks, clearly clocking the situation same as I did.

His daughter's lips remain shut, and no one else seems inclined to voice a thing, so I clap my hands together once, garnering everyone's attention. "All right. Let's head in and break into the ice pops in the cooler. A little shade and hydration will do us good. C'mon now."

Everyone but Wendy gets off the float. Lawson shoots me an appreciative half-smile, and I nod in return before herding the teens toward shore and some sugar. I keep my eye on Koda as everyone grabs ice pops, the other chaperone reminding the kids to reapply sunscreen.

Lawson and Wendy join us before long, Wendy heading toward the spot where her friends are sunbathing. Lawson meets me at the periphery of the group.

"Well?" I ask. "Do I needa kick the kid's ass or what?"

Lawson huffs a laugh, but there's reprimand in his eyes, as if he's warning me to behave. "Apparently, Koda was making fun of the fact that Wendy is on her period."

My gaze shoots Wendy's way. Of course, being seventeen, Wendy is old enough to have a menstrual cycle. I just never thought much about it, likely in part because I haven't been here the past few years.

I shuffle that guilt off to the side for the time being. "How'd he even know?"

Lawson's lips pinch. "Guess he saw her tampon string and decided to point it out to the crowd."

My mouth drops slowly open.

"Oak," Lawson warns. "You can't beat the kid up."

"We sure about that?"

"Very," he says, tone flat. "I'll mention it to Liv. She'll make sure he's given a warning about his behavior."

"A warning?" I ask harshly. "What does that even mean? He'll get a slap on the wrist if we're lucky and go right back to being an insensitive douchebag?"

"Oak," he says again, stepping close enough to block my view of Koda off on the other side of the sandy beach area. My eyes snap to Lawson's face when he places his hands on my cheeks, gently redirecting my gaze. "As much as I appreciate your outrage on my daughter's behalf, you can't go off on the kid. He's only seventeen. And Wendy will be okay. You know she's tough."

My gaze slips Wendy's way again. She already looks relaxed, chatting with her friends as if the incident on the float never happened. But that can't be an easy thing to discard, having several of her peers laughing at her expense.

Lawson lets out a soft chuff. "You gonna be good?"

"Sure," I mutter.

He sighs but releases my face, giving my cheek a gentle pat. "You've got a good heart, Oakley Beaumont."

"Uh-huh."

Lawson shakes his head as he walks away, checking on the group, giving the go-ahead to head back into the water if they'd like. My gears turn.

Maybe I can't reprimand the kid myself, but there has to be something I can do. For Wendy's sake if nothing else.

I catch her eye from across the beach, lifting my hands to sign, *'You all right?'*

She nods, shooting back a one-handed, *'Fine.'*

'Need anything? Chocolate? Advil?' I pause, racking my brain for an ASL equivalent of *nunchucks* and coming up blank. I act out the motion best as I can, and Wendy laughs before pressing her lips quickly together, giving me a reproachful look that reminds me of her father.

'I'm fine,' she repeats. *'But thanks.'*

I nod, gaze finding Lawson, the man stunning in his swim trunks with his hair still wet and his broad body on display. I try to ignore the deep well of *want* that swamps me at the sight of him. The fact that, despite my question about him dating, I don't want Lawson experimenting with other men when he has me. That it's a terrible, bad idea to even entertain the idea of continuing the casual friends-with-benefits situation that was supposed to be a one-off but didn't stop there. The realization, even, that I don't want it to stop. Not even close.

But all...*this?* It began as a way to help Lawson understand his sexuality. To make him feel good when all he'd had was a lifetime of *not quite right.*

I want to make up for every year Lawson spent with Laura. Want to rewrite every touch with my own. I want to give him things I never dared dream of. Cravings that, now unearthed, won't leave my head.

Hindsight is a funny thing. How, like Lawson said, a truth can be so obvious when it was nothing but murky before.

If only I could see the future as easily as the past.

Chapter 17

LAWSON

Oakley has a bug up his ass all day.

He denies it, but I can see him keeping a close eye on Koda, just waiting for the kid to step out of line.

Shortly before dinner, he asks for my truck keys, saying he's grabbing more tampons for Wendy. I don't think to question it until the man comes strolling into the mess hall with four grocery bags full of feminine hygiene products in his hands and a smirk lifting his lips.

Oh boy.

"Liv," Oakley says, coming right up to the chaperones' table and stopping before the camp leader. "Permission to give the camp attendees an educational demonstration on tampon use?"

I nearly choke on my spit.

Liv appraises Oakley, the rest of the adults wearing amused expressions. "Can I trust you to be purely factual?"

"You absolutely can," Oakley answers.

Liv shrugs. "Permission granted."

I watch in shock as Oakley proceeds to dump the contents of the bags onto a nearby table, the boxes of different kinds of tampons scattering. The kids are starting to look over at him now, no one seeming like they quite know what to think.

"May I have your attention?" Oakley calls, the hall quieting at once. "It recently came to light that not everyone of your age may be familiar with this product. And since menstruation is absolutely nothing to be ashamed of, I'll be giving y'all a tutorial. This"—he cracks a box open and holds up a single-use package—"is a tampon."

"Gross," one of the boys mutters. "We're trying to eat here."

Oakley tosses the tampon over to the kid's table, ignoring his squawk and grabbing another out of the box in front of him. "By all means, keep on eating. No one's stopping you."

A few of the girls snicker, the boys looking decidedly uncomfortable.

Flashing a grin, Oakley faces the room at large. "Now, a typical period can last up to seven days. That's seven days every *month*. Women or other individuals with uteruses spend approximately one quarter of their menstruating lives bleeding. That's twenty-five percent of the time, folks. One out of every four days, they are *actively. Shedding. Blood.*"

Several of the kids groan, but nearly every girl is smiling now. The chaperones, too. I shake my head, feeling a fierce sort of pride swell in my chest.

"Now, I'm not even gonna touch on other accompanying symptoms one might experience during a period," Oakley says, "because there's simply no way to understand it if you don't go through it. What I am going to do is talk about this arguably brilliant, convenient, and empowering invention: the tampon."

Oakley peels the wrapper of the tampon open to a silent, rapt audience. The gleam in his eye is all the forewarning I get before Oakley's gaze zeroes in on Koda.

Ah, Christ.

"I'm gonna need a volunteer for this," Oakley declares gleefully. He doesn't give anyone a chance to shoot their hand in the air. His eyes never leave Koda. "You. Yep. Come on up here and hold this tampon for me."

Koda, having absolutely no choice unless he wants to look chickenshit in front of his friends, gets out of his seat and approaches the table Oakley is standing in front of. The teen gingerly takes the tampon between his thumb and forefinger, looking like he'd rather be anywhere else.

Oakley pats Koda's shoulder before clapping his hands together. "All right. First, we're gonna use a water bottle to learn how to insert a tampon, as well as discuss the benefits and risks involved. And guys? Take notes. You never know if this will apply to your future partner or child one day."

Wendy catches my eye from across the room, the expression on her face one I recognize well. Overwhelming love.

Oakley spends a half hour in front of the room of teens, lecturing them on proper tampon use and disposal, talking about other feminine hygiene products, and even discussing what people used to do before many of these modern conveniences were invented.

Maybe it's not world-changing. But to a select group of seventeen-year-olds, Oakley is normalizing a conversation often avoided or treated as downright taboo, all because a young girl he loves was teased by a boy who's never had to deal with the stigma surrounding periods.

I've always known Oakley to be a good person. A kind one. Strong in spirit and possessing a moral compass that's never once failed.

But I didn't realize until right this moment the magnitude of what that means to me.

Seeing the man stand up for my daughter as if she's his own? Seeing him take away a bully's power without so much as hurting an ounce of the boy's pride?

I can't even express the gratitude I feel for that. For *him*.

The kids attend a survival course after dinner, one of the camp employees having been booked for the group. He shows them how to start a fire, how to ensure drinking water is sanitized if you're out in the wild, how to make a temporary shelter, even, and what to do if you find yourself lost.

By the time eleven o'clock rolls around, not a single soul complains about heading to bed. The campsite is quiet, the wind the loudest thing around as it ruffles the bushes and trees. Oakley and I head to the bathroom together, his phone lighting our way. Our noises echo in the barebones building, the sounds almost eerie.

When Oakley joins me in front of the sinks to brush his teeth, my eyes run over him. How many times have we stood like this throughout our lifetime? How is it possible to know someone so deeply, to know their ins and outs, and still be amazed by them?

Oakley's eyes catch mine in the mirror, although it's too dim to see the unique coloration in here. He spits out his toothpaste. "What?"

I shake my head a little. "That was really smart, what you did."

"You think so?" he asks, sounding almost sheepish. "I thought there was a good chance you'd chew me out considering you all but told me to back off."

"No," I say softly, my throat tight. "That was perfect. I feel like...like I don't have to worry quite so much when you're around, Oak. You always make me feel safe. And you do the same for Wendy."

Oakley turns to face me, meeting me eye to eye instead of through the glass. He's quiet for a long beat. "I'd do anything for the two of you. You know that."

"I do. Still surprises me sometimes to see the depth of your love."

"Jesus," he mutters, letting out a heavy breath. "The things that come out of your mouth sometimes."

"Good things, I hope?"

"Honest things." He looks as if he wants to add something else, but in the end, he only shakes his head. "C'mon. Let's get to our tent before these mosquitos eat us alive."

Not about to argue, I nod, and we head out of the bathroom, the wind warm yet wild as we walk the short way back to our campsite. Oakley's phone lights our path again, but he shuts it off once we're zipped inside our canvas shelter. There's not much moonlight tonight, so it's hard to see, but I can hear Oakley shuffling around like he's getting comfortable. There's a tightness in my chest as I lie down beside him, an emotion that feels a lot like fear rattling around in a hectic, fizzy sort of way.

"Oak," I bring myself to say.

"Yeah?"

I pull in a small, steadying breath. "Could we... I mean, would you mind if I lie down with you tonight?"

There's a pause, short but weighted, before Oakley speaks. "Not at all."

Expelling the air in my lungs, I edge closer to feel out Oakley's position. He's lying on his back, chest bare, his skin hot to the touch as I settle against him, my head at the crook of his shoulder.

My tension abates almost instantly, muscles going lax.

Oakley's voice is quiet. "I probably don't smell the best."

"You smell fine."

After a moment, his hand comes up to run lightly through my hair, the rhythmic glide of his blunt fingernails soothing. My eyes slip shut, my own hand over Oakley's heart, that pressure in my chest gone like dandelion fluff on the wind.

I'm nearly asleep when I hear Oakley murmur, "I feel safe with you, too, Law."

I should maybe wonder at the way my heart skips with that. At the warmth that blankets me. But I'm too tired to hold on to the thought, slipping instead into a dream-filled sleep that reminds me of sailing through the skies as a child.

When I wake, it's dark. Rain is pattering softly onto the top of the tent, the air muggy but cool. It takes me a second of foggy thought to figure out what roused me.

Oakley is plastered half over my body, his face pressed to my neck and soft words leaving his mouth that are too quiet for me to discern. He's clearly still fast asleep.

He's also hard. His cock is nestled against my hip, the feel of it ratcheting my pulse between one beat and the next.

For a long moment, I don't move a muscle. If I were to wake Oakley, he'd shift away from me, ever respectful. But I don't want him to. Not in the least.

Slowly, I slide my hand down between our bodies, the fit tight. Oakley's breath stutters when my fingers curl loosely over his cock through the material of his shorts. I wait, my pulse feathering, Oakley's soft groan and the unconscious flex of his hips causing my desire to bloom, like a reactionary storm, quiet as it is.

Oakley comes to consciousness quickly, his indrawn breath preceding his voice, rough like gravel. "Is that your hand on my dick?"

"It is."

"Did I put it there?"

"No, you did not."

He lets out a garbled sort of moan as he ruts once against my palm. I take it as permission, slipping my hand into his shorts, the heat of him, the feel of him filling my grip making my gut clench in the best of ways. Oakley's breathless sigh speaks of deep satisfaction, his stubble like electricity as he brushes his lips up and down the side of my neck.

I arch my head further, wanting Oakley's lips everywhere they can reach. Wanting him to cover me in sparks.

The rumble Oakley lets out in response is barely audible over the patter of the rain. I stroke my hand up and down his shaft as he scrapes my neck near raw. "You tryna make me come?"

"I didn't have a plan," I tell him truthfully. "Just wanted to touch."

Oakley hums, the sound one of approval, before reaching down to pop the button on his shorts. It gives me more room to maneuver. "And you? Do you wanna be touched?"

"Think so," I say, my own need like a distant thrum rolling closer.

Oakley doesn't hesitate. He shifts over me, straddling my waist and opening up my shorts. He must shove his own lower because, all of a sudden, there's no barrier at all as I map the shape of him with my fist. His cock is hard in my grip, hot, and I like the weight of it there, the way his breath hitches when I run my thumb over and around his cockhead.

Oakley's fingers drag over my own cock like a tease, waking me quickly up. He wraps his hand around me once I'm semihard, pumping with just the right pressure. I can't see his features or even the movement of his arm, but I can feel him looming over me, his face close to my own, his panting breaths and quiet exhalations a whisper against my ear.

"Open your hand," he murmurs. When I do, Oakley settles lower, his grip closing over my own to trap our cocks together. "Just like that, princess."

My pulse stutters as Oakley rolls his hips once, twice, before letting go, the friction and rub of his cock on mine making me wonder why I never tried this before.

I know why, of course.

But it doesn't change the fact that this, right here, is so much more than simply chasing a physical high. It's deeper in my chest, singing through my very bones. I don't have to think or encourage myself to react. There's no worry that I'm doing something wrong. Or that *I'm* wrong.

I'm not broken. I finally, *finally*, found someone who's right for me.

I lock my hand in Oakley's hair, holding him close, my other hand fisting our cocks as Oakley drives against me. He's not inside of me, but he's still fucking me, and there's no room for anything in my mind but joy and aching relief and a vicious sort of protectiveness for what I've found.

It's humid in the air of the tent, and Oakley's breath on my neck is damp. But I welcome the building heat, tugging him even closer, nearly jolting when he takes the hint and sucks against the bend of my shoulder. He keeps at it, kissing me with an open mouth as if trying to devour me, the softness of his tongue and the coarseness of his stubble a contradiction that has my nerve endings on fire. My dick starts to leak, and Oakley sucks harder.

Ah, fuck.

He shifts, shoving some sort of fabric—a shirt?—between our bodies, his mouth barely leaving my skin. "Can you come like this, princess? With my cock on yours?"

I huff a breath, feeling so damn light I'm fairly sure I could fly. "Why don't you do your best and find out?"

He lets out a short laugh, a smile on his lips I can feel as he nuzzles roughly against my neck. My back arches, a distant part of my mind reminding me where I am, but it's lost the next second as Oakley pulls my head to the side and tugs my earlobe between his teeth. The teasing nip of pain, the weight of him over me, his cock grinding against my own and the smooth glide as my hand gets wet with precum. It's too much. Too raw. Too real. Too goddamn good.

I come on a grunt, the fabric making perfect sense now as Oakley shifts his grip, using the material to catch the mess. His breathing stutters against me, his hips jerking, his cock throbbing against my palm before he muffles his moan into my shoulder. I can't bring myself to let go. Not for a long time. Oakley's chest heaves against me, his cock softening in a way I'm fascinated by simply because it's not my own. It's still dark through the tent window, not yet dawn, the rain coming down in a sheet of sound that thankfully muffled our noises, quiet as they were.

Even so, I realize how damn carelessly we acted. It's hard to regret it when I have Oakley's body plastered to my own, the man's dick in my hand a reminder of what it feels like to *want*, his breath near my ear the same.

It's Oakley who breaks the silence. "You owe me ten bucks."

It takes me a second to remember his comment about camp-goers sneaking away to fool around. I give his side a halfhearted shove. "I never took that bet."

Oakley shakes in near-silent laughter. "I didn't think it'd be us."

"No. I didn't either."

He pulls back some, but I still can't make out his face in the dark. "No one's close enough to have heard us," he says, sounding as if he's reassuring me.

"I know. I just... I feel like you've woken me up, Oak. There's so much I wanna try now. So many things I wanna do."

He sits back after a moment, taking the spare shirt with him. "Well, you've got lots of options. You can try whatever you want. With whomever you want."

My pulse kicks at the idea of being with anybody but Oakley. Not because I don't think I'd enjoy those things with another man. I'm almost certain I would, the prospect of it not something my mind instinctually shies away from. Not like when I think about being with a woman again.

But I've got Oakley. And I don't want to give this up. Give *him* up. Not yet.

So I simply hum.

And Oakley and I spend a quiet morning together in a tent as the world around us slowly, slowly wakes.

Chapter 18

Oakley

The last day at camp is filled with nonstop rain. The kids spend most of their time in the mess hall, playing games and avoiding the downpour.

I spend most of my time eyeing Lawson.

What are we doing? What am *I* doing?

I know better than to let myself fall down a rabbit hole with the man. There's a good chance any single step will send me tumbling too far to ever come back up again.

I *know* this. And yet I can't bring myself to tell him no or discourage him from seeking me out when he wants touch and comfort and to feel good.

But I haven't told him about my own feelings. How they've changed, or maybe simply made themselves known now that they're not buried under years of carefully placed dirt. I haven't even admitted it to myself, not fully.

I can't keep that up forever. Sooner or later, it'll slip or need to be said.

And what then?

Do I lose this? Him? Do I watch my best friend find someone else to make a life with yet again?

Lawson gives me a nudge as the kids start filing out of the mess hall, our time at camp coming to a close. "Ready?"

I guess it's back to the real world we go.

I offer the best smile I can manage. "Ready, Teach."

We're quiet on the ride back to Darling. Wendy is on her phone in the back seat, catching up on whatever social media the kids are using these days. My eyes keep straying to Lawson.

His hair is a bit unkempt after camping for three days, not his usual style in the least. It makes me want to haul him into my shower and then my bed, curling around him while we catch up on much-needed sleep. And then wake him up with my mouth wrapped around his cock, showing him how damn good a blowjob can feel when it's my lips doing the worshiping.

Fuck, I want to know what the man tastes like. His cock. His cum. His *lips*.

I forcibly tear my gaze away from Lawson's resting pout, the man clearly preoccupied by whatever thoughts are in his head.

What would he think if he knew my own?

This is such a disaster. How did I think I could remain impartial about all this?

How did I think shacking up with my friend of forty-three years wouldn't be the most monumental thing to happen to me in...well, ever?

Lawson drops Wendy off first at her mom's. I grab her bag from the back of the truck as Lawson heads to the door. Wendy gives me a fierce hug when I hand her things over.

"All right?" I ask, smoothing down her somewhat messy hair.

She nods against me before letting go. "Yeah. Just... You're pretty great, Oak."

"Shit, kid."

"Language," Lawson calls.

I huff a laugh, and Wendy rolls her eyes before heading for the door. Laura is there now, her gaze on me before it flicks to her daughter. Lawson exchanges a quick word with his ex before hugging Wendy goodbye.

I get back in the truck as Lawson comes my way. "All good?" I check.

He nods, buckling in and starting the vehicle. "Fine. Let's get home."

I eye Lawson before my gaze returns to the front of the house. Laura is still standing there. I raise a hand in greeting, and she shuts the door.

Well, then.

Lawson doesn't drop me off and leave for home like I expect him to. He hops out of the truck, grabbing his own things before making for my door.

My pulse is erratic as I follow after him.

He heads through the house to the back hall, opening the door to the yard and calling for Bell. My cow tromps inside, her tail swooshing, her nose immediately pressing against Lawson's bag in search of goodies. He rubs between her fuzzy black ears, the two trailing into the kitchen. When Lawson pulls a box of crackers out of the cupboard, Bell perks up.

"The fuck," I mutter as Lawson proceeds to give my cow treats like she's a dog. "What are you doing?"

"She asked nicely," he answers.

"She did not. She didn't say a goddamn word. Those are my crackers."

"You've got plenty."

When the hell did this man decide he would just start...playing house with me and my damn cow? Except...it's always been like this, hasn't it? Lawson inserting himself into my life, not that I ever tried to stop him. Claiming my home as his own, claiming my free time, claiming nearly every ounce of my attention and, unintentionally, my *affection*.

I knew, I always knew, Lawson and I had fewer boundaries than most. But I never let myself think too hard about it. Because Lawson was—*is*—my closest friend. He never wanted anything more.

Except now he does. Or at least he wants *something* from me.

Which makes him acting like he's right at home inside *my* home so much more complicated than it ever was before.

Lawson's voice pulls me back to my kitchen, the crackers put away now and Bell wandering toward the living room to sniff the bags I dropped there. "Wanna start us something for dinner while I go wash up? I'll finish cooking so you can do the same."

I stare at him for a long moment, wondering what's going through my best friend's head. Wondering if anything at all has changed for him. Or if, to Lawson, this is all just...rote. "Sure," I finally manage. "You can, uh, use my soap."

"Yep."

He's already walking down the hall.

Christ.

As Lawson strips down in my bathroom, I pull sausage links out of the freezer and get handmade biscuits started. By the time the man emerges, hair damp and cheeks rosy, I have our breakfast dinner mostly complete.

"Scramble the eggs?" I ask him, sliding the bowl his way. "And take the tray out when the timer goes off."

Lawson rumbles out an, "Mhm," before stepping up right behind me. I freeze as his arms come around my chest, my heart beating furiously. "If I didn't say it before, thank you."

"For what?" I croak, trying to keep my breaths even.

He lets out a soft sigh, smelling of cedarwood and amber from my soap, another scent I can only describe as *him* mixing in to create a heady combination I wish I could bottle. "For coming with me this weekend. I know you're happy to, but having you around makes everything better. So thanks."

Well, fuck.

"I'm surprised you're not sick of me yet," I joke, hoping my tone doesn't sound as strained as it feels.

"I couldn't ever get sick of you, Oak. Not possible."

It takes everything in me not to turn around and kiss him. Not to take his mouth with my own and ask—*beg*—that he stay, then. That he stay *with* me. Choose me. 'Cause I will never, not ever, have enough of Lawson Darling.

I want all of his soft, thoughtful smiles and the way his voice rolls through me like a gentle earthquake. I want his body pressed to mine and under mine, want to lick and kiss and nibble every inch of his skin until I know it all by heart. I want him to look at me like he can't imagine losing me. Not because I'm his friend, his...*person*. But because he knows no one in this entire universe could love him the way I could.

I love him. I *love* him.

And I was kidding myself if I ever thought otherwise.

Lawson steps back, the loss of his body heat feeling like the worst thing. "Go," he says. "I've got the rest of dinner."

I nod stiltedly, not quite meeting his eye. My mind runs circuits as I shower off the grime of camping. Possibilities. Contingencies. Every scenario, good and bad. They sit like a ball of lead in my stomach.

Lawson has dinner on the table when I get out of the shower. I join him, the kitchen quiet as we start to eat. Bell is lounging in the last of the evening sun.

"Was Laura upset earlier?" I ask, her disapproving stare still on my mind.

Lawson rocks his head side to side, finishing his bite of sausage before speaking. "Just doesn't get it."

"What?"

"You," he says plainly.

My heart thumps. "What about me?"

"Why we're so close. She's never understood it. It's a double standard. Laura has plenty of friends she's close with."

Right.

I clear my throat. "Does she know about..."

Lawson's whiskey eyes meet mine. "The sex?"

I nearly cough, amusement warring with my incredulity. "Yes, the sex. Jesus."

He shakes his head. "No. Haven't told her any of it. Not sure I want to."

"Why's that?" I ask, working on a biscuit as Lawson thinks over his words.

Finally, he heaves a sigh. "I don't owe it to anyone. To explain myself. To try to...justify how I feel. I'm not even sure I understand half of it. Physically, I'm not attracted to anyone. Sexually, I feel comfortable with men, with you, in a way I now recognize I never did with women. Romantically, I don't know what I am. If I even...feel things the way other people do. I'm realizing so much of what I thought I knew was other people's experiences told to me from the outside. I need the chance to figure it out for myself. To trust what I feel and find my own words for the person I am. Trying to explain all that to Laura with three simple letters—gay—feels like only a partial truth. And she'll see it as me giving an excuse for why we never worked, not me finally...finding myself. Does that make sense?"

"Yeah," I say thickly, my chest so tight I have to hold back my impulse to rub the ache away. "It makes sense, Law. You're more than someone else's interpretation of a label."

His gaze holds mine, so much appreciation there I'm floored by it. His voice, when he speaks, is nearly a whisper. "Yeah. We all are."

I manage a nod, that lead ball in my stomach twisting. *"Romantically, I don't know what I am."*

I give Lawson a tremulous smile and go back to my dinner. It's hard to finish, the food tasting ashen on my tongue.

It's not exactly a surprise when Lawson makes it clear he's staying the night. He brushes his teeth in my bathroom, picks out a pair of pajama pants from my dresser, and then grabs a t-shirt. Dressed comfortably, he climbs into my bed without a care in the world.

I'm slow to follow, taking my time in the bathroom, my pulse quick and a million different thoughts flitting through my head.

Could I be happy with what we have now? We're practically acting like a couple already. Do I need it to mean *more* to Lawson?

Is this enough?

When I get back to the bedroom, Lawson looks halfway to sleep already. He turns his head my way, watching almost passively as I tug off my shirt. There's no heat in his gaze, not that I expected there to be. No perusal of my body as my shorts join the pile on the floor.

"You mind?" I ask, indicating the boxer briefs I'm wearing. Frankly, I don't know how Lawson sleeps with so many clothes on, especially in the heat of summer.

He shakes his head. "Why would I mind?"

Jesus, this man.

I climb onto the bed, the comforter already tossed down near the bottom, a sheet covering Lawson's hips. The lamp is still on, but Lawson doesn't turn over to shut it off. I can feel his stare like a palpable thing, and I finally turn my head to meet it.

It never ceases to amaze me how much life has passed while looking at this face I know better than anyone's. I know every curve of Lawson's cheeks and brow and jaw. Know how his beard hair grows and which spots are toughest for him to shave. I know that he's never much thought about his eyebrows, yet he's meticulous about keeping his hair tamed and off his face. I know which locks curl stubbornly in front and every line beside his eyes that grew over time, like a marker of the years he's lived.

I know, now, how his cock feels when he's hard. Know the way every muscle in his body relaxes when I'm getting him off, like he can finally, *finally* let go of all the tension and responsibility in his life and let himself enjoy a few moments of pleasure. I know how his neck tastes. His sweat. I know the sounds he makes are masculine, grunts and hard breaths, and that he gives himself over wholly and fully, as if there's no thought in his head I might harm him.

I've known Lawson for ages. From the time he was a young boy with more wisdom in his brown eyes than maybe a kid that age should possess. Through adolescence, teen angst, college, marriage, having a kid of his own. We've gone through so many changes, together, separately, but never once has he lost his sense of dreamlike wonder. That conviction that fairy tales are real because magic can be found anywhere if you look for it.

I can see it now in his eyes. That he's witnessing something I don't think any of the rest of us are even capable of seeing.

"What is it?" I ask, my throat dry.

"Nothing," Lawson says, his hand coming up to run along my temple. It's a fleeting touch, soft, warm, and then gone. "It's just... You have the most gorgeous eyes I've ever seen, Oak."

It takes me a long, long time to answer him. "You think so?"

"Always have. Everything is right in the world when you're looking at me."

Lawson doesn't glance away as he says it. Isn't self-conscious about the admission or embarrassed to have revealed something so absolutely...raw.

I can feel it, the whoosh of air past my ears as I fall clean down that rabbit hole. I'm gone. Utterly tumbled. And there's no going back.

I'm head over heels in love with my best friend.

Chapter 19

LAWSON

"Hold this," my dad says.

I take the honeycomb frame he hands me, a few bees crawling over the surface. "Will they try to sting me?"

"Nah. And even if they do try, they won't be able to."

Right. I suppose the suit my dad instructed I put on before he all but dragged me out of the ranch house is good for keeping the bees at bay. Even if I'm starting to sweat under the layers.

My dad makes a thoughtful sound as he checks another of the frames. "Better give it another week before I collect the honey."

"How do you know when it's ready?"

"Ah, well. See the honeycomb cells here? Most of 'em needa be capped on top. It's the bees' way of storing the honey that's ready. We're nearly there. Looks like we'll have a good harvest this year."

My dad audibly praises the bees, slipping both frames back into the hive. Beekeeping is his current fixation. He's always had one hobby or another to entertain him, for as long as I can remember. He started this hive not that long ago with the sole purpose of harvesting honey in order to make my mom lavender-honey cookies from scratch, a favorite treat she tried years ago but can't buy around here.

He's always shown his love through action more than anything. Not that he doesn't tell us he loves us plenty. But hearing it and feeling it your entire life are two different things.

"Why are you and Mom divorced?" I ask.

My dad stills for just a second before finishing the task of closing up the hive. Turning away from it, he waves me into step next to him. "Walk with me."

My dad pulls off his beekeeper's hat, so I do the same, the two of us looking ridiculous in our all-white attire. The sun overhead is hot today, the dairy barn not far off from the beehive setup. It's peaceful out here. Quiet and a little more secluded than my dad's cabin-style home near the ranch house.

"Did I ever tell you the story of how your mother and I got engaged?"

I nod slowly, the memory of it a distant thing. "It was spur of the moment, right? While y'all were...outside somewhere?"

"At a friend's pig roast, that's right. Doesn't sound the most romantic, I know." My dad lets out a soft chuckle before his voice turns almost wistful. "But I remember the moment clearly. Your mother was laughing, the sun shining behind her. I thought to myself, 'this woman right here is the most important person I will ever meet.' I asked her to marry me. Just two words. And she said yes."

My dad smiles, stopping in the shade of a large tree. I see a lot of Jackson and Remi in his face. The more angular features. Colton and I have always looked more like our mom.

"Your mother never let me live that down," he says, sounding fond. "There was no ring. No finesse whatsoever. We were young and rash and foolish at times, me more than her. But we were in love. We got divorced so I could do it right."

I nearly trip over my own foot, despite the fact that we're standing still. "What?"

My dad laughs, his smile crinkling his eyes. "You heard. We got divorced so I could propose again. I know that probably doesn't make sense to a lot of folks, but it doesn't need to. It made sense to us."

I shake my head, hardly able to believe I've never heard this story before. But my parents have always been somewhat private when it comes to their relationship. They're not...cold to one another. Never have been, despite them being divorced for so much of my childhood and beyond. But I thought that was part of the problem. Their heated bickering.

"It wasn't because of the fighting?" I ask my dad.

His eyes widen in clear surprise. "What? 'Course not. Your mother and I fight because we care. So damn much. There's not a single person on this earth I'd fight as hard for."

For a second, I'm reminded of Colton and Noah and their less-than-amicable start. "And the separate houses?"

My dad shrugs. "Works best for us. We're both stubborn. I don't have to tell you that. A little space reminds us of what we're missing when we're both being too hardheaded to apologize." At my staring, my dad lets loose a laugh. "What, did you think your mother and I had fallen out of love?"

"Well, yeah," I admit. "I figured your feelings had to have changed, and, maybe, you stuck close to one another for the family's benefit."

My dad's lips twitch into a small smile. "Relationships look different for everybody. Some people are meant to find one another. To stick through thick and thin. I truly believe that. There's no mistaking when you've found a connection so rare. A person you can't imagine living your life without."

My chest tumbles and swoops, painted eyes, like earth and air, flitting to the forefront of my mind. I look out toward the far fields leading to the base of the mountains, the knowledge of Oakley so close a comfort, even if I can't see him right this instant.

It wasn't the same when he was thousands of miles away. When I couldn't see his face without a phone screen or feel the vibrations accompanying his voice. When I didn't have the assurance that he was within my reach if I needed him. To know his arms were available for a hug.

I've always wanted Oakley close. Wanted him for my own. Even when we were kids facing the unstoppable tide of time, I didn't want to lose what I'd found with him.

Someone who understands me. Who listens and makes me feel light. Someone who loves me without a single condition.

Oakley has always loved me. And I've always loved him.

Which is why him leaving Darling, leaving *me*, cut worse than anything else I've ever faced.

I find my dad's gaze, the man watching me patiently. My throat feels hoarse when I speak. "Why did y'all divorce the second time?"

My dad lets out the tiniest hum. "Well, now, I can't be telling you all my secrets, can I? Oh, look. It's lunchtime."

I follow his gaze toward the fields, the ranchers riding in for the lunch hour. My dad is already walking toward the main house, his beekeeper's hat at his side. I catch sight of Oakley at the back of the group, the lingering pain over his absence lifting into something contented and bright.

Oakley must spot me, too, because he heads in my direction. There's a grin on his face when he reaches for the rope at the side of his saddle.

"Oak," I call out, taking a single step back. "Don't you dare."

"You better run," he shouts.

Cursing, I drop the beekeeper's hat and take off toward a nearby fence. It's low enough I could hop over, but the sound of horse's hooves is fast approaching. A *whoosh* cuts through the air before I can reach the barrier. It's all the warning I get before Oakley's lasso tightens fast around my chest.

I go careening to the ground, coming to a stop on my back and staring up at the cloud-dotted sky as Oakley jogs my way, laughing all the while. The moment he's close enough, I give the rope he's still holding a firm tug. He goes down, catching himself on his knees as he falls over my torso, my best friend continuing to cackle as if he's having the time of his life.

"Caught you," he manages, sounding winded.

"If my arms weren't tied to my sides right now, you'd be getting smacked upside the head."

Oakley seems to find that amusing, levering up enough for his gaze to rake down over me. "Huh. You look pretty good all tied up."

"Oak. I swear to God."

"Why are you dressed like a marshmallow?" he asks, apparently only now clocking the white beekeeper's suit my dad outfitted me in.

"Untie me, will you?"

"I kinda like you like this," he muses, his eyebrows bouncing ridiculously.

Oh, good grief.

"How about this," I say evenly, my gaze drifting over Oakley's face, those blue-and-brown eyes so close I can see every fleck of color. "Later, when we don't have half the ranch surely watching us, you can tie me up for as long as you want. And do whatever you want."

Oakley's breath catches, the man stilling. He licks his lips, and my gaze drops there. "Do you...*want* to be tied up?"

"I don't think I'd mind it," I tell him truthfully, my stare stuck on his mouth. There's some stubble there, which I knew, of course. But his lips look soft. I've only ever felt them on my neck and back. What would they feel like elsewhere?

Oakley clears his throat before shifting off of me, his cheeks flushed under the midday sun. He sets to work loosening the lasso, helping me to sit so he can tug it off over my shoulders. "All right?" he checks.

"Fine," I tell him, glancing at the ranch house. Remi waves from the deck, a couple of the ranch hands beside him. I sigh. "Gonna get you back for this."

"Yeah?" Oakley asks, tone light if not a little strained. Amusement dances in his eyes as he re-coils his rope. "And how do you plan on doing that?"

"Oh, I can think of many ways for you to make it up to me. And I don't think you'll complain about a single one of them."

Oakley's mouth drops open, the man staring at me for a second. "Jesus Christ, are you..."

"What?" I ask, hefting myself to my feet and shoving down the beekeeper's suit, more than ready to be out of it.

Oakley shakes his head, swiping his hat off the ground before standing. "I just didn't realize you had such a mouth on you, Law."

"Oh, you know I have a mouth. You just aren't used to me talking about sex."

"Fair enough," he says around a huff of laughter. "It doesn't...feel weird to you?"

"Talking about it?" I ask, the two of us heading in the direction of Oakley's horse, Clover, who's waiting patiently for him to return. "No. Why would it?"

"I dunno. Just different for us, isn't it?"

I consider that as we walk toward the stables, Clover in tow. Most everyone else is ahead of us, inside the house already. "Logically, yes, it's different. But it feels like the easiest thing."

"Christ," Oakley mutters, grabbing an apple from the fridge before glancing at me, something almost hesitant in his gaze. "How, uh, do you see this going?"

"The rope? I figured I'd show up, you'd tie me up, and then you'd fuck me or do whatever else you think would feel good until you're too tired to keep going any longer."

Oakley misses a step on his way to Clover's stall, his answering groan sounding pained. "Fucking hell. That's not what I meant, but *damn*."

My eyes flick downward as Oakley discreetly adjusts himself. "Are you...hard right now?"

He shoots me a sharp look. "D'you have to bring it up?"

"I just... That's all it takes?"

He groans again, passing the apple to Clover, who happily chomps the fruit. "Don't let it go to your head, Law."

"I think I'm gonna. You like the idea of fucking me that much? Is it because I'm giving you blanket permission to do whatever you want? Or is it the bondage that gets you going?"

Oakley bends over, his hands on his knees as he lets out a heavy breath. "Lawson, I swear to all that is holy and not, you needa stop talking, or I won't be able to go inside that house full of people for lunch. Can we just...revisit this at a later time?"

"All right."

He eyes me dubiously. "You gonna be good?"

"For now," I concede.

"Lord," he murmurs, straightening.

I keep my mouth shut as we make our way to the ranch house, but I can't help but sneak surreptitious glances Oakley's way. Knowing I can push the man's buttons so easily is...satisfying, if I'm being honest.

When we get to the back deck, Oakley veers off toward the adjoining outdoor washroom. I head inside, passing through the dining room full of people and into the hallway bathroom to wash up. I'm on my way to drop the beekeeper suit off in the mudroom when I nearly run into Jackson. My brother is muttering to himself, his gaze on the ground as he passes.

"Oh, Jesus. I did *not* need to see that. Nope. No. Nuh-uh."

Curious, I peek my head into the living room, where I find Hank Darling dipping his ex-wife Marigold in a kiss. A smile plays at the corner of my lips, the sight one I'd happen upon from time to time in my childhood, whether my parents were married or not. I've seen it less these past twenty-some years, having lived away from the ranch house for so long.

"What was that for?" my mom asks the moment she's upright, a few inches taller than my dad when standing.

He hums. "Someone reminded me today of the importance of holding close the good we've found in our lives."

My mom sets her hands on her hips, her voice turning deceptively soft. "Good?"

"Oh Lord, Mari. You know that's not what I—"

"I would *think* having spent over forty-five years with the person who birthed four of your sons—*four*—would rank higher than *good*, but what do I know? Apparently, I'm at the same level as a decent slice of mild cheddar cheese."

My dad sputters.

My mom, apparently having noticed me in the doorway, sends a quick wink my way before refocusing on her ex-husband, her expression screaming *now what do you have to say for yourself?*

Shaking my head, I leave them to their bickering, realizing... Christ, it's foreplay? Not wanting to think too hard on that, I join the lunch crowd in the dining room, my eyes finding Oakley.

He's smiling as he chats with Remi, hands flying along with his spoken words, his leather cowboy hat hanging off the back of his chair. There's an overwhelming rush of fondness that floods me as I stare at my friend, this man I've known all my life, who's so much a part of my existence it's hard to see where he ends and I begin.

Can I imagine spending my life without Oakley?

No. No, I can't.

Chapter 20

OAKLEY

I set my empty pint glass down on the bar top, the dull thunk barely audible over the chatter inside The Barrel.

Virginia raises an eyebrow. "Another?"

"No thanks," I say.

I'm not looking to get drunk. I'm just...

I don't know what. Trying to figure out how to broach the topic of relationships with my longtime friend I happen to be fucking who admitted he doesn't even know how he feels about the idea of romantic attachments right now?

Christ.

"Is it the Darlings?" Virginia asks, her voice low enough not to carry.

My eyes whip to her. "What?"

"I know that look," she says, waving a finger in front of my face. "It's the *I'm in over my head when it comes to a Darling brother* look. I've seen it before, you know."

"With Ash?" I ask, accepting the water she passes me. She and Ash were friends from before he came to town, as I learned from the man himself. They met back in college.

Virginia nods. "With him. And with Noah."

I grunt, sipping the cold water.

"Y'all have been friends forever," she says, not even needing to name Lawson. We both know. "Have things changed recently?"

"Is this not a little cliché?" I joke. "Me airing my problems to the bartender?"

Virginia's lips quirk. "Pretend I'm still your neighbor if you want. Either way, I'll keep my mouth shut about it. Even to Ash."

I nod slowly, fingers getting wet from the condensation on my glass. I draw a little horseshoe in the moisture before wiping it away with my thumb. "Here's the thing. I haven't spent my life pining. I really haven't. I've been *fine*. Lawson was my friend and nothing more. I didn't feel like...like I was missing out on my one true love or anything like that. I..."

God, how do I even explain it?

"I lived my life, and I was fine. Until Lawson changed everything, and now I've got feelings, and there's no shoving them back down again."

"And the problem?" Virginia asks.

I swallow down another gulp of water. "The man just got out of a nineteen-year marriage. He's figuring himself out, and he's not there yet. I know he's not. So I either push the issue for my benefit, knowing he's not ready, I wait, or..."

"Or?"

"Or I protect myself," I say, the mere idea of ending things with Lawson filling me with heavy dread. I don't want to do that. Not in the least.

But if Lawson decides he wants to date men who aren't me? Or...if a relationship isn't something he's interested in at all?

What then?

Could I let Lawson keep a hold of my heart, knowing he couldn't offer the same?

Virginia hums softly, the sound barely audible. "What would be the worst-case scenario if you told him how you feel?"

"He'd do everything in his power to make me happy, even to the detriment of his own well-being and happiness, 'cause the man is too damn loyal for his own good."

The second the words are out of my mouth, I freeze.

I... I hadn't even considered it as a possibility, but it's the absolute truth. If I told Lawson I wanted more from him, he'd give it to me, even if he wasn't ready. Even if it wasn't what he wanted inside his own heart.

I'd become his next Laura.

The thought is enough to have a cold sweat breaking out over my body.

I can't rush him in this, can I? Either he'll love me in his own time and his own way or...he won't.

"Fuck," I mutter, dropping my face into my hands.

Virginia gives my shoulder a squeeze. "Love's a bitch, huh?"

"It's the absolute best and worst thing."

A vibration from my phone has me pulling the device from my pocket. Virginia shoots me a small, sympathetic smile before moving off down the bar to serve other customers. It's a text from Lawson. Of course it is.

Law: Where are you?

Jesus, is the man at my house?

Me: Just grabbing a drink. I'll be home soon.

Lawson sends me a picture. It's him and Bell...on my goddamn couch.

Me: Lawson Darling, you get that cow off my furniture!

Tugging out my wallet, I throw a ten down before giving Virginia a goodbye wave. Another text comes through as I'm heading out the door. One that has my feet drawing to a stop in the middle of the sidewalk.

It's a picture of a coil of rope lying casually over the top of my couch.

Jesus fucking Christ.

My pulse is a swift staccato as I head toward my truck. He wants me to tie him up? Truly?

I wish I didn't want that as damn badly as I do. It's not even the thought of Lawson bound that has my blood pooling hot. It's the fact that he trusts me. That he wants to lie on my bed, boneless with nowhere to go, while I turn his world inside out.

And *fuck*, I want to give him that. I want to give him *everything*. I want to take care of his pleasure, soothe his pain. I want Lawson to rely on me, to know he's not alone in this world. I want to tuck him in at night, my body surrounding his, the man's heart beating beneath my palm.

I want till death do us part with Lawson Darling.

I'm his. And no matter what else, there's simply no changing that.

The drive home is short, even as every scant mile seems twice as long as usual. The lights are on inside my house, Lawson's truck waiting in the spot beside my own. The stars are out tonight, faint flickers, reminding me of Peter Pan and flying on until morning.

My front door is unlocked, Lawson seated on the couch but Bell absent.

"That didn't take you long," he says in greeting, the rope still draped over the couch next to him, anything but innocent.

"Well, I had to make sure you weren't letting my cow ruin the damn house."

"Really? It didn't have anything to do with this?"

Lawson taps the rope, his face impassive enough but a slight gleam in his eye.

"You've gotten cheeky," I note, letting my boots hit the front mat.

He shrugs, tracking my movements. "Maybe I'm curious to find out what you'll do to me when I'm tied to your bed."

It feels as if my lungs have forgotten how to function. "That so?"

"I think if I asked for anything at all, you'd give it to me."

I swallow, the motion rough. "I think you're right."

"But I'm not gonna ask."

"No?"

"No," he says, turning my way as I round the couch. "Because I know I'll like whatever you do to me, Oak. You'll make me feel good."

I breathe through my racing pulse, his faith in me causing my head to swim. "Do you needa take care of anything first?"

In answer, Lawson stands, swiping the rope and heading toward my bedroom.

Fuck.

He's undressing when I enter the room, the bedside lamp already on. Seeing the man revealed piece by piece is an exquisite kind of torture. The small of his back as he lifts his shirt. His shoulder blades, flexing with the upward movement of his arms. The back of his neck, an arm free and then two. He drops his shirt to the floor before reaching for his pants. The swipe of a button, a zipper being lowered. A push, and then his ass, covered by his boxer briefs. Hairy thighs, thick calves, pants hitting the floor.

My breath is harsh in my lungs when Lawson hooks his thumbs under the band of his underwear and tugs.

He's entirely unabashed about his nudity. Not cocky. Not presenting his best angles or even seemingly aware of my appraisal. He simply doesn't care. And perhaps part of that is his own viewpoint on physicality. He doesn't find people appealing in that way. Or, maybe more appropriately said, a person's appearance isn't what turns Lawson on.

But I wish I could tell him how beautiful he is to me. Every scar, every imperfection. Every line that makes up the person I've grown alongside for the past four-plus decades.

Lawson said loving someone means loving all of them, past, present, and future. It means protecting who they are. Being a safe space for them, always.

Maybe I can't say the words yet, but I can show Lawson I'll protect every single piece of him. I'll worship him. Love him. For as long as he'll let me.

Lawson tosses the comforter down before settling in the middle of my bed, the rope lying beside him. His cock is soft, and I never realized how appealing I'd find that, but there's something about being the one to coax him to hardness that makes my protective instincts go into overdrive. I don't want anyone else to have that privilege.

I want Lawson to trust me with it. Only me.

Lawson watches as I get rid of my clothes, tossing my t-shirt beside him on the bed instead of elsewhere. My own cock is hard as I approach. There's simply no avoiding it where Lawson is concerned. His gaze catches there, an appreciation in his eyes that makes me want to beat my damn chest. His focus returns to my face as I kneel at his side, picking up the shirt.

"The rope isn't the smoothest," I explain. "So I'm gonna wrap this over your wrists first so you don't get hurt."

He nods once, offering his hands.

My heart beats like a drum as I wrap the soft cotton around him, tying it into a gentle knot to keep it in place. The rope is next. I secure Lawson's wrists with a knot I can release quickly, making sure the rope is sitting comfortably over the shirt, not pressing into any one spot too hard. Lawson nods his approval once I raise an eyebrow. Looping the tail end of the rope around the headboard, I pull it taut and tie it off.

Lawson's arms are stretched high above his head, only an inch or so of wiggle room in which he can move. I grab a pillow, and he automatically lifts his head. Wedging it beneath him while Lawson looks up at me with nothing but utter trust has my chest squeezing so tight I have to work hard not to do something stupid. Like kiss him and never, ever stop.

"All right?" I ask.

Lawson nods in a slow roll, even as there's a slight pinch between his brows.

"What is it?" I prod.

"You don't... I mean, you don't want me turned on my stomach for this?"

I inhale a short breath, surprised by the question. "That'd be pretty uncomfortable with your arms raised above your head, don't you think?"

"It's just... I figured you wouldn't want to be face to face. We haven't been before."

My mind rushes through our past encounters, and I realize...he's right. The first couple times I fucked him, in my kitchen, in our tent while camping when it was too dark to even see his face...

Has that been intentional on his part? Because he, what, thought I wouldn't want to see every damn flicker of pleasure that crossed his features? Because he figured it'd be too personal for what we are?

Which is friends. Who fuck.

I take Lawson's chin in my hand, my hold gentle but unyielding. "I want your eyes on me, Law. I'm not pretending it's anyone but you in my bed."

His chest rises with his breath. "All right."

I can't help but huff my amusement as I let go, easing down Lawson's body. "You start to cramp, you tell me. I don't want this hurting you."

His eyes never leave mine. "I'll tell you, Oak."

"Good," I murmur, running my palms up Lawson's thighs, his hair bristling my skin. "And feel free to use that mouth of yours, princess. I'm at your service."

Lawson's indrawn breath is sharper this time. Liquid brown eyes hold mine, flaring wide when I dip my head to run my tongue along the length of his cock. His thighs tense, the man jolting and his mouth popping open when I do it again, soft, wet brushes of my tongue sending blood through his body to stiffen his cock. I take him into my mouth, wanting to feel him lengthen on my tongue. Lawson's responding moan sounds as if I caught him off-guard.

"F-fuck," he mutters, a disjointed sound.

I grin, sucking gently until Lawson is filling my mouth, the man by no means small, erect or not. His head rolls back as I slide my lips to the tip of his cock and back down again.

"Jesus," he says, his arms tugging against the rope before he lets them hang loose. "Why the fuck does that feel so much better when it's your mouth?"

I pop off of him, sliding my fist up and down his cock, feeling a fierce sort of pride at his words. "Two fucks in under half a minute. You must really like it."

"I do," he says easily, his head coming back down to see me better. "So carry on."

My laugh feels a little wild. A little joyous. "As you'd like, princess."

Lawson groans when I replace my fist with my mouth, his hips bucking out of reflex. I don't hide an ounce of my enthusiasm, wanting him to see how much I like this, wanting him to, maybe, realize this is so much more than friends fooling around.

I let my hands wander as I bob my head, blunt nails raking over his thighs, his stomach, tweaking a nipple and then two. Instead of getting tenser the longer I tease him, Lawson melts into the bedding. It's a remarkable thing to witness, how something as simple as physical touch and affection can relax him, body and mind.

As much as I'd love to suck his cock until the man empties down my throat, I don't want this over so soon. Lawson grunts as I lever off his dick, dragging my tongue along the sensitive tendon of his inner thigh and up to his hip before biting lightly. His eyes slip shut at the nip of pain, as if he finds it just as relaxing as a gentler touch.

"I can't decide what I want to do with you," I mutter, dragging my lips up to his belly button. His stomach muscles flex, the tiniest twitch, but the man remains limp on my bed.

His response is somewhat slurred. "Yeah?"

"Mm. Which is why I think I'll do it all."

"All?"

"Kiss every inch of you I can reach. Your cock, your chest, your elbows. Finger you for a while until you start dripping onto your stomach. Find each spot on your body that makes you moan. And then fuck you until you come for me. How's that sound, princess?"

Lawson's eyes find mine, the man looking dazed as I drag my lips over the dips of his stomach. "Sounds like I must be dreaming. If I am, stay here with me, Oak?"

My breath stutters out of me, Lawson's skin warm and solid and real beneath my touch. I promise him what I know to be the absolute truth. "I'm not going anywhere."

Chapter 21

LAWSON

Oakley's lips blaze a path across my skin, his stubble scorching with the way it heats my flesh. He makes good on his word, kissing across my chest, his mouth softly scraping as it trails up my arms in turn, kisses laid against my elbows.

He's everywhere. In my field of vision, in my head, his touch on my skin, his scent in my nose, the sounds of his satisfaction filling my ears. It's overwhelming in the best possible way, and a near-frantic alarm takes up residence in my chest, so sudden I'm left lightheaded. I don't want this to end.

I don't want this ever to end.

Oakley's mouth travels back down my arm, the man clearly taking his time and enjoying it. I don't mind that one bit. I love every single thing he's doing to me. But I'm also desperate to feel those lips on my neck again. On my cock.

"Oak," I groan, tilting my head to the side, hoping he gets the hint.

He chuckles hoarsely, his lips traveling along my shoulder inward. They stop, hovering near my neck, so close but not close enough. "Here?"

"Do I needa draw you a map? Yes, there."

His laughter ghosts over my skin, and then his lips follow, prickling pain and pleasure a single entity as he presses a kiss to my neck. His fingers in my hair tug my head further aside, stubble rough, tongue smooth as he lays waste to the last of my brain cells.

"Fuck, princess. I could torture you like this for hours."

"Not torture," I manage, his fingers skipping featherlight down my cock.

His huff is small. "Only you would think edging is a damn walk in the park."

"Edging?"

He hums an "Mhm," his mouth leaving small kisses down the column of my throat. "When you prolong the period before an orgasm, making arousal last as long as possible before, finally, you or your partner allows your climax to take you over."

My brain whirs. "I don't see how that's a bad thing."

His laugh is louder this time. "It's not. Some people just don't have the patience for that kinda thing."

"Well..." My words cut off when Oakley's fingers wrap around my cock, the man tugging slowly as his lips press to my Adam's apple. It takes me a moment to find my voice. "I like this part best. Orgasms come and go so quickly. But this...this feels better than getting off for the heck of it."

Oakley's head comes up, his eyes meeting mine, the marbling of his irises taken over by so much pupil. There's a seriousness in his gaze at odds with the toying of his fingers on my cock. "It should. You deserve to feel good, Law."

"You make me feel real good. Always do."

He swallows, his eyes pinging between my own. "In that case, spread your legs for me, princess. I know another good place to torture."

I let out a soft laugh, widening my legs and hitching up my knees. Oakley leans down again, his lips traveling across my torso like a paintbrush. They bypass my dick, his breath ghosting lower before there's pressure against my balls. Air puffs from my lungs, Oakley's tongue a tease more than anything, the tip of it swiping against my sac and making my toes curl.

"Don't move," he murmurs.

"Where would I go?" I counter, giving the rope binding me to the headboard a purposeful tug.

Oakley's smile is wicked as he pops off the bed, his hair falling over his forehead in a messy wave. He grabs supplies from his nightstand, returning in almost no time at all. Wet fingers drag over my hole once he's resituated, and a sigh escapes my lungs.

"I love how much you love this," he says, rubbing against me, not yet pressing inside.

"I'm guessing that makes me a bottom?" I ask, having been wondering about that.

He hums, sliding one finger inside of me, constant upward pressure making my hips tilt further off the bed. *Ah, fuck.* "Does the idea of fucking a man appeal to you?"

"Not as much as this," I admit.

I nearly jolt when Oakley's tongue runs a path up my cock. "You only need to pick a label if you want one, Law. Top, bottom, side, vers—they're just words, and preferences can change. I think respect and communication in the bedroom is more important than a term that may mean something different to each person who uses it."

The fact that Oakley has two fingers inside of me now, stroking rhythmically, makes it hard to focus on what he's saying. "And you? This works for you?"

Oakley's eyes meet mine as his tongue flicks across the top of my dick. "I do prefer to top, so yes, this works for me real well. But if you ever want to try having me sink down over your cock, I'd be happy to oblige, princess."

Fuck.

"What, uh...what's a side?"

Oakley's chuckle curves his lips into a smile, the man looking damn happy as he slides three fingers into my ass. The stretch has my neck arching back for only a moment, my eyes returning to Oakley as soon as I can manage it. "Someone who prefers sex without penetration."

"Ah," I rasp, the thickness of Oakley's fingers making me ache for the man's cock. "Oak."

"Getting desperate?" he asks, his tone both playful and smug.

"You telling me you're not ready to have my ass clamping down around your dick? You haven't even touched it."

The man grunts, heat blazing in his eyes as he slips his fingers free. He leans over my stomach, tongue swiping along my abdomen, right below my cock. "Told you I'd get you leaking."

"Mission accomplished, cowboy. Now suit up and put that horse to stable."

"Jesus," he mutters, a laugh in his tone as he grabs a condom. He gives his cock a slow stroke as I watch. "I think I'll take it as a compliment that you're calling my dick a stallion."

"Take it as you'd like. Just fucking ram him home already."

"Good God," Oakley says, grinning now as he rolls the condom on. "Isn't this supposed to be my penance for roping you earlier? 'Cause I can't say I'm upset about any of it."

"Told you you wouldn't be," I point out. "And you know I'm not actually mad about that, right?"

"I do," he says, easing forward, one hand on his dick as he notches against me. He pushes in ever so slowly, even though I can tell he's hanging on by a thread himself. "You just enjoy giving me shit for the heck of it. Always have."

"That's not true."

"It is," he says, pressing further forward, his cock opening me up the same way his fingers did. I focus on the feel of it, the fullness a unique sort of pleasure that makes my mind blank and every inch of my body tingle, as if enveloped by a comforting haze. Oakley goes on, his voice husky as he sinks deeper. "You like... toying with me because I'm the one person in your life you don't have to be responsible around. You can let loose, and you know I'll never judge you. I'll never... think less of you for finding joy in the littlest things."

My breath catches, his words throwing me temporarily off-kilter, despite me knowing it to be true. All of it. "Because I trust you," I tell him needlessly.

Oakley swallows hard, his hand on my thigh, his hips pressed flush against my ass now. "I know you do."

"So you can't leave me again."

His face falls in an instant, the sorrow in his eyes making me wish I could take the words back. But I've never been good at filtering myself around Oakley. The one time I tried, he went and left Montana. Left *me*.

I can't let that happen again.

"God, Law," the man murmurs, tucking my leg around his hip before closing the distance between us, his weight pressing me down against the bed. "I'm so fucking sorry for that."

"I know you are."

"And I'm not leaving again," he says, his eyes imploring me to believe him. "I didn't realize this was still weighing on you."

I don't have a thing to say in response, knowing it shouldn't still be. The man is back. I believe him when he says he's not going again.

But the years I spent without Oakley were arguably the worst of my life. The thought of losing him a second time is terrifying. I'm not sure how I'd cope.

"God," Oakley mutters again, his head falling beside my own as he tucks himself firmly over me. His hands slide up the outsides of my raised arms, Oakley's elbows on the bed to either side of my head. "I'm sorry." The words are accompanied by a slow roll of his hips. "I'm sorry, princess."

"Don't," I manage, my voice coming out hoarse. "Don't fuck me like an apology, Oak. You already did your sorries. I don't want this to be...to be *that*."

He puffs out a breath, turning to press his lips to my jaw. "You're right."

"I know I am."

He snaps his hips a little harder, the glide of his cock making my back arch. "This better, princess?"

"Mhm."

Oakley burrows his face into my neck as he starts fucking me in earnest. There's an urgency in the way he's coiled around me. A pleading in every rut and touch, although for what I can't figure out.

I'm too quickly lost to the euphoria, the passing of time ceasing to exist, no troubles able to touch me while I'm suspended here. One of Oakley's hands glides up and down my arm, each fingertip trailing electricity, his mouth finding spots on my neck to abrade. Down to my clavicle. Near my armpit. My ear, Oakley's chuckle when I groan like a pleasant sort of static in my head.

"You're gone, aren't you?" he murmurs, his voice whisper-soft, although everything sounds a little fuzzy.

"'S'good, Oak."

"I know, princess. I don't wanna touch your cock yet. I'm not done torturing you."

I open my mouth to respond, but Oakley beats me to it.

"I know, not torture. I'm not done *worshiping* you. Enjoying every piece of you."

My heart kicks. "However long you want."

His groan is pained. "I wish you could hear the words you say."

I try to run back through them now, but Oakley plants a hand under my ass and lifts at the same time as he punches inside of me. My breath stutters out as he ruthlessly pegs me again and again.

"F-fuck," I groan, my cock bucking, all that haziness I was floating in coalescing into a sharp point. "Too...*ah*, too good."

"Is that possible?" he asks, his words breathy.

"Need..."

"A little longer," he says, slowing right back down, the shallow roll of his hips having me panting. I can feel every inch of him, every slide into me, the thickness of his cock keeping me open and the man himself a blanket of sensation I want to curl up in.

I know he's trying to draw this out, but I'm so close. *So* close, and every minute shift of his body against mine, inside of mine, has me creeping ever closer to that edge.

I don't want to trip. I want to fucking fly.

"Oak," I husk out, turning my head to catch his gaze. Blue and brown stares back at me, the man's cheeks and forehead flushed, his mouth slick and parted, so close I could catch his lips with my own if I wanted. *A kiss*. A token. It wouldn't mean the same thing now as it did when we were eleven. I force my voice to work. "Make me come for you, Oakley."

Gaze never leaving my own, Oakley picks up his pace, wraps his hand around my cock, and strokes. My orgasm hits me like the summer sun blasting out from around a cloud. When the sky is dreary and the air feels cold, but your face is still turned toward the sky, waiting, waiting. And then there it is, a wave of heat, a swelling in your chest and a lightness of your very being. It's bliss. A world dark having gone light. It's fleeting, you know it is, but you savor every single second of it for as long as you can.

Prickles run along the corner of my mouth, soft lips brushing featherlight against my skin. Oakley's lips. His exhalation is stuttered, an excruciating ecstasy I understand, his hips jolting against me as he comes undone. His mouth is right there. *Right* there. And *God*, I just want...

But Oakley turns his head before I can finish my thought, his face tucked against my neck, his breaths sawing out, one hand still clutching my arm. My heart beats erratically. I don't want the clouds to return yet. I want to bask in Oakley's sunlight.

Which is why, when the man says, "Stay tonight," I have only one response.

"Yeah."

Oakley draws back, his gaze snagging on my mouth for a prolonged moment before he pushes up onto his hands. He slips from my body, discarding the condom and making quick work of untying my arms. He lowers them back to my sides slowly, rubbing each as if to help the flow of blood return.

"All right?" he checks.

"Fine."

Oakley wipes me down with the corner of the sheet before falling next to me on the bed, too tired maybe to bother with anything more. I don't mind. I scoot up the mattress with my pillow, finding Oakley watching me, expression serious.

"It's not weird," I assure him, wondering if that's what he's concerned about. He did ask the other day if talking about sex with him was odd. None of it is. "Does it feel weird to you?"

"No," he answers quickly. "That's not what I was thinking."

I wait, but he doesn't volunteer more. "Would you get over here then? I'm getting cold."

With a huff and a twitch of a smile, Oakley scoots closer. He wraps his arm around my chest, bristling the side of my shoulder almost aggressively with his lips before I reach over and swat him. His sigh sounds happy, his hand wandering down to my forearm before stilling. He brushes a fingertip along the scar I got there when I was sixteen.

"I remember when this happened," he says, tracing the crescent shape slowly.

"I should hope so. You were there."

Oakley hums. "I've seen that old ass wandering around the ranch a couple times. The Darling Donkey. Why is that?"

I chuckle. "Jackson could tell you the story better than I could. The donkey helped him find Ash when he went missing."

"Ash was missing? Shit."

"More like stuck. In the woods. Jackson's been giving the donkey treats ever since as a thank-you."

Oakley snorts, his finger continuing to run along my forearm, over the bite mark. "I still haven't forgiven him."

"It's a donkey, Oak. Let it go."

"A donkey who bit you for no good reason," he says hotly.

My chest warms at the consternation on Oakley's face. "At least I had you there to run him off, didn't I? My protector."

Oakley goes motionless for just a second before his hand slides up to my chest, his fingers and palm skimming lightly over my skin. "I don't like seeing you hurt. Not then. Not now."

"I know," I say softly, feeling the same. Of course I do.

His hand splays over my heart, voice solemn. "I'm not leaving again, Law. I need you to know that. To trust in it."

My pulse skitters. Oakley follows my draw when I pull him close, curling around me, my protector still, chasing away the clouds whether or not he realizes it. "I know, Oak. Because I won't let you go."

Chapter 22

OAKLEY

Lawson is at the school today, the teachers having gone in to get their classrooms ready before the students return next week. I saw him off this morning after dropping him back at the ranch house, seeing as he spent the night at my place. Again. As he's been doing most nights for the past two weeks.

There's no way that hasn't been noticed by his family, not that any of them have said a word about it to me. I've seen a few looks, though. From Jackson. Remi. Marigold, even. The only two who've seemed somewhat oblivious are Colton and Hank, although I don't know if it's a matter of not noticing or not being the overly interfering types.

And there's Wendy, of course. She's come over with Lawson a couple times for dinner. I can't tell for sure if I'm imagining her looking a little longer at me and her dad or if she's figured it out.

Christ. What would I even say to her? *Yes, I'm shacking up with your father. Practice safe sex.* That might be a minefield better left to Lawson.

When I turn in for the day, I run into a familiar farrier inside the horse barn. One that isn't Colton. Noah King is bent over a hoof, fixing new shoes on Hazel, the mare I used to ride before I left Montana. He gives me a nod when I pass with Clover.

"Heard she's yours now," I say in greeting, stopping outside Clover's stall.

Noah huffs, an amused if not short sound, his tattoo-covered arms flexing as he works. "She is."

"Heard Colton's yours, too."

He lifts his head, a bemused grin on his face. "I'd love to watch him hear you say that."

I chuckle, pulling Clover's saddle loose and lifting his saddle pad off his sweaty back. "It's a mutual thing, I'm sure."

"That it is," Noah says, sounding fond. Which, considering he and Colton were at each other's throats last I was here, is incredibly odd to bear witness to. "You and Lawson now?"

"Well, shit," I mutter, staring at the top of the man's head. "No beating around the bush, huh?"

Noah laughs. "I'm not one for subtlety."

"No, I guess not. I dunno," I tell him truthfully. "Still figuring it out."

He makes a sound as if he gets it. "These Darling brothers need a minute. Don't take it to heart."

"What d'you mean?" I ask, swapping Clover's bridle out for a simple harness.

Noah hems for a moment, his rasp a rhythmic metronome to the brief silence. "Colton took a long time to admit his feelings for me. From what I know, Jackson was the same when it came to Ash. I think obstinance runs in this family's veins."

I hum.

Lawson sure is stubborn when he wants to be. But I'm not sure that has anything to do with...*us.*

It could be wishful thinking on my part, but I swear, I *swear*, something is changing for him. It's small things. Seeking intimacy outside of sex. Little touches that occur far more frequently than they used to. Sitting close on the couch instead of in his own space. The way he's been looking at me, like he's thinking hard. Hell, sleeping in my bed even if we haven't fucked.

I don't think Lawson is avoiding any feelings he might have on purpose, if they're there at all. I think, like he said, he's had other people's voices telling him what's *right* when it comes to sex and romance his whole life, so he needs the time to listen to himself. To replace those voices with his own.

And I can give him that time. After all we've been through, it's the least I can do.

"Thanks, Noah. I'll keep that in mind."

The man gives me a nod, and I finish getting Clover settled in his stall. Instead of heading straight home, I make my way to the ranch house, wanting to catch Lawson when he gets back from his first day at the school. I leave my boots on the deck and head to his room to wait, knowing he won't mind. I even change into fresh clothes—Lawson's, of course—so I don't leave dirt all over the place.

Spotting his old, ratty reprint of *Peter and Wendy*, the original novel written by J. M. Barrie, I snatch it off the bookshelf and start to read.

And that's exactly how Lawson finds me a good hour later, still sitting in his chair at the corner of the room. He pauses in the doorway, but his surprise doesn't last long. "Hey."

"Blast from the past," I tell him, holding up the book.

A smile quirks his lips as he closes the door, setting his laptop bag down. "Finish it?"

"Not even close. Good first day back?"

He nods, even as he all but falls on top of his bed. I huff a laugh, getting up to join him. Lawson doesn't complain when I start rubbing the tension from the nape of his neck.

"Can't believe the summer is nearly over," he mumbles. "Just one more year, and Wendy will be gone."

My chest pinches in sympathy. "She won't be gone, Law. Just spreading her wings for a bit."

He nods, rolling to his side, his eyes running over the book I set onto the bed beside us. "Do you know why I picked the name Wendy?"

"Because you love the story," I reply easily.

The corner of his lips turn into the briefest of smiles before he shakes his head, one finger tracing the old cover of the novel. "It makes me quite sad, actually."

"Wait, really? Why?"

Lawson turns onto his back, a sigh escaping his lips as he stares up at the ceiling. "Peter... He's a representation of youth. He can never age, can never grow up. He's so often depicted as being happy, as any child ought to be. But do you remember that time he was looking through Wendy's window, watching her from outside, thinking...what a lovely sight? A lovely sight he wasn't a part of. Peter loved Wendy in his own childlike way, but he knew at that moment he could never join her."

Lawson lets out a short, shuddering breath before going on.

"Every single person he loved moved on, Oak. But he was trapped playing pretend. I pity Peter Pan. And that's why the story has always stuck with me."

My heart aches at the sadness in his voice. "I didn't know that."

Lawson turns his gaze my way, warm brown eyes holding mine. For a second, time stalls. And then Lawson opens his mouth. "That story? It's the best reminder I have to *live*. You and Wendy are proof that I have."

My breath leaves me in a rush, the absolutely astounding impact of those words nearly knocking me to the floor. Have I been that pivotal in shaping Lawson's view of his life? That important to him?

Lawson lets out another sigh, completely unaware of how he's cracked me right open. "You smell like cattle."

My chuckle is more than a little hoarse. "I, uh...haven't showered yet."

"C'mon, then."

Lawson drops his feet to the floor and stands, making his way out into the hall, presumably to start the shower. I stare at the open doorway, knowing I shouldn't follow him. Not when I feel like this. So fragile. Like one wrong press could crack me clean in two. But my feet carry me forward nonetheless.

Lawson waits for me to join him in the bathroom before closing the door and shedding his clothes. He tugs my shirt—*his* shirt—off over my head. Then he pulls down my jeans and underwear and drags me into the shower like it's the simplest thing.

I wash myself with Lawson's soap as the man watches me passively, his eyes tired. He shampoos his own hair before tipping his face into the spray, letting the soapy suds run down his back. I take my turn rinsing next, Lawson shaking his head slightly at my routine.

"Never understood why you do body first and then hair," he mutters.

I shrug. "Does it matter?"

"Yes, it matters. You're dirtying your already clean body with the shampoo."

"It's just a different kind of soap," I point out. "It's not dirty."

He grumbles something I don't catch, so I collect some of the foamy suds from my head and wipe them across his cheek. Lawson's eyes come alive as he backs me into the wall, wrestling my arm down as I try to cover him in more shampoo bubbles.

"Stop it," he gripes.

"Nah. But thanks."

"Christ." He grunts, grabbing my arm again when I get free. "*Oak.*"

I flick his forehead, snickering at his scowl. "Admit I'm right and I'll stop."

Lawson slips an arm around me, snagging my hair and tugging my head back. My breath whooshes out of me, my heart beating fast as he pins me to the shower wall with his bulk, nearly equal to mine. He stops as quickly as he started, no doubt feeling my cock swelling against his hip. His eyes ping from my face down to my neck, my pulse firing rapidly beneath his gaze.

"Does it feel the same for you?" he asks.

"Does what?" I respond roughly, not following, all of my attention on Lawson's wet body crowded against my own.

He leans forward, warm lips brushing lightly against my neck. My eyes slip shut, a whisper of breath leaving me.

"This," Lawson says in answer, brushing his lips against me again, his stubble bristling. "Does it affect you the way it affects me?"

Ah, fuck.

"Yes," I admit, any part of Lawson touching me as close to heaven as I've ever been.

He hums, a pleased sound. When he slips a hand between us, reaching for my cock, I have to stop him, much as it pains me.

"Law... You can't get me off when there's a houseful of people a mere fifteen feet below us enjoying their dinner."

"No?"

My groan is half laugh. "No."

He hums again, his touch feathering away. "You kinda taste like shampoo."

After a beat, I boom a laugh.

My heart rate settles as we finish rinsing off, Lawson stepping out of the shower ahead of me. It gives my body some much-needed time to cool down.

Once we're dressed, me once again in his clothes, he raises an eyebrow. "Dinner?"

I huff. "Why not?"

With my hair as dry as it'll get, we head downstairs. The dining room is still packed, although the food is dwindling this late in the dinner hour. A couple of the ranchers are heading out, and no one pays us much mind as we join the fray. Mealtimes are always a bit hectic.

Ash seems to be the only one who catches our arrival, his eyes bouncing quickly from me and my damp hair to Lawson's equally damp locks. His smile flickers, eyes going wide. Lawson doesn't notice, sitting down and tugging me into a chair next to him. He spoons a heaping portion of pasta onto my plate before reaching for a platter of breadsticks.

"Evening, Oakley," Marigold says from down the table, her voice light. "Lawson dear."

Lawson tosses his mother a nod, preoccupied with filling our plates.

"Evening," I tell her, smiling as casually as I can.

She looks amused, and I glance Lawson's way again. I don't think he even realizes how obvious we are.

Or maybe he doesn't care?

Hope blooms in my chest, and I take a bite of the breadstick he passed me, the top covered in garlic, parsley, and parmesan.

"So, Lawson," Marigold tries again. "Is everything ready for the start of school?"

"Not quite," Lawson answers, pouring water into his glass and then my own. "But there's not much left to do."

"I bet Wendy's excited for her final year," Ash says, the blonde man's free hand resting on the back of Jackson's chair beside him. Remi is sitting nearby, too, watching the conversation as he eats his pasta, the simultaneous signing from several occupants of the table like second nature. Even Colton and Noah are present for dinner, the pair situated on the other side of Ash.

Lawson's smile is slight. "She is. Yeah."

Marigold's expression softens. I have no doubt she understands Lawson's conflicting emotions over his daughter growing up. My chest aches again at the thought, Lawson's words about Peter losing everyone he loved still fresh in my mind.

God. No wonder Lawson was so upset with me for leaving. I was the one person he could depend on. The one who promised I'd never go.

And I did just that.

I give the man's leg a squeeze under the table, feeling like no apology will ever be enough. His eyes meet mine, questioning, but I only send him a smile, not about to dredge up our history right here at the Darling Ranch dinner table.

Colton's voice breaks through the quiet. "Law, think you'll try dating again now that you're single?"

I swear my heart plain stops. Time does, too. A few wide eyes turn Colton's way, Remi's included. Other gazes dart from me to Lawson. Lawson himself is sitting frozen with his forkful of pasta halfway to his mouth.

"Colt," Noah says quietly from beside his boyfriend.

Colton looks from Noah back to Lawson. "What? Wendy would understand. Wouldn't she?"

"Uh," Lawson says, lowering his fork to his plate. "Wendy would be fine with it, I'm sure. But... No, that's not something I want."

My inhale is short but sharp, cutting through me like glass. I pull my hand off Lawson's leg, feeling eyes on me. I don't meet a single one, my entire focus on appearing as impassive as I can.

In my periphery, I can see Remi's gaze on his oldest brother.

Marigold makes a curious sound. "Lawson, dear..."

"It's my choice," Lawson says, his voice firm. "I know what I need to be happy. No one knows that better than me."

"You're right," his mother says, her tone conciliatory but sad.

Noah whispers something to Colton, who doesn't seem to understand why his question was so loaded.

And me?

I'm fairly certain that future I'd been envisioning, the one where Lawson and I were finally more than friends, just got shattered to dust alongside the shredded remains of my heart.

Chapter 23

LAWSON

The remainder of dinner is quiet.

The last of the ranchers start dispersing before long, heading home after a busy day of work. Jackson, Remi, and my mom bring dishes and silverware into the kitchen to be cleaned. Beside me, Oakley is eerily still.

"All right?" I ask him, keeping my voice low.

He nods in a sharp jerk that doesn't reassure me at all.

I feel bad for causing the mood to drop after shutting down conversation about my love life, but, frankly, it's not something I want to discuss with my family right now. Especially considering I haven't had the chance to discuss it with the one person it matters most to.

I make to grab our plates, but Ash beats me to it. "Go on," he says, canting his head toward the exit. "There are plenty of us to clean up."

"You're not supposed to," I point out, knowing Ash is officially off the clock at this point in the day.

He rolls his eyes. "It's no trouble. You two get."

Not about to argue against relinquished dish duties, I stand. Oakley joins me as Ash mutters something to himself about *turning into a real damn cowboy*.

Oakley wanders toward the back door, so I do the same, both of us stepping out onto the deck. There's a jitteriness to Oakley's movements as we stop along the glass at the back of the house, but when I reach for his arm, he skirts my grip, turning to face me.

"Did you mean that?" he asks, a frantic sort of gleam in his eyes that makes the blue look bright amidst the brown.

"Mean what?"

He tosses his hand toward the dining room. "What you said in there. That you're not interested in dating."

"Well, yeah," I say slowly.

Oakley blows out a short breath, bending at the waist before nodding several times. "Yeah, okay. Wow. I really thought..."

"You thought what?" I ask. "What's going on?"

"I just, uh... *Shit*. I don't think this is a good idea anymore."

"What's not?"

"Us," he practically spits, his hand flicking between him and me. "Fucking around."

My gut sinks like a stone.

Is that what it feels like to him? Fucking around?

"Oak..."

"I can't, Law." He shakes his head quickly, disrupting his already unruly hair. "I know I said I was okay with it. With this. Well, now I'm not."

My throat closes up real fast, this conversation not one I thought we'd be having. Ever. "I don't... I don't get it. What changed?"

He huffs an incredulous laugh that feels all sorts of wrong. "Really?"

"Yeah, really."

"Jesus Christ, Lawson. I know you can miss what's right in front of you sometimes, but surely you see it?"

I take a reflexive step backwards, hurt flaring in my chest. Oakley's eyes go soft, instant regret there.

"I'm *sorry*, Law. Fuck, I'm making a mess of this." He paces a step away, looking out over my family's land. The dairy cattle are moving about, some sheltered in the shade of wide-branched trees. When Oakley turns back, his face is resolute. "You talked about choice in there. I get a choice, too. I needa be done."

My mouth opens, but Oakley steps past me without another word. I grab his arm, my alarm ratcheting. He doesn't pull from my grip, but there's wariness in his eyes. And what looks a lot like a whole lot of pain.

"The fuck, Oak? You...you can't just leave me."

The sound he lets out is wounded. "I'm not leaving you, Law. Not ever. I'll always be here. I'll always be *yours*." He slowly plucks my hand off his arm. "But if we keep this up, I'm the one who ends up getting hurt. And I know you don't want that, either. Find someone else to have fun with."

With that, Oakley rounds the corner of the deck toward the dining room door. He shoves his feet into his boots as I rush after him, my pulse racing fast.

"How does that hurt you, Oak?"

He ignores my shout, passing through the dining room with me at his heels. A few of my family members stop what they're doing, watching us pass. I don't look away from Oakley's back.

"Hey," I call, the man barreling through the front door now. "How does it hurt you?"

Oakley stops at the bottom of the porch stairs, the look on his face when he turns around carefully shuttered. He's nothing but stone when he's always been utterly transparent with me. Warm and bright. Not now. Now, there's ice in his eyes that chills me to the bone. "The fact that you don't even know says everything, Law. I'll see you later, all right?"

I don't move an inch as Oakley gets into his truck, the man pulling down the drive before long, dust kicking up behind his vehicle.

How the fuck does it hurt him, what we are? How is my not dating other men a reason to end things? Because...

Because I'm holding him back?

Because we're only *fucking around*, as he said, and if Oakley is with me, he can't find the person he wants to build a life with?

The person who, apparently, isn't me.

Fuck.

"Law." Remi's voice is gentle. I turn, finding my youngest brother standing on the porch, the door open behind him. "You all right?"

"I... I don't understand what just happened," I admit, my chest so tight I can barely breathe.

"Colton's an ass. That's what."

I huff a laugh entirely devoid of humor, scrubbing a hand over my face. "It's not Colton's fault. I don't think."

Remi seems to weigh his words as I glance out toward the dust in the driveway that's yet to settle. "You really don't feel that way about him?"

"Feel what way about who?"

He cocks his head when I look back at him. "You and Oakley. We all thought... Well, we all thought y'all were dating already. Except maybe Colt. Like I said, he's an ass."

That leaves me entirely confused. "What are you talking about? Colton didn't ask me about dating Oakley. He asked..."

I fall silent as the implication of my own words tumbles into place.

Remi blinks at me, shock on his face. "Law... Don't you think Oakley would have taken what you said to mean you didn't want to date *him* either?"

"Jesus fucking Christ," I bite out, having come to the same conclusion myself. "That sonofabitch."

"Holy shit," my brother whispers. "The swearing."

"I gotta go. Where the fuck are my keys?"

"Here," Jackson says, tossing my keyring through the open front door. "Go get 'im, brother."

I take a step before remembering I'm not wearing any shoes. Jackson tosses my boots out the door, Remi laughing as I shove my feet hastily inside.

"What's happening?" Colton calls, but I'm already stomping down the porch stairs, and I don't stop.

Remi's voice is light as he answers. "Lawson's on his way to get his man."

"Wait..." Colton says. "Lawson has a man?"

Jackson grumbles out a, "Good Lord," and I leave my brothers to it, my mind firmly on Oakley and his incorrect assumptions.

The drive to his house feels endless. I pull the old acorn Oakley gave me when we were kids out from the center console, cradling it in my palm, my thumb rolling over the cap as I curse a good dozen times inside my head.

He thought, after everything that's changed between us, after everything that hasn't changed at all, he could end things that easily? He thought I wouldn't care? That I'd just let him go? That I don't want him with every fiber of my being?

I can tell even before I park that Oakley isn't home. His truck is missing, the living room dark. Bell saunters over from behind the house, looking at me through the fence, her tail swishing.

Frustrated, angry, and real damn hurt that Oakley wouldn't fight harder for me, to *keep* me, I turn my truck around and get back on the road. I call my best friend before I've even left the gravel of his drive.

It rings and rings before going to voicemail.

"Goddamn it," I mutter, the acorn rough against my palm as I take a turn.

I call again.

This time, Oakley picks up, sounding wary. "Lawson?"

"You think it didn't mean anything to me?" I spit out.

His voice echoes throughout my truck's cab. "What are you—"

"You thought I could be so careless as to cast aside your feelings, as if how you feel isn't the most important fucking thing to me?"

"Jesus, are you pissed off?"

"Yes, I'm goddamn pissed off. Because apparently you thought I don't feel a damn thing for you."

He sucks in a harsh breath. "Do you?"

"Yes, I do."

There's a long beat of silence. "Like..."

"Yes, like that. Exactly like that."

Oakley puffs out a breath rife with both relief and exasperation. "Why the heck didn't you say something, Law?"

"'Cause I just figured it out! What you meant when you said you'd get hurt. The fact that I want to kiss you, Oak. I can't stop thinking about it. About your lips on mine."

"Jesus, Lawson."

"The fact that, yes, I have feelings," I go on, my anger still burning hot. "I have a whole fucking lot of them, Oakley

Beaumont. I don't want to date *other people*. I already know who and what it is I want. And I'm guessing, based on the way you left, you feel the same."

"I... I didn't think..."

"No, you didn't. You were reacting. 'Cause you were hurt. And I get that. I do. But you don't get to leave me, Oak. I thought we already covered that."

He huffs out a breath, the sound mildly amused. "You think you just get to boss me around, don't you?"

"Yes, I do. Because you made me a promise. Remember? You said we'd always be together."

I roll my thumb over the acorn again, willow branches swaying in my mind's eye. Bright painted eyes and pixie dust floating on the breeze. My friend's voice telling me *always*, that very promise in the token he gave to me.

My voice is hoarse when I speak. "Which means you're mine, Oak. You always have been. You're *my* person. And now..."

I don't finish my sentence, knowing that's something we need to decide together.

Oakley's own voice is hushed, barely audible over the sound of my truck on the road. "I'm at my parents.'"

I ease out a breath. "Figured. I'm nearly there."

"Lawson, I..."

"Tell me when I get there. And then I need you to kiss me, all right, Oak? 'Cause—"

My words cut off when there's a screech of wheels in front of me. I don't have time to say a single thing more, barely have time to react, before my world is upended, Oakley's cry nothing but a distant ringing quickly snuffed out.

Chapter 24

OAKLEY

"Lawson," I shout, jumping to my feet as there's an ungodly crunching sound followed by the call disconnecting. "Holy fuck."

"What is it?" my mom asks, her and my dad looking at me wide-eyed from across the living room.

"Phone," I say quickly, holding out my hand as I redial Lawson with my cell, my feet bringing me quickly my parents' way. "Phone, please."

My mom hastily grabs her cell phone, passing it over. Lawson doesn't answer, but I try again, putting my own phone on speaker as I dial 911 with my mom's.

"I gotta go," I tell them. "It sounded like Lawson was in a crash."

"Oakley—"

"I know," I tell her, already shoving my feet into my boots. "We'll follow you," my dad says.

I don't argue, simply push open the door and sprint toward my vehicle as the emergency services dispatcher answers my call.

"911, what is your emergency?"

"I think my friend was in a car crash," I tell her quickly, starting up my truck, my phone ringing again and again on the passenger seat beside me. "I didn't see it happen, but we were talking, and..."

I trail off, my breath stuttering.

"Do you know your friend's location?"

"Um..." I will my brain to cooperate as I pull down my parents' drive, my mom's phone tucked between my shoulder and ear. "He was somewhere between my house and my parents'."

I give the dispatcher our addresses, praying I come across Lawson quickly yet dreading what I'll find. I don't allow myself to think about it. I can't.

I *can't.*

My voice shakes as I go on. "He's not picking up now."

"I have police and ambulance on the way," the dispatcher tells me. "Sir, it sounds like you're in your vehicle, so I'm going to remind you to please remain calm and follow all rules of the road. It won't do anyone any good if you crash yourself."

"I know," I say, even as I speed down the paved backroads toward my house.

"Sir, can I have your name and your friend's?"

I inhale a ragged breath. "Oakley Beaumont. That's me. His name is Lawson. Lawson Darling."

"Okay, Oakley. I'm going to ask you to keep our call connected. If you arrive before emergency personnel, I'll have you tell me what you see."

"Okay," I say hoarsely, setting the phone on speaker before dropping it beside my own. I use my thumb to unlock my phone screen and redial Lawson, but it doesn't connect.

Goddamn it, Lawson. Pick up. Pick up. Pick *up*.

Be all right. You have to be all right.

I try to be cautious as I drive, cognizant of my dad keeping up behind me and, yes, my own safety. But it's hard not to skip every stop sign when I need to know if Lawson is okay. What if he's not? What if—

I cut that line of thinking off at the head, refusing to go there. It's another minute before I see a car askew in the road up ahead.

My pulse sprints, my gaze swinging about wildly until, finally, I spot a truck half in a ditch at the side of the road.

Lawson's truck.

Upside down.

"Fuck, fuck," I utter frantically, fairly certain my heart has stopped beating. Time, too, has slowed to a crawl, every nerve ending in my body on high alert, my hair standing on end as if waiting for lightning to strike.

When I see a head of dark brown hair, my breath whooshes from my lungs.

"Ah, God."

"Oakley?" the dispatcher says, her voice small from beside me. "What are you seeing?"

"He's okay," I rush out, my breath catching repeatedly as I slow my truck, my eyes locked on Lawson, who appears to be digging around in the dirt beside his vehicle. "He... He seems to be okay. There's another person here, standing beside her car. They both seem okay."

"That's good. The ambulance is less than two minutes out."

I think I mutter something in response, but there's a loud ringing overtaking my ears, my entire focus on Lawson as I pull my truck to a swift stop at the side of the road. I jump out, jogging toward Lawson, my newfound hope mixed with a heavy fear I haven't yet sloughed off.

"Lawson," I shout, the sight of his truck on its top making my pulse skip anew. I glance quickly at the woman nearby. She has her hand in front of her mouth, her other tight around her stomach. "Are you all right?"

The woman, realizing I'm talking to her, nods. "Fine, fine. He won't stop. I thought, *God*. He got out of the truck, but he won't stop."

I don't have time to decode her words before I'm reaching the area where Lawson crashed. The man himself looks unharmed, but he's down on his knees, hastily searching through the leaves and debris beside his vehicle, glass shattered on the ground all around him.

"Jesus," I curse, practically skidding down the short incline into the ditch. "Lawson."

He doesn't look up, shaking his head, his hands raking over the ground.

"Lawson, fuck."

A siren sounds off in the distance, my mom's voice behind me calm as she talks to the other woman involved in the crash. I put it out of my mind, the sight of Lawson whole in front of me hitting me with enough force to nearly have my knees giving out. As is, I stagger the last few steps to him. My boots crunch over glass and leaves before I drop to a crouch in front of the man who doesn't even seem to clock my presence.

"Lawson," I try again, my voice breaking as I reach for his face.

He startles when I redirect his gaze my way, his eyes wet and unfocused. I nearly sob out my relief, my eyes running over him quickly, looking for any injury that might be there.

"Are you all right?" I rasp. "Jesus, Law, are you hurt?"

He doesn't answer me right away, his hands shaking as he goes back to brushing leaves and small pieces of glass out of the way. "I can't find it, Oak."

His voice is so small I nearly miss it.

"What?" I ask.

He shakes his head again, his movements frantic as he crawls toward the passenger door of the wrecked truck. He drops low, sweeping his hand inside, so much broken glass everywhere I wince, sure he must be cutting himself.

"Lawson, c'mon, let's get you to the road. You might be hurt."

"Oak... I can't find it."

"Can't find what?"

My dad's voice drifts over. "He all right?"

"Think so," I call back, trying to guide Lawson away from the wreck, but the man is immovable. "Law, you needa get checked. The ambulance is nearly here."

If anything, he searches faster, his breaths starting to come in short pants. "It's not here. I can't find it."

"What are you looking for?" I ask again.

The sirens cut off as the ambulance arrives, Lawson refusing to budge, his reticence scaring me.

"Hey," I say as soothingly as I can, my hand on Lawson's arm squeezing. "It's okay. Would you look at me, princess? Please? Look at me?"

That seems to get through to him because he finally does, stalling long enough for me to see the shine of tears in his eyes. His voice comes out choked. "Oak."

"Yeah, I'm right here. You're okay. Everything's okay."

His stubble is rough on my palms as I take his face in my hands, letting loose a slow, measured breath in the hopes Lawson will follow. He does, inhaling shakily before easing out his own breath. I can hear the medics approaching from behind us, but their voices don't register.

"I think I lost it," Lawson says, sounding gutted.

"Lost what?"

"My acorn. The acorn you gave me."

My brain stutters and restarts, my pulse joining the fray. "It's okay. It's just an acorn."

"It's not," he says vehemently, his hands coming up to hold my wrists. They feel damp, and I'm fairly sure it's not sweat. "It was your promise, Oak. And I lost it. I can't find it."

Ah, God.

"Law..."

The paramedic's voice is closer now. "Are we okay down here?"

Lawson's eyes hold mine, the whiskey-brown imploring me. I pull him into my arms, my lips pressed to the side of his head, Lawson shaking as he hugs me back tight. The man smells like earth and iron, the latter having me squeeze him tighter, as if I could somehow call back his wounds.

"It's okay," I promise him. "I'll find you another, Law. It's okay."

My heart breaks right down the middle when I hear Lawson start to cry. I'm pretty sure the man is in shock, but he doesn't let go of me as the paramedic starts to look him over. It takes a long minute before I can persuade Lawson to unlatch his arms, not wanting him to go but knowing he needs medical attention. I pray his only injuries are the small cuts on his hands, but there's every chance he got banged up when the truck tumbled over. The airbags clearly deployed, and although there's no blood on his head or body that I can see, bruising or whiplash or, hell, even a concussion could be a concern.

I stick right by Lawson, my hand in his vise grip as the paramedic finishes examining him. My parents are waiting up on the road, the police here now, talking to the other woman who has her own paramedic nearby. Everything passes so quickly, and, before I know it, Lawson is being loaded into the ambulance.

"You can ride with him," the paramedic tells me, nodding down to my hand still wrapped firmly in his.

"Thanks," I say, belatedly recognizing the man as someone Lawson and I graduated high school with. "Appreciate it, Duke."

Duke gives me a nod and a smile before stepping back to grab his supplies, his partner getting into the front of the vehicle to drive. The police remain with the woman, although it's clear there wasn't a collision. Her car isn't damaged in any way, and I catch her telling the cops that Lawson managed not to hit her when she swerved to avoid a deer. He drove off the road instead, risking himself in the process, the damn fool.

I make a mental note to chew him out later, even though, realistically, I know it's no one's fault. Only an accident born from split-second reactions on both the woman's and Lawson's part. No one's to blame, not really.

But fuck if he didn't terrify me all the same.

I brush Lawson's hair back as we wait, the dark brown messy atop his head, threaded through with a few silver strands these days. He's staring up at me from his position on the gurney, tiredness starting to show on his face and in his eyes. A good bit of pain, too, although the paramedic found nothing but cuts on his palms and a few on his knees from the glass that tore through his jeans. The neck brace is only a precaution.

The man escaped so many worse fates.

"You scared the shit out of me," I tell him, my voice wobbling.

Lawson's hand tightens in mine. "Didn't mean to."

That has a rough laugh jumping out of my throat. "Jesus, you think? I need to call your family."

He looks as if he tries to nod, but the neck brace doesn't let him.

Duke hops up next to us, grabbing hold of the door to shut us in. "Ready?"

I catch my dad's eye. He waves me on, pointing to my mom and then our vehicles. Understanding they have it in hand, I give Duke a nod. "Ready."

He shuts the door, and the ambulance sets off.

There are so many things to take care of. Getting my phone from my dad once they join us at the hospital. Letting Lawson's family know what happened if they haven't already heard. Making sure Lawson himself is given a pristine bill of health after rolling his damn truck while trying to find *me*. Apologizing for leaving the way I did in the first place, when all I could see was Lawson telling me he wasn't interested in a romantic attachment with me, even though that wasn't the case at all.

He has feelings. He told me so himself.

He asked me to kiss him.

My eyes trace the man's lips now, so full, even set in a straight line as they are. I brush his hair back again, the ride minimally bumpy as the ambulance brings us toward the hospital.

"You're not allowed to leave me, either," I tell the man, my voice scraping on the way out. "You don't get to leave me like that."

Lawson's eyes stay locked on mine. "I'm not going."

"For a long fucking time," I demand. "Promise me."

His lips tip up the tiniest bit. "I promise, Oak."

I know it's not a promise he can truly control or keep. But I nod all the same.

Because Lawson Darling is finally mine.

And like hell am I willing to give him up.

Not ever again.

Chapter 25

LAWSON

"I'm *fine*," I tell my mother for the hundredth time.

She shushes me, fluffing my flat-as-can-be hospital pillow as Remi stands at the foot of my bed, a frown on his face.

'A little help here?' I sign discreetly his way.

'You're on your own,' he shoots back, lips twitching ever so slightly before his concern returns.

"I know you're talking about me," our mother says, even though she didn't see our conversation.

"Where's Oak?" I ask, trying to keep the whine from my tone. "He was supposed to be back by now."

Wendy, for her part, is sitting in the corner of the room, her eyes on me as they've been since she and the rest of my family barreled into the hospital. Oak stepped out to talk to his parents, but that was a good fifteen minutes ago.

"Is there a reason you want Oakley here instead of your own mother?" my mom asks, her amusement slipping in beside her dry tone.

"I assume that's a rhetorical question?" I deadpan.

Remi barks a laugh before coughing when our mom shoots him a halfhearted glare.

"At least you'll live," she says to me. "Which is good because there are some things we need to discuss."

I let out a sigh, knowing exactly what she's talking about. "You're a bunch of meddlers."

"This is news?" Remi mumbles.

My mom steps back from my hospital bed, apparently satisfied with the fluffiness of my pillow. Her eyebrow raise is pointed.

"Not before I've talked to him," I tell her.

Something lights in her eyes, happy and tear-bright, before she blinks it away. "Fair enough, dear."

There's a knock on the door, followed by Oakley stepping back inside. He must see the stark relief on my face because his expression softens. "Hey."

"We'll send the next two in," my mom says, waving for Remi to join her. "Oakley, make sure he gets some rest tonight?"

"I'll tie him down if I need to," Oakley responds, the shit.

My mom blows me a quick kiss, Remi sends me a one-hand *'I love you,'* and then they're out the door, leaving us in relative quiet.

"How long have I been here?" I ask Oakley.

He checks the clock on the wall. "Few hours."

"Sure you don't mean days?"

He huffs a small laugh, walking over to the side of my bed. There's a pinch in his brow I wish wasn't there. "How's the neck?"

"Stiff but not too bad," I tell him truthfully. "When we get home, I want beef stew."

That pinch smooths out, Oakley looking faintly amused. "That right? As it happens, I know a perfectly good cow."

"You're not talking about Belladonna," Wendy says from the corner of the room, her tone indignant.

Oakley winces, his back to Wendy before he turns ever so slowly. "No?"

Wendy huffs, grabbing her phone and looking busy, even as there's a tiny smirk on her face.

I chuckle, giving Oakley's hand a tug. "When can I get out of here?"

"Nurse said you'll need to stay the night—"

"Oak," I groan.

He huffs again. "Lawson, it's not my decision. Christ, don't give me those fucking eyes."

"My eyes?"

"You know damn well what they do to me," he says. My heart patters, and Oakley lowers his voice, his gaze running softly over me. "As soon as I can get you home, I will. Just sit tight and rest."

"Home," I repeat, not sure if Oakley means the ranch or...his house.

Before I can ask, there's another knock at the door. Jackson peeks his head in, Ash behind him.

"Oakley?" my brother says. "There's an officer in the waiting room who'd like to get your statement real quick if you have a minute."

"Sure," Oakley answers, turning back my way and running his fingers through my hair, the simple touch making flutters set off in my stomach. He goes to step back, but I grab his hand before he can get far.

"Don't be long?" I all but beg.

His smile is warm, eyes bright with something that looks a lot like hope. "I'll be right back. Promise."

I nod, and he steps past Jackson and Ash, the door shutting behind him.

"Well," Ash says, a cheeky grin on his face. "Does this mean we can stop pretending nothing is happening between you two?"

"Ash," Jackson groans.

The blonde man's shoulders deflate. "What? I've been *so* good. But come on—we all saw that."

Jackson walks to my bedside, a serious set to his brow. His eyes run over me quickly. "How are you? Truthfully?"

"It was unexpected, but I'm fine. Healthy enough and whole. You didn't all have to come."

Jackson's blue eyes hold mine. "I think you can excuse us for wanting to see for ourselves that you're all right after hearing your truck flipped end over end."

"It wasn't end over end," I point out. "It was a single 180-degree horizontal twist."

"Oh my God," Ash mutters. "Every one of you. Stubborn as can be."

"You flipped," Jackson retorts flatly. "Your truck is totaled. You're stuck with our concern, so deal."

"I think what Jackson means to say," Ash cuts in, joining him at the side of my bed, "is that we're all glad you're okay, Lawson. Isn't that right?"

Jackson lets out a sigh as Ash elbows him none too gently. "Just don't scare us like that again."

My own exhale is heavy. "I'll do my best."

Jackson and Ash stay for a while before heading back to the waiting room to join the rest of the family. While the reprieve lasts, I take in my daughter. She's staring out the window into the parking lot.

"Doing all right?" I check.

She jolts slightly before a frown settles on her face, reminding me of Remi. "Of course. Are you?"

"I'm fine," I assure her.

I'm a little sore, that's true. But apart from the mild cuts that have already been bandaged and some minor whiplash, I'm relatively unharmed. A blessing, all things considered.

Wendy gets out of her chair and approaches my bed, her eyes darting once to the door before settling on me. "You told Grandma you and Oakley need to talk about some things."

"We do," I agree.

"Like...relationship things?"

"Would you be okay with that?"

She huffs a breath. "Are you kidding? Of course I would be. Has this been going on since camping?"

"You could tell?" I ask, not exactly surprised she caught on. I can't say I was trying all that hard to hide the way things had shifted between Oakley and me.

My daughter raises an eyebrow. "Dad. Everybody could tell."

Well, Christ.

Maybe we were more obvious than I thought.

Wendy glances at the door again, perhaps checking for Oakley. He's yet to return. "Do you love him?"

I pull in a breath, but my daughter goes on.

"He's in love with you, Dad. He's always been in love with you."

My throat is so tight I have to clear it before I can speak. "How do you know that?"

"Because of the way he wouldn't look at you," she answers. "I didn't even realize it until recently, but... When you were still with Mom, Oakley was always so careful not to stare at you for too long. He'd avoid certain parts of your body or turn away when you weren't wearing a shirt. I don't know if he was hiding it for your sake or maybe his own, but now... Now he looks at you all the time. He doesn't even try to hide it."

I swallow roughly.

"That's how I know he's always loved you," my daughter says. "You don't have to hide something that's not there."

I turn her words over as I try to compare the Oakley of *then* to the Oakley of now. I haven't noticed what she has, but... I think I've missed a lot. Oakley might have been right about that, much as his words hurt at the time.

"Do you ever feel like everyone else has some key you were never given?" I ask. "And you're just trying your best to pick your way through an endless series of locks into rooms you don't even know?"

My daughter laughs lightly, her eyes creased with her smile. "Yeah, Dad. That's life. We're all faking it 'til we find the right rooms."

"That's terrifying."

Her expression warms, my daughter of seventeen who's grown up to be so much more than I ever could have known to hope for. "It kinda is," she agrees, offering me her hand. I squeeze her tight. "Good thing none of us are alone, huh?"

I nod, my eyes stinging. "I'm so proud of you, Wen."

She rolls her eyes, but I go on.

"I am. You're smart and kind and cautious, which isn't a bad thing. You're observant and hold others to high standards. But you're also forgiving when it counts. You genuinely want the best for those around you. You're creative. Grounded. But you're not scared to dream. I'm so proud of the person you are. I'll always be proud of you."

Wendy presses her lips tightly together, her eyes wet. "Thanks, Dad."

Another knock at the door has Wendy quickly wiping her eyes. Oakley steps in, looking between the two of us.

Wendy gives me a smile before letting my hand go. "I'll be in the waiting room with the rest of the family."

"You sure?" I ask.

"I am. Love you, Dad."

"Love you, too, Wen."

As Wendy leaves the room, Oakley gives me a chagrined smile. "Bad timing?"

"No," I assure him. "C'mere."

He does, and I raise the head of my bed some, putting myself into more of a sitting position. Oakley's eyes run over me, as if the man is assuring himself I'm well. That I'm here.

I keep my tone soft, knowing we both went through a lot today. "I'm fine, Oak."

"Need anything?"

"Just you."

His breath leaves him in a rush. "Jesus, Law."

"What is it?"

Oakley looks down at where my arm is resting, at the crescent-shaped bite scar he runs a finger along. "I don't know how I'm supposed to get used to you saying things like that."

"You'll manage," I tell him, sure of it.

He snorts his amusement, but his expression quickly sobers. "Law... I shouldn't have left the way I did. If you hadn't come after me—"

"No," I tell him, not wanting him for one second to blame himself for what happened. "It's not your fault, Oak. It was an accident that could have happened anytime to anyone. And I'm *fine*. Yes, it could've been worse. But we're not playing the *what if* game. It does no one any good."

He nods, although his face is still downcast. I catch his wandering hand, the man finally meeting my eye.

I steel myself for what needs to be aired. "What I want to know...is why you were okay leaving things like that. Why you would have rather ended things than tell me how you feel."

He swallows, the motion heavy.

"I don't usually have to encourage you to speak your mind, Oak."

"I know," he says at a rasp. "I do, I just... I didn't think you wanted me like that, Law. And I couldn't bear it. I thought maybe it'd be okay. That I could keep on like we were, even if you didn't feel...the way I did. But coming face to face with it, I... I knew it'd slowly eat away at me. It wouldn't have been fair to either of us."

"So you ran instead of talking to me about it."

His laugh is humorless. "I'm not always perfect, okay?"

"I never said you were."

"Well, shit. And here I thought the sun rose and fell with me."

I chuckle, and Oakley graces me with the ghost of a smile. It slips when I say, "I don't want you to run from me, Oak. I want you to stand up to me. To stand *with* me. Like you always have."

He blows out a slow breath, blinking rapidly. "I didn't want to push you toward anything you weren't prepared for. Anything *you* didn't want for yourself."

"And you thought I didn't want you?"

His eyes ping between my own, a slow back-and-forth. "Lawson. I never would have forgiven myself if I became your next Laura."

My inhale is sharp. "Oak..."

A knock at the door has the both of us stilling. It opens to my ex herself looking in with worry in her gaze. She opens her mouth to speak when her eyes slip from me to Oakley and down to our joined hands.

So much for a moment of peace.

Chapter 26

OAKLEY

"Lawson," Laura says, letting the door close behind her. She hesitates for a moment before stepping forward. "I'm glad to see you're okay."

"I am," Lawson tells her, not letting my hand go when I try to give the two some space. He only grips me tighter.

Laura notices. Of course she does. She clears her throat once before finally meeting my eyes. "Oakley."

"Evening, Laura."

"Nighttime now," she says.

I hold my tongue.

She returns her gaze to Lawson. "I won't stay long. Just wanted to stop by. I assume you have all the help you'll need?"

Lawson nods. "I'm all set."

Laura glances at me again. "Well, then. I really am glad you're all right, Lawson. Let me know if there's anything I can do."

"I appreciate it, Laura. Thanks for making the trip."

She lets out a soft sort of sigh before turning for the door. Before going through, she pauses, looking back at us. "Is it...official now? You two?"

A beat of tense silence passes. I look to Lawson, unsure how much he wants to say on the matter.

He's holding Laura's gaze. "We're figuring it out."

Laura's lips purse. "I always suspected, you know."

I go still, but Laura keeps on.

"You don't have to keep hiding it from me."

Lawson's responding tone is calm. "We're not hiding anything." He holds up my hand, as if to make his point. "But I don't owe you information about me and Oakley."

Laura looks taken aback. "We were married. You don't think that gives me some right to know?"

"Who I'm involved with now?" Lawson counters. "No, I don't."

"Law," I say quietly, squeezing the man's hand. "She's talking about before."

"What?" Lawson asks, brows drawn together.

I meet Laura's gaze, some fire in her eyes that wasn't there when she first walked in. "You're talking about when you were still married, aren't you? You think he knew then."

She doesn't say a word, but Lawson's head whips her way.

"He didn't," I tell her, trying to control my anger, even as I can feel it welling fiercely inside my chest. "It was never like that, Laura. Not once. Not even close."

"You..." Lawson's voice cuts out before starting again. "You thought I was cheating on you?"

"Not sexually," she says, arms crossing, as if daring Lawson to come to his own rescue.

"Emotionally?" he asks her, sounding shocked.

She shrugs, the silence heavy between us.

Lawson's hand flexes in my own, his voice coming out like steel. "I was always faithful to you, Laura. Maybe I wasn't the best husband. But I tried. I loved you as well as I knew how. My failing in that regard doesn't mean my intentions weren't pure."

"It wasn't a failure," I interject, not wanting Lawson to think that way. But he's still watching his ex.

Laura's voice is choked, real emotion there. Hurt. "Are you really going to tell me you never thought about it? About him? All those times you asked me to—"

She cuts off, but it's not hard to guess what she was going to say. All those times she pegged him.

I've officially had enough. "You need to leave, Laura. This isn't the place for this."

She doesn't argue, only looks from me to Lawson one more time before heading out the door, cheeks bright red.

"Excuse me," I say to Lawson.

"Oak."

I lean down to kiss his forehead before jogging out the door. I catch Laura in the hallway next to a nurses' station, thankfully empty of people. She hears me coming and stops, unshed tears in her eyes that she doesn't bother wiping away.

"What?" she says, tone flat.

I work to steady my breathing, my anger still far too close to the surface. Despite my best efforts, it still bleeds into my voice. "How long did you suspect something?"

She pulls in a breath, looking off to the side as she shrugs. "I don't know. Years? It was obvious, Oakley, once I could accept the signs. I mean, what straight or even bi man wouldn't enjoy fucking his wife?"

My inhale is a shuddering thing. I don't bother telling Laura it's so much more complicated than that. That not all men, regardless of who they're interested in, crave sex. That people can be allosexual or ace or any number of varying things. That just because a man enjoys being fucked, that doesn't automatically make him queer.

But I don't say any of that. Like I told Laura, this isn't the place.

There's one thing, however, that I can't let slide. It's been boiling inside of me from the moment Laura said she *suspected.*

I keep my voice low, even as every part of me wants to rage. "The moment you figured it out, you should have let him go."

Laura pulls in a short breath, even as she meets my gaze.

"But you didn't do that, did you?" I ask, no more than a whisper. "You kept that man by your side because you knew he'd stay."

"Tell me," she says, just as quiet. "How was I supposed to let go of the man I loved?"

"Selflessly," I bite out, turning away.

"I did let him go, Oakley," she calls at my back. "You don't get to judge me for what happened during my relationship with my husband."

"And you don't get to interject yourself into ours."

Laura says nothing to that, and I walk down the hall toward Lawson's room. I pace outside of it for a moment, not wanting to go inside while my anger is still broadcast across my face.

I used to have sympathy for Laura. And I still do, to some degree.

But she knew. She knew Lawson was gay, and she held on to him anyways.

I don't think I can forgive her for that.

Once I'm feeling calm enough, I crack open Lawson's door. His head turns my way, his gaze skipping behind me as if expecting Laura to return.

"She left," I tell him, walking over to the man who's spent so much of his life living for others. I don't want him to sacrifice a single thing for me. I want him to have everything he's ever wanted. I want him *happy*. Loved. I want every dream of his to come true, no matter how big or how small. There's not a thing I would deny him. "Beef stew, you said?"

His head cocks. "Yes?"

"I'll make you beef stew."

Lawson reaches for me, a soft smile settling on his face amidst the exhaustion of this day. "You'll need to get me home first. Your place? Or..."

"If you want," I say quickly, my heart thumping at the idea of Lawson coming home with me. Staying, maybe.

He nods, letting out a sigh. His eyes trace down my face, stopping at my mouth. My breath hitches when his gaze rises back to my eyes. "Oak."

"Not here," I say, my voice sounding like gravel. "My first time kissing you isn't going to be in a hospital room after you flipped your truck."

"Rolled it," he mutters, even as his lips twitch.

"Semantics."

"But you will?" he checks, eyes on my mouth again.

Fuck.

I clear my throat. "Oh, I will. Many, many times."

"Is that a promise?" he asks, longing mixed in with that cheekiness I so love.

In answer, I hold out my pinkie. My friend of forty-three years stares at it for only a beat before looping his pinkie with mine. I bring his hand up to kiss the side of his little finger, whiskey eyes staring at me all the while.

"It's a promise."

Lawson is released from the hospital the following day with a prescription for extra-strength pain relievers he doesn't bother filling—because *"Christ, Oak, I can just take four regular pills. Why do I need to pay more for a horse pill I don't wanna swallow?"*—as well as a good dozen text messages and voicemails from his family members checking in.

"I'm *fine*," I hear Lawson telling Marigold over the phone, his voice exasperated.

I head to the back door, unlocking it for Bell, unsurprised when she wanders in to see us.

"Yeah, I'm at Oakley's," Lawson says. "Yes, I have clothes. Jesus, what is this? I was in a car crash. I didn't fall back in time."

I chuckle, earning a glare from the man. "Just invite them over."

Lawson tells his mom to hold on for a second before pulling his phone away from his ear. "What?"

"Tell them to come over for beef stew. They'll see you're fine, you'll deal with the lot of them for an hour or two, and then you'll be done with it."

Lawson's brow remains pinched.

"There will be plenty of stew," I assure him. "I'll make a triple batch."

Sighing, Lawson nods. "Ma? Y'all wanna come over for dinner? Yes, to Oakley's. Of course Noah's uncle is welcome. Yeah, okay. Six-thirty?"

I realize Lawson is asking me and nod.

"Six-thirty," he tells his mom. "Yep. See ya soon."

Lawson drops his phone on the couch with a deep sigh. Bell takes the opportunity to stick her face against his, startling Lawson. He rubs behind her ears, a line of drool on his cheek that has me smirking. I walk over with a washcloth and wipe it away.

"Thanks," he murmurs, eyes soft as he looks at me. "Once they go, I'm sleeping for ten years."

"I'll join you."

"Tell me again what I did to deserve a family like that?"

I drop the washcloth in the sink. "You're an amazing son, brother, and father?"

His head rolls on the back of the couch to see me better. "Was that my mistake?"

I bark a laugh, and Lawson looks pleased.

His expression shifts, though, into something more pensive. "What'd you talk to Laura about?"

I heave out a breath, not surprised by his question, even as I'd hoped he wouldn't ask. "If I ask you to let it go, would you?"

He looks at me for a long time. "You want me to?"

"Please," I tell him, not wanting to dredge up bad memories from a past none of us can change. Lawson said himself, thinking about that time he tried so hard to fit with a woman he never could fit with is painful for him. It wasn't at the time, and I believe him in that. But that doesn't mean he'd do it again given the chance.

Maybe he should know Laura suspected he was gay and said nothing. Or maybe it'd only hurt him worse. Given the choice,

I know Lawson would do anything he could to protect the people he loves.

I want to do the same for him.

"I'll let it go," Lawson says. "But if it's ever something that involves Wendy—"

"I'll tell you right away," I cut in. "I promise."

"Lots of promises lately."

"And I intend to keep them."

"Is that so?" he asks, watching me move around my kitchen. I check the crisper to see how many carrots I'll need to buy.

"You doubt me?" I ask, checking the pantry for potatoes next.

"No," he says simply. "Just wondering."

"About?"

"When things changed."

That has me pausing. Lawson and I haven't had a chance to talk about the phone call. Not really. There hasn't been time for it, what with him at the hospital and now a whole host of Darlings to feed in mere hours. But I don't doubt the conversation is one we'll be having soon.

"I think," I say slowly, "you asking me to dick you down might've been a turning point in our friendship."

Lawson laughs so hard Bell startles, her cowbell tinkling as the disgruntled bovine lifts her head off Lawson's lap and stomps away. "It is a very nice dick."

"Oh, Lord. What have I done?"

"I mean, it's not like I've had a lot of comparison... None, really. But you sure know what you're doing with it."

"Ah, fuck. *Law.*"

"What?" he asks, trying to look innocent.

I point an accusing finger his way, hiding my crotch behind the kitchen counter. "You can't get me hard right now. I needa buy beef for your family, all of whom will be here very fucking soon."

"And whose fault is that?"

"Yours," I declare. "All of it, yours."

He huffs a laugh, smile warm as he stretches his arm along the back of the couch, the bandages on his hand making my chest clench tight. "Not everything has changed, has it?"

"No, it hasn't," I agree, my throat hoarse.

"I'm glad for it, Oak."

Well, fuck.

"Groceries," I say again, grabbing my keys. "Take a quick nap if you can. I'll be back soon to make the stew. And Law? For God's sake, don't let my cow up on the furniture while I'm gone."

He sends me a salute.

As I close the front door behind me, the man I'm closer to than anyone tucked inside with my damn cow, I realize this is it. Isn't it?

This is the one that's going to stick.

Chapter 27

LAWSON

Oakley's backyard is filled to the brim, his patio furniture accompanied by a couple folding tables and a dozen chairs brought over from the ranch. Everybody is deep into their stew, no one complaining about the hot dish on a still-hot day.

Especially not me.

The stew is perfect. Oakley's always is, even though he does it on the stove, not in a slow cooker. How he manages to create such tender beef alongside carrots and potatoes with the perfect texture, I'll never know.

The rosemary from his new windowsill herbs adds a nice touch, as well.

"Gonna propose?" Oakley says under his breath, an amused glint in his eye. He's clearly teasing me for enjoying my meal so much.

"To you or this stew?" I joke back. "Either way, the answer might be yes."

Oakley breaks into a sudden coughing fit, and Colton slaps his back. "Wrong pipe," Oakley manages to tell my brother.

"Did I hear Benson is back in town?" my dad asks no one in particular.

Remi shoves a spoonful of stew in his mouth as my mom nods.

"Got back yesterday," she says. "Louise is over the moon."

Louise is my mother's closest friend. August, Louise's youngest son, is Remi's age, and the two have been thick as thieves since they were kids. Benson, her oldest, is the same age as Jackson.

"Didn't know he was planning to come back," Jackson says, not that he and Benson were ever all that close. No more than Jackson is close to anyone else in town.

"Don't think it was planned," my mom says. "Colton, dear, you lost a carrot."

"What?" my brother nearly shouts.

Everyone stops to look at him. Colton's eyes are wide.

"Your carrot," my mom says slowly, pointing her fork at a piece of carrot lying on the table beside Colton's bowl.

"Right," he says, huffing a nervous laugh. "Bell!"

The cow trots over upon hearing her name, her cowbell jingling softly. She snatches the softened carrot from Colton's palm.

Oakley groans under his breath. "Y'all gotta stop giving my cow a taste for people food."

"Oakley, you play chess?" Noah's uncle, Walter, asks from the table next to ours.

Oakley turns his way. "Can't say I do. Why, you looking to kick my ass?"

Walter chuckles, and the next thing I know, someone is pulling an old chessboard out from the game cupboard in Oakley's living room. After that, our impromptu family dinner turns into a game night. As Colton and Ash duke it out in a rather brutal game of *Jenga*, I start collecting dishes to bring into Oakley's kitchen.

My mom finds me before long, her tone gently accusatory. "Shouldn't you be resting?"

"I'm fine."

She heaves a sigh, forcefully pulling the plates from my hands to load into the dishwasher. "Go. Sit."

Not about to get into an argument, I plop down in the living room, tiredness weighing my limbs.

My mom hums softly. "Lawson. You understand why we care, don't you?"

I turn my head to see her better, my neck stiff still but not terribly so. "Of course I do. Doesn't make it easier to accept being coddled."

She huffs, grabbing a cutting board to clean. "You, my son, have always been stubbornly independent. Probably comes with the territory of being firstborn. You're so set on it, you see everyone here showing up for you and assume it's because we think you need help."

"And that's not it?"

My mom grabs a towel to dry her damp hands before joining me in the living room. She sits opposite me, expression serious. "Lawson, dear. It's because we love you. Yesterday, we got a call that you'd been in an accident. That your truck flipped, and Oakley was with you at the hospital. We're here because we need to see for ourselves that you're okay. It has nothing to do with your capabilities and everything to do with our love for you."

I pull in a slow, steadying breath. There's probably some merit to what my mom is saying. I have always been independent when it comes to my family. Partly because I felt a responsibility growing up to look after my brothers, all of whom are younger than me. And once they were grown themselves, breaking that habit wasn't easy.

I know my family loves me. That they want to be there for me. And I can't begrudge them that.

But the Darlings have always been a loud bunch. Not just in volume. But in opinions. In actions. They're loud with their love.

Telling them when it's too much has never been an easy thing for me.

Before I can explain that to my mother, the door opens at the back of the house. Remi and Jackson walk in, catching sight of our mom and me in the living room.

"All right?" Jackson asks.

"Yeah," I tell him. "Would you get Dad and Colt? We gotta talk."

Jackson's eyebrow pops up, but he turns back around to do as I asked. Remi's frown accompanies him into the living room.

"It's nothing bad," I assure him, signing simultaneously.

He sits beside me on the couch, eyes pinging our mother's way.

It doesn't take long for Jackson to return with Colton and our dad. Everybody settles in the living room, the silence heavy for a moment before I break it.

"First, I want to say I'm sorry. I realize yesterday was scary for all of us. I don't even want to think about how I'd feel if it were Wendy in my place. That must have been hard for you, and I never meant to scare you like that."

Remi huffs, his eyes moving from my hands to my face. "As if it was your fault, Law."

Colton grimaces. "It was mine, wasn't it? What happened at dinner—"

"What?" I cut in. "Colt, that wasn't your fault."

"But if y'all wouldn't have fought, you wouldn't have left like that, and—"

"And I might've gotten in a car crash anyway," I point out. "Why is everyone trying to take credit for me driving off the road?"

My mom winces, and I send her a one-handed apology.

"Even so, I *am* sorry," Colton says. "I didn't realize you and Oakley were a thing. You never said anything."

Remi looks at Colton, incredulous. "You didn't see how close they've been?"

"They were always close," Colton defends hotly.

"He's right," I put in before my brothers can start bickering. "I didn't say anything about it to anyone."

"And why is that, dear?" my mom asks, her voice and movements soft.

I puff out a breath. "Because it was mine," I explain to them. All of them. "And I was still figuring it out. *Am* still figuring it out. I know y'all mean well where it concerns my happiness. You always do. But sometimes a person needs the space to learn on their own. We're always learning about ourselves. I don't think that ever stops. What I need right now is for y'all to listen when *I'm* ready to talk about what's going on in my life. Not to tell me things I haven't figured out for my own yet."

A beat passes before Jackson mutters, "Well, shit."

Remi's hands move swiftly. *'Sorry, Law, if we haven't been giving you the space you need.'*

"Y'all care," I answer with a shrug. "I can see that."

Colton nods slowly. My mom's eyes look a little wet.

My attention moves to my dad when he sits forward in his seat. "Is there anything you want to tell us now?"

My gaze skips around the room, everybody waiting patiently. "I'll be staying here for a while. Oakley isn't just my friend anymore. And I'm gay."

Another brief silence falls.

"Well," my mom says, a tiny smile on her face. "I think I speak for everyone when I say I hope you find what it is you're looking for."

I give her a nod. But I think I already have.

It's late when my family leaves. Hugs are passed around, my mother whispering a quiet *I love you* before she's out the door. Once every vehicle has disappeared down the short drive, I help Oakley clean up the rest of our mess, putting the last of the apple pie Ash brought over in the fridge.

"Little bit left," Oakley says of the beef stew. He sets a small container of it on the countertop. "All yours tomorrow."

I give him an appreciative smile. "It's my favorite, you know."

"Oh, I know. You and Wendy both. You're two peas in a beef stew pod."

"That makes absolutely no sense, Oak."

He huffs. "I take it back. That stew is mine. I'm eating it for breakfast."

"You wouldn't."

"Maybe not," he agrees. "But—"

A sound has both of us looking over. The container Oakley set on the counter is now tipped on its side, stew covering Bell's nose as she uses her long pink tongue to scoop as much of the leftover meal into her mouth as she can before sprinting hurriedly from the kitchen. The container, following Bell's momentum, falls to the floor, bits of the leftover stew splattering in an impressive arc as Oakley and I stare on.

"Oak..." I say slowly.

"Belladonna!"

The man jogs to the back door, Bell's cowbell already quieting, the bovine surely far out of Dodge by now. I can't stop my laughter as Oakley comes storming back into the kitchen.

He tosses a hand toward the backyard. "Your stew, Law. Your *stew*. Can we eat her now?"

"We're not eating the cow."

Oakley lets out a big huffing breath, sounding a bit like Bell himself. He grabs a towel to clean up the splatter, the sight of the man down on the floor grumbling about my poor stew making my chest ache in the best way.

"Oak," I say quietly. "I don't want to date you."

The man freezes, turning his head up to look at me.

"I already know everything I need to about you. I know your smile and your heart and the fact that you're a morning person. I know how you sound when you laugh and the way it hurts me when you cry. I know *you*. I don't need to date you to know what I want."

He swallows heavily, leaving the towel on the ground as he stands. His eyes move slowly between my own, the blue and brown so familiar I'm fairly certain I could draw the mottled pattern by heart. "What if I want to take you out? To The Barrel or something?"

I shrug. "Then we'd go."

"And what would we call it?"

I walk the few steps over to him, tracking the way his breathing picks up. How long has it been like this? Me affecting him this way? "We'd call it a date, I suppose."

"But we wouldn't be dating?"

I run a hand up the side of Oakley's neck, his skin warm, his stubble prickling my thumb. "We're past that, don't you think?"

Oakley breathes shallowly through parted lips, the crook in his nose reminding me of pirates and bandana eye patches. Of sunny summer days and pixie dust on the breeze.

We're not those boys anymore.

No, we've grown to be something much greater.

"You made me a promise," I remind him.

His voice comes quiet. "I didn't want it to be like this."

"Like what?" I ask, bringing my other hand up to frame his face.

"Us in my kitchen," he says roughly. "With beef stew all over the floor. There's nothing special about this."

"Oak, I don't need special or extraordinary. I like ordinary quite a lot. I think this is perfect."

He doesn't move an inch, his hands still at his sides. "Law..."

"Are you scared?" I ask him, the panic in his eyes taking me off guard.

"A little bit. This is *you*."

"We've done this before. Don't you remember?"

He shakes his head, a slow movement. "Was I conscious?"

I let out a short laugh, my hands sliding to the nape of Oakley's neck. His shoulders come down some. "You gave me my first kiss when we were eleven."

I can see the moment he gets it. "The acorn?"

"Mm."

His face falls, the man surely remembering only yesterday when I lost the acorn he gifted me so many years ago. "I'll give you another."

I squeeze the back of his neck, not wanting him to worry about that right now. "Give me your lips, Oak. That's what I want."

Oakley's hands come up slowly, shaking as they settle to either side of my face. His thumb ghosts over my jaw, stroking gently, much as I had done to him. His Adam's apple bobs, eyes fixated on my mouth as the seconds stretch into many.

When Oakley leans in, it's on a broken breath. I meet him in the middle, the first brush of his lips on mine so soft I'm not convinced I didn't imagine it. But then he's there again, cedarwood and warmth, smelling like my childhood and my now, feeling like all the things I've been searching for, not realizing they were right here all along.

I don't let Oakley move away, not that he tries. He holds me tight, shaking still, his lips urging mine to open and fitting perfectly against me the moment they do. The snag of his lip on mine, the soft swipe of his tongue like an invitation and promise all its own, even the way his stubble stings like a vow I'll feel him long after he's gone...

It's nothing I've felt before. But I know it, like a dream I've had many, many times.

One kiss becomes two. And then three. Oakley's body presses to mine, not in suggestion but simply as if the man can't hold himself away any longer. It doesn't matter that we're in his kitchen. It doesn't matter that there's stew spread across the floor. The only thing that exists is him and me in a moment we're making our own.

I'm breathless by the time our mouths part. Oakley tugs me close, his head pressed against the side of my own, his chest rising and falling like a slowly ticking clock. I run my hands down his back, up again, my lips still tingling, my chest filled with sparks.

Oakley pulls in a breath, his voice soft as he whispers a single word into the air between us.

"Fireworks."

Chapter 28

OAKLEY

Lawson sleeps in, not that I'm surprised. He's already been excused from work for the week, the timing not ideal considering school starts up again in a matter of days. But there's little Lawson can do about that, and the man needs the rest.

Jackson told me to take some time off, too, in order to look after his brother. I didn't consider arguing.

Lawson's mouth is soft in sleep, the lines of his face relaxed and one bandaged hand tucked under his pillow. The sight of it has my chest twisting, the memory of Lawson scrambling around on the ground through broken glass with his truck tipped on its top still fresh in my mind.

I have no doubt Lawson was running on a good bit of adrenaline after the crash, probably not even feeling the cuts he was collecting. Luckily, none of them were severe: shallow only, no stitches required. Even so, knowing he was so torn up over the lost acorn I had no clue he even still had...

Fuck.

I brush my fingers ever so lightly through Lawson's hair, the strands somewhat coarse from the gentle curl they have. It's difficult to force myself away, but I want breakfast to be ready when Lawson wakes so he can take his pain meds.

The house is quiet, Bell out back. I get the pills prepared first, laying them next to a glass of water. My mom calls as I'm pulling bacon from the fridge.

"Morning," I say, setting my phone on speaker so I can keep cooking.

"How is he?"

"Good. Resting," I answer, pulling a pan from the rack. "Thanks again for following me that night. And for keeping Lawson's family fed at the hospital."

My mom hums. "Of course. You want to talk about it?"

I start the stove heating, knowing exactly what my mom is asking. It still takes me a moment to speak.

"I was terrified. Because what...what if..."

"But he's okay," my mom cuts in gently. "He's perfectly fine. You've seen it for yourself."

"He flipped his damn truck."

"He did," she says, her voice calmer than my own. "And he walked away from it."

"But what if he hadn't? What if the last time I spoke to him, we were arguing? What if I'd gotten there and found him—"

I can't say it. Can't even think it.

I exhale shakily as my mom's voice pipes into the kitchen. "Fear is normal, honey. It's healthy, even. You just can't let yourself linger on it. Do you remember when you were fourteen and your dad fell off a ladder?"

It takes me a second, but I nod, even though she can't see it. "I'd forgotten actually, but yeah, I remember now."

"That was one of the scariest moments of my life. You know what another was?"

"What?"

"The moment I first held you in my arms. I was terrified something was going to go wrong. You were so little, and there were so many things in the world that could have hurt you. So you know what I did? I hugged you close. Your father, too. You can't fixate on all the bad. Hold on to the good, Oakley. Let that fill you up instead."

I lay the bacon into the pan as Lawson's resting face comes to mind. The strong lines of his body in sleep. The way he asked me to kiss him just yesterday in this kitchen. And how nothing could have prepared me for what it felt like to press my lips to his.

A simple kiss.

And the lighting up of my very being.

I'd never kissed someone I was already undoubtedly and irreversibly in love with. Not until him.

"Why did Dad fall off that ladder?" I ask, my voice hoarse.

My mom chuckles. "Spider crawled on his hand. That man can climb up on the roof like it's nothing, but one little bug and he's done for. It's why I hide the good cookies in the garden."

"You do not," I say around a laugh.

"Oh, I sure do. Got an airtight lockbox out there."

"My *God*. I never knew you had such a villainous side."

She laughs, the sound light. I can't help but smile in response.

"Thanks, Mom. For calling. For checking in."

"Always," she says simply. "Let it out and then let it go, Oakley. And give Lawson a hug for me, would you?"

"I will," I promise.

When my mom hangs up, I flip the bacon in the pan. I'm not expecting arms to snake around my middle, but I manage not to jolt too hard when they do.

"You hear that?" I ask Lawson, the man nuzzling against my neck. My eyes slip shut.

"Just the part about hugging me."

Spinning slowly in Lawson's arms, I wrap myself around him tight. He lets out a soft breath, the two of us fitting together like those ceramic salt-and-pepper shaker sets in ridiculous designs. My chuckle has Lawson pressing a quick kiss to the side of my cheek.

"All right?" he asks.

I nod against him. "Mhm. Just thinking you'd be pepper."

Lawson pulls back to look at me. "Oak. Did you hit your head this morning?"

I bark a laugh. "Nope. I'm right as rain. Breakfast is on the way if you don't mind waiting a few more minutes."

"I don't mind," he says. "Although I have a question for you."

"Oh boy."

I peck a kiss against Lawson's lips with the intent to get back to cooking, but that quick peck becomes another and another, and then Lawson's hands are slipping into my back pockets, and I'm gone.

He tastes minty, telling me he used my toothpaste this morning. I didn't realize I have a kink for the man helping himself to my toiletries, but apparently, there's a lot about Lawson I'm still learning.

Like what his mouth feels like curved against my own. The pleased sound he makes in reaction to the moan that slips past my lips. The fact that I'm more than certain he's ruined me for all others, but I can't find it in me to care or worry.

Because if I have my way, there won't *be* any others.

And isn't that a remarkable thought.

"You're dangerous," I mutter against his mouth.

"I thought I was pepper."

"Good God, he's got lip."

"Two of 'em," Lawson says, proving his point quite nicely.

Thankfully, the man steps back before the bacon can burn. I clear my throat, licking my lips as I turn back around to pick up the tongs. The strips of bacon are cooked, so I turn off the burner and start the oven on quick preheat, having forgotten before. "Your question?"

Lawson leans his hip against the counter as I collect flour and the other ingredients to make biscuits. "You said something I didn't get a chance to ask about."

I shoot him a quick nod so he knows I'm listening.

"You said you didn't want to be my next Laura."

I still for only a second before continuing to mix up the biscuit dough. "I did."

"What does that mean?"

Lawson waits patiently while I cut up the still-warm bacon, folding it into the biscuit mixture with some cheddar cheese. I start dropping the biscuits onto a tray after.

Voicing this is harder than I expected it to be.

"I was afraid if I pushed you into something you weren't ready for, you'd stay out of obligation. Not because it was what you wanted or needed. And I didn't want you to be unhappy, Law, even if it meant I got you."

Lawson is quiet for a long moment. Long enough I get the biscuits in the oven and am starting on the eggs when he finally speaks. "Oak. Did you forget the part where I drove over a thousand miles to drag you back here? You *are* my happiness. Don't you get that? I'm never happier than when I'm with you."

I draw in a ragged breath and chance a glance at Lawson. The expression on his face leaves me no room for doubt.

"I'm not ever gonna feel stuck with you," he says. "I can't get enough of you. Pretty sure I'd chain us together if I could figure out a way to manage it."

My laugh is hoarse. "Shit, Law. We went from rope to chains pretty fast."

There's amusement in his voice, albeit a gentle sort. "I don't think it was all that fast. It took us a long time to get here."

I can't argue that.

"I don't want to step back from this, all right?" he says, more serious. "When I think about what it is I want and what I *need*, the one constant is...you."

"Jesus," I manage.

"Something I said?"

"Everything," I tell him truthfully. "You have this way of just...cutting deep. Not in a bad way. You're just so damn honest, it makes me feel splayed open, too."

"And that's a good thing?" he asks, a smile tipping his lips.

"Where it concerns you? Yes."

"'Cause I'm your person." It's a factual observation he's confident in.

"Mmph. You're gonna, uh, need to give me a minute to find my feet again."

Lawson's smile is wider now. Smug. "You're standing just fine."

I pointedly eye the counter I'm gripping. "Am I, though?"

"You look good from here."

It takes me a beat. "Fucking hell, you *are* flirting."

Lawson chuckles, the sound one I'm not likely to ever forget. "I've found I like knocking you off-kilter."

"Why's that?" I ask, not sure if my heart is ready to hear the answer.

He hums. "'Cause you've always held me up, Oak. I guess it's nice being the one to pull you to your feet now and again." After the briefest of pauses in which, yes, my heart thumps erratically, he says, "*Plus—*"

"Oh Lord, help me."

"I've found it's real easy to get you hard. And when you're hard, you fuck me."

"Nope," I tell the man, aiming a stern finger his way. "Nuh-uh. You're recovering from whiplash. You're an injured man. *Behave.*"

Lawson chuckles again. Thankfully, I'm saved by a knock at the door.

"I'll get it," he says.

I pull the eggs off the stove as Lawson heads to the front door. When I hear who it is, I grab three plates from the cupboard instead of two.

"What are you doing here so early?" Lawson asks his daughter.

"Morning, Wen," I call.

"Morning," she calls back, toeing off her shoes. "Figured I'd bring this by. I know you still have a little work to finish, and you'll just be anxious until you get it done. Even though your doctor told you to rest."

I keep my amusement to myself as Lawson accepts his laptop bag from Wendy.

"Also," she adds a little shyly, "I wanted to see you. 'Cause I love you or whatever. What's for breakfast?"

"Bacon-and-cheddar biscuits plus eggs," I tell her, catching Lawson's eye as the two near. He's doing his best to keep it together, but I can see the emotions he's battling. "Orange juice?"

"Please," Wendy says, pulling out a chair at the table. "So... You two?"

Lawson and I exchange a look.

There's a lot we still need to figure out. What we're calling this. How this change will affect our lives, separately and together. Whether or not we'll be living in one house or two. Or if Laura is going to be a problem.

But it's clear we're on the same page when it comes to *this*.

"Yeah," I tell Wendy, my lips curving into a smile as Lawson's brown eyes hold mine. "Us two."

Chapter 29

LAWSON

"I was wondering when you'd come by," Laura says, holding open the door.

I step inside her house, once *our* house, and take off my boots. Laura leads the way into the kitchen, pouring me a glass of water without asking if I want it.

"Feeling better?" she asks, waving me toward the living room.

"I am," I tell her. "Neck stiffness and headaches are mostly gone."

"Just in time for the school year."

I give a nod, the both of us sitting down, half the room between us. Laura looks out the slider door for a moment, jaw tight.

"I suppose you want me to apologize," she finally says.

I set the water she gave me down. "I wasn't going to ask that."

She looks at me, surprised.

"You're entitled to your feelings, Laura. I just wish you would've talked to me instead of assuming Oakley was what came between us."

There's a look in her eye I recognize as disbelief.

"You don't believe me?"

"You really never thought about him?" she asks. "Not even once?"

"Not like you're thinking. It never occurred to me until after we'd split."

She shakes her head a little. "You have feelings for him, Lawson. It's clear to see. How are you telling me that's new?"

I ease out a breath. "That's not what I'm saying. What I'm telling you is I wasn't hiding anything back then. I wasn't lying. We just didn't fit, Laura. We tried for a long damn time, and there was some good that came from that. But we agreed our separation was best, and I don't want what *was* to come between what *is*. Not for either of us."

She rubs her temples, some strain present at the corners of her eyes. "Oakley hates me."

"He's upset with you," I agree. I could ask Laura why, but the truth is I trust Oakley. There's a reason he doesn't want me to dig. That's enough for me. "But I hope y'all can be civil. He's not going away."

Laura falls silent for a long minute, her eyes on her lap. "For what it's worth, I am sorry, Lawson. About a lot."

"I am, too," I tell her truthfully. I have no doubt Laura loved me. And I loved her, as well, although not in the same way. I realize that now.

But not every relationship ends in happily ever after. Not every one is meant to.

Laura doesn't say a word when I stand. I walk from her house, ready to move forward with my life.

Oakley isn't home from work yet when I get to his place. I unlock the back door, opening it a crack and giving a whistle so Bell knows I'm here. She comes trotting in before long, leaving a few dirt clumps on the floor from her hooves as she stops in front of me, waiting patiently. Big black eyes surrounded by a snow-white face watch my every move as I pull a box of crackers from Oakley's cupboard. I remember those eyes staring up at me when Bell was only a calf, so much smaller than she is now, even being a miniature breed.

My chest squeezes tight when I think about the way Oakley stepped in—stepped *up*—to adopt Bell when Wendy needed it. He's loved us for so long, me and my daughter both.

Was he truly *in* love with me, even back then? Wendy seems to think so. If that's the case, it couldn't have been easy for him to be intimate with me, not knowing whether or not I might ever return his interest.

But I think there was a reason I wanted so badly for it to be him, more than simply trusting him as my closest friend.

Maybe Oakley was right about me missing the obvious.

Bell carefully nibbles the crackers from my palm, some drool left behind I wash off in the sink. I leave the dirt on the floor for the robot vacuum to deal with, Bell settling onto the rug in the living room as I pass. I've finished showering and am lying on Oakley's bed when I hear the man come through the front door.

He murmurs something quietly to Bell, the man gentle with her, loving, despite claiming she's nothing but a nuisance. His footsteps come closer, a steady rhythm that has a smile quirking my lips.

Oakley stops dead once he reaches the doorway, his breath rushing from him when he sees me lying naked on his bed. "Jesus, Law."

"I'm not injured anymore," I point out.

He grunts.

"And I've been thinking about you all day."

"Yeah?" he asks hoarsely, his eyes trailing over me, as if he doesn't know where to focus his attention.

"Mhm. Remi said something recently that stuck with me. He said attraction doesn't have to be only physical. That it can be mental, too."

Oakley's eyes are on mine now, curiosity there.

"I think maybe I'm gray-ace," I tell him. "Because I don't get turned on by you naked or understand your obsession with ears—"

He huffs a throaty laugh, stepping closer.

"But I know I want you something fierce, Oak. Maybe it's not how you want me. Not exactly. But *God*, do I want you. All the time. I want you near. I want to hear your voice, feel you, spend my time by your side. I want you to fuck me all the goddamn time, and not just because it feels good, but because it's *you*. I want *you*. If that's not attraction, what is?"

His throat bobs in a rough swallow, a sheen in his eyes as he stops beside the edge of the bed.

"But truth be told," I go on softly, "I'd want you even without the sex."

"If you ever aren't interested—"

"Then I'll be honest about it," I cut in, understanding the direction of his thoughts. "You've never initiated anything, Oak. Don't think I haven't noticed. But you can. I'll tell you if I'm not in the mood."

"I'd never pressure you," he says vehemently, bending down until his hands are planted on the bed to either side of me, his face a foot away, the smell of the ranch and his sweat a gentle presence with his proximity. I don't hate it one bit. "I don't just want you for sex either, Law."

"I know that. I do."

"Good. Because it shouldn't ever feel like an obligation. I don't want it to. I only ever want you to feel good."

"I know," I say again, running my palms up the outsides of Oakley's arms. "Everything with you feels good. That's what I'm trying to tell you. You with me...it feels better than good."

He lets out a shaky breath, his eyes dipping down my body again, a heat in his gaze he doesn't try to hide. "And right now?"

"Right now," I say, my words measured, "I'd really like for you to join me on this bed. Preferably naked and with some part of you inside some part of me."

He laughs, a roughened sound. "In that case..."

Oakley leans closer, dipping his head at the last moment to brush his lips over my neck. I arch my head to the side, and Oakley sucks a gentle kiss against my skin. He doesn't stay long, leaning away to open the nightstand drawer beside the bed. He pulls out a bottle of lube and sets it beside me.

"If you want, why don't you get a finger or two inside of yourself while I shower," he suggests. "It'll give me something to think about in the next three and a half minutes before I can make it back to you."

"Should I time you?" I tease.

"Not necessary," he assures me. "There's no keeping me away."

I pick up the lube as Oakley backs steadily toward the door. He groans when I slide my heel closer to myself, the move hitching my leg up. He doesn't stay to watch, even as it looks like he wants to. His shoulder clips the doorway in his eagerness to get away so he can return to me. Ten seconds later, the shower turns on.

I take my time, wetting my fingers before rubbing over myself slowly. When something hits the shower floor, possibly Oakley's shampoo bottle, I huff a small laugh, the man's haste making my chest warm. I have two fingers inside of myself when the water turns off, my cock half-hard and a steady thrum of anticipation lighting my veins.

Oakley is still damp when he steps back through the door, nude and hard himself. His hair is mussed, as if he ran the towel over his head a couple times and called it good. Some water is dripping down his chest and legs he doesn't seem to notice, his entire focus on me. Specifically on the fingers I have curled inside of myself.

He steps forward without a word, one knee on the bed beside my bent leg. He swipes the lube, the look in his eyes almost predatory. It's the same look he gets every time he edges me, as he called it. Intense concentration and a sort of hunger that makes me feel like maybe it wouldn't be so bad, being eaten whole.

When Oakley's finger joins my own, I can't stop the sound that breaks from my lips.

"Too much?" he asks.

I shake my head. "No. Not at all. I like the stretch."

He rumbles a low sound, his finger working a rhythm opposite to my own. The sensation has my breath stuttering, and when Oakley brings his other hand to my cock, thumb rubbing up the underside like a caress, I nearly lose track of what I'm doing.

"Love getting you like this," he says, his finger toying with me continuously, his thumb doing the same. "When you melt against the bed, boneless and trusting. You look like you're in heaven."

"'Cause I am," I manage. "Everything you do to me is heaven."

Oakley crooks his finger, pressing my own against my prostate. My leg shakes.

"Ready for me to take over now, princess?"

In answer, I slide my fingers free, and Oakley chuckles. He presses a kiss to the inside of my bent knee, another to my thigh. His hand slips up my leg, following the touch of his lips, his other moving inside of me, two fingers now pressing relentlessly in that slow *come hither* motion that both feels wonderful and stretches me at once. His lips continue upwards, a kiss pressed to my abdomen, one to my cock and then two, another to my pec. He stops there, his tongue slipping up the underside of my nipple in a teasing flick.

I curse, and Oakley chuckles again, likely pleased to have pulled a *fuck* from me. His stubble brushes against my chest as he lays kisses, what feels like a hundred of them, a hoard of promises I'll keep close.

By the time he reaches my neck and, finally, my mouth, I'm trembling. He's not hesitant this time. Not scared by what this could mean or scared, maybe, of all the unknowns up ahead. His mouth meets mine as if we've always been saying hello this way. It's a dance of sorts, not that I've ever been particularly good at that. But this is natural. Electric.

I slide my hands down the rough planes of Oakley's chest and stomach, hair bristling my fingers, the man's muscles jumping beneath my touch. His cock jumps, too, when I wrap my hand around it. His groan comes from deep within, and I want more of that sound. I stroke him firmly, the rhythmic tug of it mesmerizing. The feel of Oakley's cock in my grip. The man's reactionary moans and the bite of his teeth against my lip when I find a particularly sensitive spot to rub near the head.

"Oak," I breathe out. "Want this in me."

"Do you?" he asks almost lazily, three of his fingers inside of me now, the glide effortless as they fill me again and again. "I could make you come just like this."

"You could. But we both know you won't. You're gonna give me exactly what I want."

He lets out a softly amused breath, painted eyes meeting mine. My heart skips a beat at the imperfect perfection of his irises. An entire world of sky and earth looking back at me.

"You're gonna pick up that lube," I nearly whisper. "Slick yourself up. You're gonna slide inside of me, not too slow because I can't handle that right now, and not too fast because you'd never hurt me. You're gonna fuck me, Oak. But we both know it's not only that. And you're gonna kiss me near the entire time. Isn't that right?"

He swallows roughly, his fingers sliding free, leaving a whisper of cold against my damp skin. "You're getting it now, aren't you? That I'm yours?"

"You've always been mine. My best friend. My person. There's no one else in this world who knows me the way you do."

His eyes slip shut as he dips his forehead to mine. "God, Law. One of these days I'm gonna get used to the things that come out of your mouth."

"I hope you don't," I admit. "I like you blushing for me."

He groans, dropping his face to my neck and biting lightly. "You gotta stop."

"Then put your mouth on mine, Oak. That's a surefire way to shut me up."

Oakley lifts his head, his eyes holding mine for a long moment. He leans over just long enough to grab a condom from the drawer, lifting it in question. I shake my head, the precaution not one either of us needs anymore. He drops it back in the nightstand, unopened. His eyes never leave mine as he settles in close. I pull my knee into the air, giving him plenty of room to get inside of me. His gaze flicks down for only a second or two, the pressure against my ass expected and welcome.

His eyes come back to mine as he presses forward. There's so much it feels like he's saying without words. I remember him telling me before, when I was tied up nearly in this exact spot, that he wouldn't be pretending it was anyone but me in his bed. I should have understood all that meant. That I wasn't interchangeable.

It may have taken me longer to catch on, but I can see it now. The rapture on Oakley's face. The way he's not hiding from me. Not trying to shy away from my gaze on him in return. He's utterly bared, and maybe it's always been this way. Maybe I really am a fool when it comes to love.

But all I see in Oakley's eyes is relief to be where we are now. There's no remorse. No pain or wishing things were different. There's joy. Warmth. A little bit of disbelief and a whole lot of ecstasy.

And knowing I can make Oakley feel as good as he makes me feel simply by offering myself? By *being* myself?

There's no greater acceptance than that.

Oakley leans over my body as his cock comes to rest fully inside my ass, not a single barrier left between us. His weight presses my own cock to my stomach, one of Oakley's hands threading through the hair at my temple as blue and brown drowns out everything else.

When he kisses me, I'm fairly certain I can hear the breeze. Feel the sun on my face. We're flying, just him and me, still lost boys in a lot of ways but, like always, together in our very own Neverland.

It never was about staying young forever. Everyone grows. We all age. All live our lives for however long that may be.

The important part is keeping close those we care about. It's *living*. It's hope and love and chasing one another through the clouds.

It's pixie dust. So much of it, there's no room for anything else.

No, I never was running after Peter Pan. It was Oakley I was running towards.

Always.

Chapter 30

OAKLEY

My chest feels almost unbearably tight as Lawson and I kiss, the man's mouth soft but his desperation clear. His leg hooks around my hip, tugging me closer, his grip in my hair unyielding.

I think there was a deeper reason I was so hesitant to return to Darling all those months ago. To return home. And it had everything to do with this, right here.

With the newly single man I didn't think I'd ever have the chance to love like this.

I suppose in the end I never could stay away from Lawson Darling for long. It was my undoing. And I'd unravel all over again given the chance.

Lawson's mouth holds me captive. I want to tell him I'm not going anywhere, but I can't seem to find the willpower to come up for air. Oxygen seems unimportant when I've got this man at my fingertips, urging me to give him all the things he's been missing out on for years.

Pleasure. *True* pleasure. Happiness, even. Admiration. Respect. Love.

When I flex my hips, Lawson groans. It's a low sound, pleading, so I do it again, the way his body hugs me tight making me want to stay here forever. He's silk inside, hard muscle out, demanding and pliant both, so many contradictions I've always been fascinated by.

"Oak," the man says, breaking from my lips to suck in air. His breaths pant from him, a sheen of sweat beading on his forehead.

"What is it, princess?"

He grunts as I sink inside of him slowly, one of his hands on my ass cheek as if wanting to feel the flex of muscle. "Need..." He puffs out another breath. "Could you talk to me? I wanna hear you."

A smile curls my lips, Lawson's eyes looking dazed already. "Yeah? You want me to whisper sweet nothings in your ear?"

"Don't make me ask twice," he groans out, giving my ass cheek a slap before hanging on again.

I bark a husky laugh, tempted to flick the man's forehead in retaliation. Instead, I draw my lips around to his ear, brushing the sensitive skin there as I roll my hips languidly. "Whenever you wanna get dicked, I'll be here for you, princess. Fast, slow, anything you want. If you want my mouth on your cock, my tongue in your ass, my lips covering every inch of your body, you'll have that, too. You were made for this. Do you realize that? You were made to be treasured and worshiped and loved."

Lawson's chest heaves beneath mine, his own hips shifting in time to my deep, measured thrusts. "And you?"

"I was made to love you."

His breath hitches, his hand in my hair flexing.

"My touch, my kisses, they're all yours," I say, my lips ghosting over his ear. "Every last one of them. Yours."

Lawson tugs my head around, claiming my mouth, the urgency in his kiss and the way he pulls at me making it clear what he wants. I slip a hand under his ass, lift his hips off the bed, and go to town.

Lawson's cock leaves a mess of precum between us as I fuck him as hard as I dare. Hard enough that he'll feel it long after. He relishes it; it's easy to see and feel and hear. Every grunt he lets out. Every bite of his teeth against my lips. Every flex of his hand on my ass or hip or back asking for *more, more, more*.

When Lawson gets close to the edge, I pull him away from it. He doesn't offer complaint, heat building between us as soft moans pepper the air. I make it last as long as I possibly can.

Fucking him slow. Hard again when I know he can take it. All the while, our mouths find one another again and again, stubble rough, kisses sweet and filthy.

When Lawson whispers my name with an edge of desperation, his breath stuttering, I reach between us and wrap my hand around his dick. His reaction is instantaneous. The hard inhale. The near-bruising grip on my back.

My voice comes out hoarse. "Take me with you, princess. There's nowhere else I'd rather be."

Lawson pulls me down into a hard kiss, his body wringing my cock as he locks in pleasure. It kicks off my own orgasm, the raw, tortured groan he lets out tugging me after him like a hook. My hips punch, Lawson sucks in air, and I can feel it. Right in my chest. That certainty that after all this time, after so many years, I've found the person I'm meant to be with.

My very best friend.

Lawson's hand soothes over my nape as I continue to shudder. He says something, but I can't hear the words past my own breaths.

"What was that?" I ask, my face tucked against the crook of Lawson's neck, where the smell of my soap mixed with *him* is strong.

He presses his lips to my ear, his voice deep and soft. "I said all of my kisses are yours, too, Oak. I gave you my first. And I plan on giving you my last."

My heart gives a great big thump as I tighten my grip on Lawson, my body weight pinning him to the bed. He doesn't seem to mind. In fact, I think he likes it with the way he's holding me to him, his hand still running rhythmically over my neck and shoulders.

"Can I ask you something?" he says.

I nod against him.

"Why do you call me princess? You said something once about pampering me. Is that why?"

I hum before pulling my face from Lawson's neck. Carefully, I slip from his body, transfixed for a moment by the cum leaking out of his ass. I settle back over him, our chests pressed together, my elbows on the bed keeping me from crushing him completely.

"There's this term," I explain. "Pillow princess. Ever heard of it?"

He shakes his head.

"It's like... I guess the best way I can think to describe it is someone who prefers receiving pleasure to giving it. Whether that's being railed against a kitchen countertop or...lying in bed comfortably with a pillow under their head while their partner brings them off."

Lawson's brow pinches. "That doesn't exactly sound like a positive."

"It's not a bad thing, Law," I assure him. "We've already established I like making you feel good."

"But you don't...you don't want me to participate more? Am I doing enough for you? 'Cause I can—"

I bring my lips to Lawson's, stopping his words before they can form. The kiss is short but steady. "I don't want you feeling like you have to perform just to make me happy. *This* makes me happy." I think of how best to explain it to him. "Try to imagine what it's like to look at someone and get mesmerized by every dip and valley of their body. Imagine getting turned on by the way they move and sound and how they react to your touch. And then imagine being told you have free rein to enjoy it. That's not a bad thing, Law."

He's quiet for a moment. "It doesn't work like that for me."

"I know. And that's okay. It just means we fit in a way that works for both of us."

I lean onto one elbow to brush Lawson's hair back from his forehead. There are subtle wrinkles carved into the skin beside his eyes, a few in the furrow of his brow.

"Law... I don't want you to be anyone but who you are. You're welcome to touch me however you want, always. But I will never tire of being the one to bring you pleasure. Frankly, I can't think of anything hotter."

Lawson lets out a slow breath. I wait for him to quarrel further, but all he says is, "All right."

"Yeah? You believe me?"

"You don't lie to me, Oak. So yes, I believe you."

"Good," I say on a sigh. "Because I quite like you being my princess."

The flush on Lawson's cheeks is a mighty endearing sight. He clears his throat. "You just like me bossing you around."

"Excuse you," I say, laughter in my tone. "I tolerate it at best."

"Love it," Lawson combats. He's not wrong. "Now run us a shower, would you? You made a mess of me again."

"Ah, Christ," I grumble, even as I dutifully lean back and help Lawson from the bed.

We make a quick dinner once showered, eating outside while the sun lasts, our hair drying in the breeze. Bell lies nearby, her tail swishing every once in a while to chase off the occasional fly.

"I saw Laura earlier," Lawson says unprompted.

I finish chewing my bite of food before responding. "Yeah?"

He nods, looking out over the expansive backyard, his gaze distant. "I didn't ask her what you two talked about."

"You can, Law. It's not anything I'm trying to hide. I just—"

"I know," he cuts in. "You're protecting me. I don't need to know the specifics. I'd like to remain friendly with Laura. For Wendy's sake. But we're not ever gonna be friends again, Oak. There's too much hurt there already."

I nod slowly, my gaze boring into the side of Lawson's head. "I'll be as nice as I can," I tell him. "But I'm not sure I can be forgiving."

Lawson's whiskey eyes meet mine, something near to a smirk on his face. "I know, Oak. You understand now why I can't excuse what Stevie did to you?"

I puff out a breath, my chest so dang tight. "Yeah, I guess I can."

He nods once, satisfied.

"Do you need to head back to the ranch tonight?" I ask, stacking our empty dishes. "First day of school tomorrow."

Lawson hums. "No. I'm not going back."

I nearly drop the silverware in my hands. "You mean tonight?"

Those eyes meet mine again. "What do you think?"

"Lawson," I breathe.

He twists in his chair, taking the forks from my grip and setting them back on the table. "Why do you think I never found my own place? The only place that felt like home was here. I didn't want to settle for second best."

My pulse skips frantically, Lawson's thumb smoothing over the side of my neck like he can tell. His eyes hold mine as he pulls the ground swiftly out from under my feet.

"I don't want to say goodbye to you at the end of the day anymore, Oak. I want you from saddle to sunup and every hour in between."

"Fucking hell, Law. You're not even gonna wait for me to ask you to move in?"

He shrugs one shoulder, his thumb running over my jaw now, as if he simply can't stop himself from touching. "You would've gotten there eventually."

I let out a hoarse laugh. "So we're living together? Just like that?"

"I reckon so. Feels right, doesn't it?"

I catch Lawson's wandering thumb with my lips, kissing the pad of it. "When do you want to move your stuff over?"

"We'll find time," he says. "But not tonight. First day of school tomorrow and all. I need my beauty sleep."

I huff a small laugh. "You do realize you'll have to tell your family, right? You can't just move out without saying a word to them."

Lawson groans. "Would they even notice?"

"Uh, yes. They absolutely would. It'll be fine. They'll hug you and congratulate us, and your dad will probably cry."

That has Lawson chuckling. "He is the crier of the family."

"Mhm."

"My brothers will throw a bonfire," Lawson adds, a small smile on his face. "Wendy will threaten you."

"Wait, what?"

"And we'll need to tell Laura. So she knows where to find me if need be."

Lawson ignores my grunt.

"It'll be good, Oak," he says, the late evening sun hitting his face in a way that causes my breath to hitch. I'll be looking at that face for a long time to come. Years. Decades. The rest of our lives, quite possibly.

"Yeah," I agree roughly. "It'll be great."

When Lawson and I get inside, we load our dishes and silverware into the dishwasher before getting ready for bed. We brush our teeth. Take care of other necessities. Lawson gives me a fond smile when I ask about his ass, assuring me all is well.

As I watch the man climb into my bed, I'm hit once again with the conviction that this is it. It really is. No more first dates. No more trying to find someone to build a life with.

I have that person. And we've already built a life.

It's all the years we've traveled together. All the truths we've shared. It's riding horses through the Montana wilderness and sitting quietly inside while Lawson reads a book. It's pages and pages of memories we've written, each one part of a bigger whole.

Lawson looks over when I open the top drawer of my dresser. I root through my selection of socks, finding the old pair I never wear anymore. Unfolding them carefully, I pull the small ceramic thimble from within.

I can hear Lawson's breath catch. The thimble was his mother's once upon a time. There are flowers hand-painted on the surface, small and delicate. The entire thimble is delicate, one tiny chip in its edge the only thing marring its otherwise perfect visage.

"You kept it," Lawson says, his voice rife with emotion.

"Of course I did. You gave it to me, didn't you?"

I set the thimble atop the dresser, a tiny piece of my heart I was always afraid to show. Not anymore.

"You remember my promise?" I ask.

Lawson swallows hard as I approach the bed. "We'll always be together."

"That's right," I tell him, one knee atop the mattress as I lean close, Lawson's face inches from mine. "The two of us."

Lawson tugs me down until there's no space between us. His lips meet mine, the answer there clear as day.

Forever.

Chapter 31

LAWSON

"Well, this is a disaster."

"It's fine," Jackson counters flatly.

Marigold Darling gives her second-oldest son a *look*. "The floor is covered in half an inch of standing milk, Jackson. Tell me how that's *fine*."

Jackson unbends to his full height, a mop held in one hand. "We're handling it," he answers, waving to the many employees and family members inside the milking barn who are helping clean up the mess made from a burst milk line. "You gonna help, or are you here to tell me I'm doing it wrong?"

Our mom clucks her tongue. "Somebody's gotta keep everyone in line. Hank! What on Earth are you doing with that shovel?"

As our mom stomps off, her boots splashing through the mess, Jackson shakes his head, grumbling about *that ridiculous woman*. Seeing as it's Saturday, I was free to lend a hand when I showed up at the ranch with the intent to tell my family I'm moving out. Technically, I've been living at Oakley's for a few weeks now, ever since the aftermath of the crash. But a good many of my possessions are still here, and it's about time I face my family to get them.

That'll have to wait, though. Seeing as we have a milking barn to set to rights.

Colton passes by with a long-handled squeegee, he and a few of the ranchers herding the milk toward a drain at the edge of the room. Remi, like Jackson, is getting the excess with a mop. I've got bucket duty. Same as Ash.

"You didn't have to help with this," I tell the man. He's the ranch cook, after all. His duties certainly don't include...whatever this is.

He lifts one blonde eyebrow, amusement lacing his tone. "Neither did you. But it's what we do, isn't it? Help out family."

I guess I can't argue with that.

"Cowabunga," Colton calls, practically running past with his squeegee held out in front of him, trying his best, I think, to make a wave. "*Cow*-abunga. Get it?"

"My God," Jackson grumbles, shaking the resulting milk splatter off his muck boots. "Are you a goddamn child? Slow down."

"Hey, Jackson," Colton says.

The moment Jackson lifts his head, Colton splashes milk his way.

Jackson goes stock-still, milk soaking into his jeans above his boots. "You did not just do that."

Backing away, Colton says, "Did."

"Get over here."

Colton turns and takes off, Jackson hot on his heels. I shake my head, my younger brothers attempting to bat each other off with the handles of their cleaning implements. A couple of the ranch hands stop to stare. Remi, I notice, has his phone out.

"What're you doing?" I ask him.

He keeps his eyes on the device. "Recording for Noah."

"Ah."

"Colt, I swear to God," Jackson says at the same time Colton swipes his squeegee handle toward the heels of Jackson's boots. Jackson goes down, landing on his back, nearly everyone letting out an *ooh* as he's covered in milk.

Colton sucks in a sharp breath before wincing. "I, uh... Whoops?"

A long beat of silence passes before Ash heads to Jackson's side. He holds his hand out, trying to hide the smile on his face but failing terribly. "You did kind of have it coming, Jack."

With a grunt, Jackson grabs onto Ash's hand and pulls him down into the mess.

Ash barks a laugh, breaking the tension in the room. The next second, Jackson is on his feet again. He takes off after Colton, whose boots slip around as he tries his best to get out of Dodge.

"Boys!" our mom yells, her hands on her hips. "Were y'all raised in a barn?"

"Help me!" Colton shouts to the room at large.

Remi is laughing uncontrollably, still recording the whole thing. "Oh my God. I'm never deleting this."

Colton, possibly having heard him or, I don't know, maybe intending to use his younger brother as a shield, heads in his direction. Remi yelps and runs off faster than I've ever seen my brother move.

Ash is still sitting on the floor, laughing and telling Jackson to *leave him be*. Colton looks scared for his life, as he should.

My dad is trying to shovel milk. And my mom unrolls a nearby hose, presumably to break up the scuffle.

"Well," I mutter to myself, an empty bucket in my hands. "Can't say it's not interesting around here."

Hours later, when I'm washing up in the ranch house, I get a text from Oakley. A smile springs to my lips. He sent a selfie, the man wearing thin-rimmed glasses with a wry expression on his face.

I call, and he answers right away. "Hey, you still at the ranch house?"

"I am," I tell him. "I take it the eye appointment went well?"

He groans. "Reading glasses, Lawson. I'm getting old."

"Had to happen sometime, Teach."

"Nuh-uh," he says. "That's your nickname, not mine."

"If you say so."

He blows out a breath. "Things go okay with your family?"

"Haven't told them yet," I admit.

"No?"

"No. Milk emergency."

There's a pause. "Do I wanna know?"

"I'll have Remi send you the video."

He snorts. "Want me to come over? While you tell them?"

"No," I say, although I appreciate the offer. "I've got it. Was just washing up first."

He hums. "Miss you, you know."

My chest squeezes so fast it takes me a second to breathe past it. "Already?"

"Doesn't take long. You coming home after?"

Home.

"'Course I am," I answer. "Where else would I go?"

"I dunno. To your other boyfriend's?"

"Other?" I question. "You really think I could handle two of you?"

Oakley laughs. "Actually, yeah, I think you could wrangle us just fine."

"There's no one else, and you know it," I grumble in mock-affront.

He huffs another small laugh, but his voice turns serious. "Is that all right? Calling you my boyfriend? Or would you prefer something else to signify our together but...not-dating status?"

I let out my own soft huff. "Boyfriend is fine. Partner. I'm not picky."

"You *are* picky, actually. About a lot of things. That's why I'm asking."

"And I'm telling you I don't mind one way or another. So choose."

"Oh my God," he says, amusement heavy in his tone. "Are we arguing about this? Really?"

"Of course we are, Oak. We argue about everything. You're the only goddamn person I argue with."

"And why is that?" he asks, sounding endlessly fond if not a little curious.

"Because I care about you too damn much not to fight for what's important."

My conversation with my dad floats into my mind. I guess I'm a lot more like my parents than I maybe want to admit.

"What's important," Oakley repeats, his voice softer than before. "Which would be?"

"You need me to say it?"

"I kinda do."

I blow out a breath, even as my chest warms. "You, Oak. You're what's important."

"Huh."

"Huh?"

"I think you, Lawson Darling, might really like me."

I chuckle, even as my smile slowly slips away. I've never said it, have I? I've never actually spoken the words.

Oakley knows, though. Doesn't he?

"You there?" he asks. "You got real quiet."

"Yeah, I'm here. I, uh... I needa talk to my family. And then I'll be home. All right?"

"Yeah. See you soon."

"Soon," I agree, pulling my phone away from my ear to end the call.

I've never said the words...

I find my family out on the back deck, everyone still hanging around after the milking-barn fiasco. Even Colton has yet to leave, although he's tugging on his boots like he's getting ready to head over to Noah's. I clear my throat as I walk up.

"You're still here?" my mom asks, a glass of iced tea sitting beside her chair.

"I live here, don't I?"

"Do you?" she counters, a sly gleam in her eye.

"That's actually what I wanted to talk to y'all about." Taking a beat, I glance around at my family before revealing, "I'm moving out."

Colton looks from me to the others. "You're not already moved out?"

"Oh, for Christ's sake," I mumble. "I'm moving out *officially*."

Remi's smile is soft. "Good for you, Law."

Ash, sitting on the armrest of Jackson's chair, speaks up. "Anything we can help with?"

"I don't think so," I say truthfully. "I'll pack up my clothes and things sometime this week or next. It won't take long."

Colton snorts. "No, it won't. You've been migrating over to Oakley's for a while now."

Remi tosses a coaster his way, which Colton bats across the deck. "How did you notice *that*, but you didn't know they were together?"

"How was I supposed to know!" Colton cries.

I clear my throat again. "I just wanted to say, well... I expect I'll still be here plenty. For dinners or just to say hi. I won't be gone for good."

"We know that," my mom says, a small smile on her face. "But we'll still miss you all the same, Lawson dear. Isn't that right, Hank?"

My dad, who's weaving what looks to be a hanging basket out of twine in the grass beside the deck, grunts. "Boy's following his happiness. It's a damn good thing."

Everyone nods their agreement.

Well, shit.

After a second, Colton claps his hands together. "Bonfire to celebrate! Tomorrow night? I'll bring the mallows."

"You always bring the mallows," Remi mutters.

"'Cause no one else ever does," Colton retorts. "Jackson?"

"We'll be there," Jackson answers. "That work for you, Law?"

I nod. "I assume Oakley is invited?"

Colton lets out a *psht*. "Obviously. Hey, is that Benson Harper over at the petting farm?"

All heads swing that way.

It is, in fact, Benson. Although he looks different than I remember. But it's been, what? Years since I last saw him? He has a beard now. And he looks a good bit bigger. Bulkier.

Remi lets out a garbled sort of choking sound.

"Jesus," Ash says. "Is he a lumberjack?"

"No, he's in corporate finance," Colton says before frowning. "Or he was."

"Didn't you used to have a crush on him?" I ask Remi, his reaction sparking a memory. "Back when you were sixteen or so?"

"What?" Remi says quickly. "No. 'Course not."

Jackson cringes. "Really? He's my age."

'There was no crush,' Remi snaps with shaky hands. He pushes out of his seat, brushing a quick, *'Excuse me,'* our way.

A few eyes follow Remi as he heads into the house.

Colton hops up, swiping his hat and fixing it into place. "I'll go say hello. Tomorrow, Law. Don't forget."

"Yep."

As Colton saunters off, my mom hums. "Well, now. Who's gonna get dinner started?"

By the time I get to Oakley's, I'm beat. I kick my boots off inside the door, drop my keys on the kitchen table, and head to the couch, all but falling into Oakley's lap. He chuckles, one hand sifting through my hair as I turn my gaze up to look at him. He's not wearing the glasses anymore. They looked nice.

But then again, Oakley always looks nice.

"I realized something today," I tell him.

He cocks his head, fingers continuing their slow passage through my hair. "Yeah? What's that?"

"Something I haven't said."

"Am I supposed to guess?" Oakley asks, his eyes dancing. "Because that might take a while."

"No," I answer softly. "Just...listen, all right?"

His humor fades, giving way to a seriousness as he nods once.

Maybe it's nothing monumental, this moment on his couch, with fatigue weighing my limbs and Oakley dressed in sweats. But as I told him before, I like ordinary. I like *this*. And I don't want to keep any part of myself from him ever again.

"When I was younger," I start, "folks would always say I'd know what love was because it'd feel different than what I felt for friends. And when I met Laura, it *was* different than what I felt for you. I just didn't realize until far too late what that meant."

Oakley swallows roughly, his hand slowing.

"Oak... I've loved you since before I knew what love was. I've been trying to pinpoint the time when things changed for me, but...they never did. That's the thing. I loved you from the very start. Back then. Now. I'm more than certain I'll love you always. And I haven't told you that."

Tears line Oakley's eyes, ones he doesn't try to hide. He's never been afraid to cry in front of me. Oakley knows vulnerability isn't a weakness. He's shown that to me time and time again. I think it's a big part of why I've been able to be so open with him in return.

It's a gift, letting someone see the deepest parts of us. Knowing we're safe to.

His voice is raspy when he speaks. "Law. You know I love you, too, right?"

"I do."

"And that's not going away. Not ever."

"I know," I tell him. "It's not fickle, you and me."

"No," he agrees, sucking in a harsh breath. "Can you come up here so I can kiss you?"

The moment I push upright, Oakley's mouth is on mine. It's hard, and it's tender, and it's all the things I know us to be. There's a lot that can be said with a kiss.

I love you might just be my favorite yet.

Chapter 32

OAKLEY

Wendy waits as I take a seat at the kitchen table, her hands clasped primly behind herself, a stern expression on her face.

"All right," I say. "I'm seated. Now, are you gonna tell me what this meeting is about?"

"In time," she says simply.

I raise an eyebrow, battling a smile at this seventeen-year-old who texted me earlier to schedule a time to meet and who's now standing in front of me very much like how I imagine her father stands in front of his classes each day.

Good grief.

Lawson was right, wasn't he? She's here to threaten me.

"My dad is a good guy," Wendy says.

There goes my other eyebrow. "You realize I've known him longer than you, right?"

"You gonna listen, or are you gonna give me attitude?"

"Jesus, there's two of them," I puff out. "I'm listening."

"Good," Wendy says, placing her palms flat on the table, her hazel-brown eyes searing into me. "My dad is the best person I know. If anyone deserves the world, it's him. Which means if you ever leave this town again without him by your side, there won't be a rock you can hide under where I won't find you."

I stare at her, flabbergasted. "Good Lord, Wendy Darling. Who the heck taught you to speak that way?"

"Prob'ly you," she shoots back. "Seeing as I've known you just as long as my dad. You realize *that*, right?"

I huff, crossing my arms as a smile stretches across my face. "If you're trying to scare me, it won't work."

Wendy steps back from the table with a huff of her own. "I'm not trying to *scare* you, Oak. I'm trying to tell you I love my dad. And I love you. And I don't think either of us would survive if you took off again. If this isn't...if it's not..."

I'm up and out of my seat in an instant. Wendy doesn't try to stop me from pulling her into a hug, but she's stiff in my arms.

"Wen... Do you know why I left Darling?"

She sniffs. "For Stevie."

"Not just that," I tell her, my voice hoarse. "I left because I was trying to make a life for myself that didn't revolve around your dad."

She pulls back some, looking up at me.

"He's been the center of my world for as long as I can remember. My first memories include him. Most of them after that, too. Your dad... He's the goddamn gravitational center of my whole freaking existence, and I thought I had to escape that, at least a little. Because how foolish would I have been to devote my life to my best friend?"

Wendy's eyes are glassy, and I run my knuckle along the top of her cheek to catch an errant drop.

"I love your dad and everything he's ever created, including you. I never thought having him love me back was an option. Not when we were young and single still. Not while he was married to your mom. Not after that. Not until...suddenly it was. There's not a single thing that could pull me away now, you hear?"

"You promise?"

In answer, I hold out my pinkie. After a long second, Wendy curls hers with mine. "I promise, Wen. I'm not leaving either of you. Not ever again."

Wendy throws her arms around me, the top of her head at my chin as she hugs me tight. I remember walking into the hospital room the day she was born. She was this tiny, wailing thing, all pink and wrinkled. Lawson had tears in his eyes as he held her out to me.

I had wondered at her then. At this miraculous little human.

Over seventeen years later, and a tear slips down my cheek, the same as back then.

Family is a funny thing. The way it grows. How it adapts. It's not the same for everybody, but I think that's what makes it so great.

You can always gain new family. Wendy joined mine long ago.

Proof, Lawson said, that he *lived*.

Proof, too, that he loved.

And so do I. So do I.

Lawson and I arrive at Jackson's house as the sun is dipping below the mountains. The bonfire is already roaring out back, his brothers' chatter drifting across the yard as we approach.

It feels like every summer I've lived in Montana. The crisp night air. The smell of the outdoors. The sound, even, of the boisterous Darling family.

It's so damn good to be home.

"Hey," Colton calls out. "You guys are finally here. Saved you a chair, Oakley."

I glance at the Adirondack chair Colton indicates, which is set apart from the others, almost like...

"Oh, good grief," I mutter. "Is this a goddamn interrogation?"

"What? No," Colton protests, even as he sits forward with his hands steepled over his knees. "We're just gonna have a friendly chat."

"Lawson?" I plead.

The man squeezes the back of my neck, tugging me in for a brief kiss that has Jackson grunting. "You knew what you were getting into, Oak."

I stare at the back of Lawson's head as he leaves me to my fate.

Ash hands me a whiskey tin, winking before he steps away.

With a sigh, I seat myself across from the others, the fire crackling between us. Ash sits beside Jackson, the man's feet crossed at his ankles. Remi has a gentle smile on his face that looks like it's meant to reassure. Colton is still staring me down with intense blue eyes, even as Noah, seated next to him, is shaking his head, bemusement on his face.

I take a sip of my whiskey before clasping my hands together. "All right. Lay it on me."

Colton knocks his hat up with a knuckle. "What, exactly, are your intentions with our older brother?"

Remi groans, Noah loses his battle not to laugh, and Ash is outright grinning now. I find Lawson's eyes, somehow knowing from just one look that I have permission—encouragement, even—to answer however I'd like.

Refocusing on Colton, I say, "Are we talking about when he's tied up or not?"

There's a beat of silence before a collective groan rings out.

Colton scrubs his face, muttering, "Nope, sure didn't need to know that."

Noah supplies a helpful, "You did ask."

Remi looks as if he's contemplating what choices brought him here.

Ash hollers suggestively, adding a, "What? That's hot," when Jackson glares his way.

I, for my part, kick my boot over my knee, enjoying the Darling Whiskey in my tin as the flames from the fire turn the night orange.

Finally, Colton says, "Are we talking rope or—Nope. No, no. I don't wanna know. Forget I asked."

"I think what Colton means to say," Remi puts in with a pointed look at his brother, "is that we're really happy for you guys. Oak, you've been family from the beginning. And I can't think of anyone better suited to look after our brother."

My throat feels tight as I find Lawson's eyes again. "I will," I say roughly. "Look after him. And take care of him. I'll love him harder than anyone else ever could."

"Oh, gross," Colton mutters.

"Love is gross?" Noah asks, amusement in his voice as he wraps an arm around Colton's shoulders.

"When it's my brother? Yes."

Lawson pulls his chair over next to mine, accepting the tin I hand him once he's seated. "Bet you missed this while you were gone," he says, a smile quirking his lips.

I know he meant it as a joke, but I answer seriously. "Yeah. I did. I really, really did."

His eyes hold mine as he takes a sip of the whiskey, his gaze as warm as the fire. A bell ringing in the night has everyone freezing.

"Is that..." I say before it clicks. "Lawson, get inside the house."

"What?" the man says, looking confused as I try to tug him from his chair.

The ringing is getting louder.

"It's the goddamn donkey," I tell him. "*Go.*"

"He's not gonna *bite* me, Oak."

"You don't know that."

"Jesus," Lawson grumbles. "You really do hold a grudge."

As Lawson remains stubbornly rooted in his chair, the donkey comes trotting into sight. I breathe a sigh of relief when the old ass walks up to Jackson, the man sighing low and long.

"I don't have any treats," he says, the donkey prodding at his pocket. "For Christ's sake, would you just—"

A loud tearing sound has Jackson jumping from his seat, the front half of his jeans, pocket downward, stripped away as the donkey takes off with the denim firmly between his teeth. Jackson stands in shock, nearly falling on his ass when the bottom hem holds tight. But that donkey yanks, and it rips free, leaving Jackson's tattered jeans hanging around his leg as the donkey's bell grows quieter.

Ash doubles over, laughing so hard he starts to wheeze. Remi has a wide grin on his face, his phone out in front of him, aimed at Jackson. Lawson lets out a single chuckle, taking another sip of his whiskey.

And Jackson? "See if you get another treat from me ever again," he shouts at the donkey, voice lowering as he mutters, "The fuck? First the milk, now this?"

"Oh my God, Jack," Ash says between breaths. "I can see your briefs."

As Jackson stomps toward his house, pant leg waving behind him, Colton loads a few marshmallows onto a stick.

"Well," the second-youngest Darling brother says. "I think it's time for s'mores."

As Colton and Noah get into the chocolate and graham crackers, Lawson passes the whiskey tin back my way. His lips are pressed into an amused line I get a little caught up in, considering the man's pout is always distracting.

"You were ready to leap in between me and that donkey, Oak."

It's an accusation I don't bother countering. "Considering you wouldn't move, you bet your ass I was."

"He's not that dangerous," Lawson says, shaking his head.

I wave a hand toward Jackson's house, where the man disappeared inside less than a minute ago to replace his pants. "Uh-huh. Which is why the residents of Darling put a bell around his neck so you could hear him coming. Where d'you think I got the idea for Belladonna?"

"*That's* why she has a bell?"

"She keeps stealing my food, Law! Even with the bell on, she manages it. I don't know how she learned to move so stealthily."

Lawson snorts. "She's a sweetheart. Admit you love that cow."

"I'll do no such thing," I reply hotly. "A cowboy. With a goddamn house cow. It's ridiculous."

Lawson hooks a hand around the back of my neck, tugging me close and planting a kiss on my lips. "Admit it."

"What is this? Some sort of new tactic—"

He kisses me again, longer this time. I'm fairly certain I hear a halfhearted complaint from Remi, but everything is so very far away. Everything except for Lawson.

He leans back an inch at most to stare me down. "Admit you love her."

I clear my throat. "I love you."

"And the cow."

"I'd like to eat the cow."

He barks a laugh. "You could never. You're the softest soul I know, Oakley Beaumont. Think about those big black eyes of hers and tell me again you could eat her."

He's got me in a corner, and he knows it.

"She's all right," I allow. "But she gets in the house—"

"Because you installed a cow door."

"—and leaves dirt all over the floor—"

"Which is why you bought a robot vacuum."

"—and honestly, it's just the principle of the matter, all right? I mean—"

My words come to a halt when Lawson tugs me in again. He offers me the taste of whiskey on his lips, and I can do nothing but indulge in it for long minutes. When there's a whistle from Ash, Lawson pulls back.

"Needa use the bathroom," he tells me, standing and heading toward the house.

I clear my throat, feeling stares on my person from around the fire.

Remi is the first to speak. "It's good to see him happy again. Smiling."

"And laughing," Colton adds. "I can't remember the last time I heard him laugh like that."

Remi hums his agreement, and my heart squeezes tight. There's lingering guilt for having been absent the past few years, unaware of exactly how badly Lawson was hurting. If I'd known, I wouldn't have stayed away. But mostly, it's relief I feel, knowing how much happier Lawson is now. And so much love for the man it physically hurts.

Colton sets his hat on the ground, his eyes meeting mine. "You know I was just playing earlier, right?"

"I do," I tell him.

"It's just... Law has always felt the need to look after all the rest of us. Maybe because he's the oldest, or maybe it's just who he is. But I want him to know we have his back, too. That we'll always look out for him. The same goes for you, Oak."

I nod, a lump in my throat. As I collect my words, Jackson returns to Ash's side, the fire between us sending occasional fits of golden sparks up into the night. "Y'all are the closest thing I've ever had to brothers. I've never doubted you'd be there for me if I needed it. Lawson knows that, too. But you have to admit... You're all stubborn in your own ways."

Ash huffs a laugh at that, smacking Jackson's chest. Not a single Darling refutes it.

"He knows you love him," I go on. "And he knows you'd move the world for him. But that doesn't mean he wouldn't still choose to go the long way around just to spare anyone else the strain. Being selfish isn't easy for him."

Remi opens his mouth, but I go on quickly.

"I know, and *you* know, it's not selfish to lean on the folks you love. But Law... He's spent so much of his life making sure everybody else is happy. I think he's only just realizing he can ask for the same. Give him some time to get used to it."

Colton nods slowly, Noah's hand resting on his thigh. "And your intentions?" the Darling brother asks, his lips tipped into a smile.

"Easy," I answer. "I intend to give that man every single thing he asks for and everything he doesn't know he needs. I'll make him happy. I swear it."

A moment of silence passes, apart from the snap of the fire and the wind slowly whistling by.

Ash breaks the quiet. "Now about that rope..."

"Nope," Remi shouts, snagging the bag of marshmallows from beside Colton's chair and tossing the whole thing Ash's way.

The blonde man laughs, Remi shaking his head all the while. I can see Lawson heading our way as his family bickers, a bottle of whiskey making the rounds as his silhouette gets closer in the dark.

Yeah. It's damn good to be right where I belong.

Chapter 33

LAWSON

"I remember when you got that," my mom says, her voice coming from the doorway.

I look down at the copy of *Peter and Wendy* I'm holding, having paused in my packing to rifle through the pages. "Yeah?"

"You were six," she says, stepping into the room. Her eyes sweep the space, this bedroom I was raised in. It looks far different now than it did back then. "It was your grandpa's first. Do you remember him?"

"Barely," I admit. My memories of Grandpa Darling are fuzzy. But I do recall sitting with him on the old couch downstairs, back before my parents replaced it, my grandpa reading to me. Most likely this book.

"You're like him in a lot of ways," my mom says, sitting at the edge of the bed. "He was always quiet. Spent a lot of time in his head. I worried for him, at times. The same I worry for you."

"There's nothing wrong with being quiet."

"No, there isn't," she agrees. "But even as a child, you were so serious, Lawson. When Jackson came along, that stayed the same. You looked out for him. Then Colton. Eventually, Remi. The only kid you ever really played with was Oakley."

I nod, my fingers tracing the aged corner of the book. "We played Neverland a lot."

"I know," my mom says, a smile in her voice. "And I was so grateful to see it. Any good parent only ever wants the best for their children. Seeing you now, the way you've been these past few months..." She blows out a quiet breath. "It's like you're a kid again. The version of yourself that would steal wooden spoons from the kitchen so you and Oakley could pretend they were swords. He's always been good for you, Lawson. He complements you. And you him. I couldn't ask for anything more for my son."

From the corner of my eye, I see movement at the door. I don't look, but I recognize the flash of Oakley's belt buckle as he steps out of sight, giving me and my mom privacy. I'm glad he heard some of that. Proof that my family loves him just as much as I do.

"He's the reason I see pixie dust," I tell my mom.

She cocks her head gently. "Lawson, dear... Is that some euphemism I'm unfamiliar with?"

"What? *No.* Ah, God."

My mom laughs as I groan.

"No," I say again, more firmly. "I just mean... If there's magic to be found in this life, he's it for me."

My mom's eyes are wet when she squeezes my hand. She doesn't say anything more, but she doesn't have to.

When I get downstairs with my last box of books, Oakley is waiting.

"Everything all right?" he asks, opening the front door for me to pass through. His truck is parked just out front, the back filled with everything I packed up from my brief time living back at the ranch.

"Yeah," I tell him. "Everything's great."

I slide the box into the bed of the vehicle before looking at the house. The cabin-style siding. The big windows. The metal roof reflecting the sun.

I know it's not the last time I'll see it. I'll be back. And often.

But I'm traveling down a new road. Isn't that what Colton said?

I have no doubt this one is right for me.

Oakley squeezes the back of my neck before tugging the tailgate up. With a quiet goodbye to the place I was raised, we head toward home.

Bell is lying in a shade spot when we park. She doesn't rouse, which tells me she's not hungry at the moment. Oakley and I haul my things inside, and it feels a heck of a lot like the beginning of the summer, when it was Oakley's possessions being unloaded inside this house. Luckily, I don't have any furniture with me. Only clothes, trinkets, books.

Oakley brings my toiletries to the bathroom, and I leave him to it, adding my collection of hardcovers and paperbacks to his bookshelf. It's fairly empty, Oakley not being a huge reader himself. Even so, I get a sense of satisfaction slipping my books in with his. I leave *Peter and Wendy* for last, unable to help but open it up again.

I find the passage where Peter is watching Wendy through the window, his sadness at being left out like a soft blanket set carefully over the words. I could sense it, that melancholy, even before I understood why the magical boy was sad over such a thing. As it says, he has countless joys in his life. More than most children. So why would he possibly be sad over one single thing he couldn't have?

I get it now. That one thing represented so very much.

"Law?"

Oakley's voice is soft as he crouches down beside me. His hand drifts over my shoulder, the touch so light, so simple, yet far more than he would have allowed himself in the past. It's a door, a window wide open, where before there was glass.

"I'm fine," I tell him, sensing his concern. "Just thinking."

He hums. "Do you need some more time? There's something I'd like to do today if you're up for it."

"What's that?"

"A surprise. And no, I'm not gonna tell you. You'll just have to trust me."

I huff. "Easy."

Oakley makes a pleased sound, waiting as I set the book on the shelf, the cover displayed. I swear, if I listen hard enough, I can hear the faint ticking of a clock. Standing, I follow Oakley out the door and into his truck.

My eyebrow wings up when he drives onto the road leading back to the ranch. "Is this surprise a dinner with my family?"

He snorts. "No, it's not."

"Hm. Horseback riding?"

"If you want," he says. "It isn't far, but we could get there by saddle instead of walking if you'd like."

I glance at the sky, so bright today, even as the evening approaches. It'll be cooling down soon, the start of fall near.

"Why not?" I answer, thinking a final summer ride with Oakley sounds just about perfect.

He shoots me a quick grin before taking the turn onto my family's drive.

Oakley parks near the milking barn, the walk to the stables shorter from here. A couple of the ranchers are inside, getting their horses settled before they leave for the day. Oakley grabs gear for Clover, and I saddle up Prairie, one of the family horses who isn't used for work. She's getting up there in age, but she perks up as I unlatch her stall, eager, it would seem, to go for a walk.

Once she's ready, I swing by the tack room and grab a spare hat. I don't wear them often, certainly not as much as Oakley does. But beyond being good for sun protection, slipping that leather on my head reminds me what it was like growing up around here. All the good parts.

Maybe I'm no cowboy when it comes down to it. But I'm a Darling. I'll always be that.

Oakley's smile turns into a grin when he sees me. "Looking good, cowboy."

"You think so?"

"Mhm. All that's missing is the rope."

A clang comes from the direction of the horse stalls. "Gross," Remi says, turning to grab a bag of feed. He hefts it easily.

"Sorry," Oakley mutters. "Didn't see you."

"I was right here the whole time," Remi grumbles, stalking off.

Oakley fails to cover his laugh.

"Don't be fooled," I tell him. "He's not as innocent as he seems."

Oakley holds up his hand. "Yeah, I'm gonna stop you right there. I don't needa know."

Chuckling, I tip my hat toward the barn doors. "Ready to take me to this surprise?"

"Sure am. About that rope, though..."

My responding laughter rings out, and Oakley looks oh so pleased with himself. Horses in tow, we head into the sun and take to the trails. Oakley doesn't seem in any hurry to get to where we're going, so I sit back and enjoy the ride.

"Did your dad mention we're going camping the weekend after next?" I ask.

Oakley's head whips my way. "What? No. My dad?"

I nod. "He hasn't gone in a while, so I suggested we all take a trip before it gets too cold for it. You're coming, too."

"Oh I am, am I?" Oakley snarks, a tiny smile at the corner of his lips. "Wendy?"

"Yep. Your mom is staying home, though."

He doesn't look surprised. "Ten bucks—"

"We are *not* betting on whether or not we have sex during a family camping trip," I say sternly. "Not happening, Oak."

His chuckle lasts a good long while. "Whiskey?"

I sigh. "Prob'ly."

I do my best not to be amused by Oakley's hissed, "*Yes.*"

When we've gone a good handful of miles, Oakley pulls Clover's reins to the side to get the horse turned around. I watch him for a moment, confused.

He looks back at me expectantly. "Coming?"

"We're turning around?" I ask, even though it's obvious. "Where exactly are you taking me?"

He hums. "I've always heard it's not the destination but the journey that's the important part."

"You saying you're happy just to spend time with me?"

"Mostly Clover," he teases, blue-and-brown eyes filled with mirth as I sidle up next to him.

I swat his leg with my hat, and Oakley takes the opportunity to flick my forehead.

"Cut it out," I grouse, no heat behind my words.

"You started it."

"Jesus Christ. We're twelve again."

Oakley titters a laugh, looking so damn happy it stuns me for a second. My throat feels tight as I replace my hat on my head. Oakley is facing forward again, smiling serenely at the trees and dappled sun around us as our horses walk along at a leisurely pace.

"Thanks for this," I tell him, his eyes meeting mine again. "For bringing me out here."

"You don't even know where we're going yet," he says, amusement still lingering in his tone.

"No," I agree. "But like you said, all of this is what matters. I've had a real damn good life with you, Oak. Even when... Even when we were just friends. I don't regret any of the time I've shared with you. And I guess I'm realizing I have a whole lot more to look forward to, don't I?"

He eases out a careful breath. "Yeah, Law."

"You got a little something in your eye?"

"Yeah. I do," he huffs. "It's my emotions, all right? You make me emotional."

"All right."

He huffs again, shaking his head. "You're such a snarky little shit."

This time, Oakley puts Clover into a trot before I can swat his leg. I chuckle, nudging my heel against Prairie to follow after him.

We slow before long, the entrance point of the trails up ahead. Oakley doesn't head back in the direction of the horse barn. Instead, we walk along the edge of the woods, past the petting farm. When Oakley steers us toward the river that cuts through the ranch land, I look his way. He's biting his lip, and my pulse ratchets.

Oakley slows once we reach the river's edge. He hops fluidly down off Clover's back and waves for me to do the same. "C'mon."

I dismount, smoothing a hand over Prairie's neck before flipping the reins to the front of her. Oakley leads me toward an old fence line that's sturdy enough to tie the horses to. Their tails swish in the shade, Clover nudging the grasses with his nose in search of something good to eat.

We walk a little ways along the river, the water shallow here. We used to play in this spot, the current nearly nonexistent, so our parents didn't mind. I can almost see a shipwreck in the broken log stuck along the river's edge, white sails blowing gently in the breeze.

I smile at the image in my head, Oakley's footsteps leaving a trail ahead of me. A crack of a twig. The imprint of his boot in the mud.

It's no surprise when he stops outside our willow tree. It's a little more gnarled than it used to be. Some of the branches are barer, and one side of it broke off years ago in a bad storm. It never quite recovered, but new branches started to grow in the scars of the old. Oakley takes a breath before setting his hat on the ground and stepping forward.

The green branches sway behind him, hiding him from view. Following his lead, I set my hat down beside his and walk into our safe little cove.

My breath catches the moment I'm through the curtain of leaves. Oakley is standing near the big trunk of the tree, the expression on his face a mixture of anticipation and...I'm not even sure what. Nerves?

But it's the hundreds of acorns lying scattered around our feet that have my eyes pooling real fast.

"Told you I'd give you another," Oakley says, his voice rougher than usual.

It takes me a second to speak. "This is a lot more than 'another.'"

His laugh is just as rough as his voice. "One didn't seem like enough. Not for the number of promises I wanna give you."

"When did you do this?" I ask, bending down to pick up one of the acorns. It's tiny in the palm of my hand. A token that's worth so much more than its weight.

"Spent some time collecting them the past couple days while you were packing," he says. "Maybe it doesn't replace the one you lost, but I figured it was a start."

I shake my head in disbelief. "What's this one for?"

Oakley's lips twist. "I promise I'll kiss you every night before bed."

I add another to my palm. "And this one?"

"Promise I'll make beef stew anytime you want it."

My chest squeezes tight. "This one?" I ask, picking up another acorn. The cap is rough against my skin.

"I promise I'll love you even when you feed my cow snacks you know she shouldn't have."

The crinkle beside Oakley's eyes belies his amusement. I try to hide my own.

I hold up another, and he says, "I promise I'll worship you, Law. Any way you'll let me."

Another. "Promise I'll do my best not to wake you each morning when I get up at three."

Another. "Promise no matter how much we argue, I'll never let you walk away."

Another. "I promise there isn't a single thing in this world that could stop me from loving you."

I stand slowly, my palm filled with acorns, Oakley watching me all the while.

"And us?" I ask. "Which one means forever?"

"They all do," he says simply. "Every one of these acorns means forever with you."

I suck in a shallow breath as the wind rustles the branches around us. The sun winks in and out, shafts of gold lighting Oakley's hair and the side of his face. There's pixie dust dancing on the breeze around him, the shimmer of it undeniable.

My gaze is drawn to the willow branches above us, the brown spreading out like a star, blue sky peeking through in a way that reminds me of Oakley's eyes. Of all the times I've looked into them and felt utterly content.

It's summers past and the warmth of sunlight on my skin. It's safety and home and the excitement of battling pirates. It's knowing my heart is safe with this man. As safe as the memory of two eleven-year-olds sharing their first kiss under the shade of a willow.

I bring my gaze back to Oakley. This man, once a child, who has always made me feel as if I could fly.

"Marry me."

Those blue-and-brown eyes of his flare wide.

It's two words. No ring. No finesse.

But it couldn't feel more right.

Oakley pulls in a shuddering breath as I step closer. His nod is a slow thing, but there's no hesitation in it.

"Yeah, Law," he says, his voice nothing more than a whisper.

I hold out my pinkie, my palm full of promises. Oakley twines his with mine.

Our kiss, this time, isn't two boys holding on to Neverland. It's men who recognize the adventure has only begun.

Chapter 34

OAKLEY

"This isn't too much?" I ask Wendy, the abundance of rings on my fingers feeling like overkill. Not to mention the bracelets tucked under my sleeves.

"It's tradition," she says, twisting one final loop onto my thumb. "There."

I look at the jewelry covering my hands, over every digit except my left ring finger. My throat gets tight.

"You didn't want to help your dad get ready?" I ask her.

She shakes her head, her brown hair held half back with pins, the rest in a subtle curl. "Colton's got him."

Taking a step back, she sweeps her gaze over me. From my freshly cleaned boots, to my slacks and light tan jacket. The sprig of lavender in my breast pocket. The bolo tie Lawson insisted on because *we're not fancy, Oak.*

My hair is neatly tidied. My beard trimmed. Every inch of me is pressed and polished. Not to mention adorned now that Wendy is through with me.

"You look great," she says, seeming as if she's trying not to cry.

"Shit, kid."

"Language," she mumbles.

I bark a laugh, holding out my arms. Wendy steps into them, hugging me back, her light purple dress covered in a thick white coat befitting the weather.

Marigold sticks her head into the room, expression soft. "It's time."

With a nod, Wendy and I disentangle, the three of us making our way toward the back door.

Winter is blanketing Darling Ranch like a scene out of a postcard. The ground is covered in fluffy white, new snow having dropped while we were sleeping. Chairs are set out not far off, the woods near the petting farm their backdrop. One or more of the Darlings already shoveled a path through the snow, and footprints line the trail from friends and family who are waiting.

But it's the man standing before it all that snags my attention.

Lawson's slacks and jacket are an earthy brown, darker than my tan. Like me, he's wearing a bolo tie, the sight of it making my throat close up for no conceivable reason, and a sprig of lavender adorns his breast. His belt buckle is showing, his hands are tucked in his pockets, and his hair, like usual, is sitting perfectly in place.

I've seen this man thousands of ways over our decades of life. I've seen him primped. Seen him wearing his rattiest sweats. I've seen him nude, wearing nothing at all.

But I've never seen him waiting to walk down the aisle with me.

Not until today.

My eyes prick as I join him, Wendy giving her dad a final hug and whispering something that has him nodding before she goes to take her seat. Our parents are standing nearby, but they don't interrupt, giving us a moment before the ceremony begins.

"Hi," I manage, the snow falling gently around us, dusting Lawson's shoulders and hair.

His smile is warm, his inhale stuttering as his gaze runs over me. "You look real good, Oak."

"You think so? Somebody wouldn't let me put on a fancy tie."

"You don't need it," he says seriously. "I like you best like this."

"Looking like a cowboy?" I tease.

"Looking at home," he replies, effectively shutting me up. Lawson reaches for my bolo tie, fist curling around the cords as he tugs me closer.

"Not sure you're supposed to kiss me yet," I whisper.

He huffs a small breath. "You gonna complain if I do?"

"Nope. Carry on."

Lawson's lips curl gently against my own, warm and familiar as he steals the breath from my lungs. It's not lascivious or brash. But it's demanding as Lawson's grip holds me in place, the same way he's always held me close.

When he loosens his fist and draws back, his whiskey eyes snag my own.

"I'm gonna be the best husband you'll ever have," I promise him hoarsely.

He snorts. "The only, Oak."

I nod in a jerk.

"Ready?" he asks.

"Damn right I am."

Lawson clasps his hand with mine, the clink of my jewelry on his making me laugh. He shoots me a wink as we get into place, our guests looking back at us now as music begins to play. Marigold and Hank walk down the aisle first, followed by my parents. It was our way of honoring tradition, just a little bit different. There's no bride to give away today, but having our families here to celebrate with us means a lot.

Our parents take their seats in the front row, and Lawson looks over at me. Together, we begin the journey down the aisle. The snow is soft underfoot, Lawson's hand snug in mine. We split apart only once we reach the officiant, Lawson looking a dream as the snow falls around him like twinkling pixie dust.

The thought has a smile curving my lips.

Our ceremony is brief. We didn't want to keep folks out in the cold for long. But every minute of it is a minute I treasure, this day one I've wanted for myself all my life. At times, when my prior relationships came to an end, I wondered if I'd ever actually get it. A wedding of my own.

A person all my own.

When the officiant guides me to say my vows, I have to clear my throat a couple times before I can speak.

"Law. When we were kids, I spent a lot of time on this land with you. These woods beside us housed a good many adventures. As we got older, those adventures looked a little different. But through it all, I never lost you."

I inhale a winter-cold breath to compose myself.

"We've been friends for as long as I can remember. I never doubted you'd be a part of my life, always, but having the chance to fall in love with you? Having you love me back? I never saw that coming."

Lawson smiles softly, a sheen in his eyes that I'm sure mirrors my own.

"I made you a promise long ago," I remind him. "The two of us. Forever. It's a promise I'll make again and again, in sickness, in health, on our good days and our bad. Nothing could change the fact that my heart belongs to yours, Lawson Darling. From saddle to sunup, and all the hours in between."

He lets out a quiet breath at his own words returned to him, the expression on his face so full of love I can feel it in my chest. The officiant gives him a nod, and Lawson begins his own vows, his voice soothing and deep.

"Oakley. There's this line in the original Peter Pan story that's always stuck with me. 'To die will be an awfully big adventure.' That passage got rewritten a lot in later adaptations. To live, they said, would be the adventure. Not to die. But I think they completely missed the point."

Lawson's eyes hold mine as he draws in a breath.

"There was one thing Peter could never do. Grow up. So what bigger adventure would there be than to grow old for a person who's incapable of it? It was never about death. It was about *living*. I've always wanted to grow old with you, Oak. To live my life at your side. And now, I'll have the chance to."

My own breath is choppy as Lawson sends me a gentle smile.

"I'm not afraid of growing older. Every year we have waiting is another to love you. It will be my honor, Oakley Beaumont, to live the rest of my days as your husband, your friend, your fellow lost boy. Not a single daydream could compare to the life I know I'll have with you."

I blink back tears as I reach for Lawson's hand. His fingers twine with mine, the officiant walking us through our *I dos*.

The ring he slips onto my only empty finger is brushed gold. His is the same.

I watch Lawson through the sparkling snow that falls featherlight from the sky. When we're announced husband and husband, it's on the softest breath. Lawson's. My own.

His kiss this time is curved around a smile. It's calm, and it's happy, and I can feel myself trembling in response, even as my chest lights with a warmth I know isn't going anywhere. Our family claps. Our friends, too.

Lawson and I return down the aisle hand in hand as the music starts up again. My nose is cold, but my smile couldn't get wider.

We're the first to walk into the ranch house, but our guests aren't far behind us, ready, I'm sure, to get out of the cold. Appetizers are already set out in the dining room. Drinks, as well. Lawson tugs me past it all.

I'm about to open my mouth and tease him for wanting to get me alone so soon when we stop in front of the kitchen and set eyes on the absolute mayhem inside. Lawson and I stare as one at Belladonna, my damn cow, who's managed to spread our wedding cake over just about every surface in the room, herself included.

She freezes when she sees us watching her, and then she streaks past.

I nearly fall on my ass as her hip hits my leg, startled gasps ringing out from the dining room as Bell races inside. Something topples. Something else crashes. There's frosting smeared across my pants.

"Oakley..." Lawson says, voice steady.

I suck in a breath. "Who the *hell* brought my cow to the wedding?"

There's a grunted, "Got her," I think is Jackson and then all is quiet.

"I thought it'd be a good surprise!" Colton finally calls. "She was shut in the mudroom."

I speak past gritted teeth. "Clearly, she got out."

"I, uh... Did she eat the cake?" Colton asks.

Marigold is the first around the corner into the hall, her hand flying in front of her mouth when she sees the state of the kitchen. She starts to laugh, my mom the next to join us. Sienna Beaumont takes in the chaos with calculating eyes before shedding her coat, rolling up the sleeves of her dress, and stepping forward.

"Marigold," she says. "Would you kindly show me where you keep the aprons?"

Mrs. Darling follows my mom into the kitchen, opening up a cupboard. "Right here. Colton! You're on cleanup. We've got a cake to bake."

Lawson's brother looks despondent as he steps into the hall. "How'd she get out?"

"That cow," I say evenly, "is the worst."

Lawson clasps the back of my neck, pulling my focus. I'm not expecting the cake he smashes down my face. There's another gasp, and more footsteps join us.

"Holy shit," Remi says in awe.

"There was cow drool on that," I put in, horrified.

Lawson's laugh is as bright as the snow outside. He bends over, clutching his side, the frosting on his hand leaving a white patch on his suit jacket. But it's the joy in his eyes that has my heart pattering anew.

I pull him upright, wiping my face against his before he can protest. He doesn't once stop laughing, his lips finding mine through the mess of frosting and cake. It's horrible and wonderful and the same fireworks I felt the first time my lips met his.

I don't care about the, "Gross," Remi affectionately mumbles. Or the fact that our reception got upended by a cow. I barely hear Ash declaring he'll get the frosting started or notice the folks moving around us to help set the house to rights.

There's only Lawson, who once gave me a thimble, a gift so much bigger than I ever knew it'd be. It was love, plain and simple. A piece of his heart he promised to me.

Promises don't always keep.

But Lawson's? Him and me?

It's a fairy tale that has nothing to do with make-believe.

"Love you, hubby," I whisper against Lawson's lips.

He smiles. Oh, how he smiles. "Oak?"

"Yeah?"

"Kiss me again? And this time, don't stop."

And what can I possibly do but give my husband exactly what he wants? A kiss.

His first.

His last.

"Anything you want, princess. I'm yours."

Epilogue

LAWSON

TEN YEARS LATER

All is warm when I wake, the surface beneath me moving steadily like the tide. It takes me a second to orient myself, the feeling of being shipborne dissipating.

I can almost remember pirates, but that, too, floats into mist.

"Morning," Oakley rumbles, his voice like thunder beneath my ear.

I pull in a deep breath, contentment secure around me like a blanket. "Morning. Your sword is poking my thigh."

Oakley snickers, his hand rubbing down my back. His fingers slip under the band of my sleep pants, a suggestive little dance that has me smiling. "Feel like dueling this morning?"

My laugh has Oakley chuckling in response. But then I remember what today is, and tension creeps into my frame. Oakley senses it, his hand slipping free.

"Everything all right?" he asks.

I nod against his chest. "Yeah, I just... I'm a little nervous about today."

"It's not the first time Wendy has introduced you to a partner."

"No," I agree. "But this time is different. I can tell. The way she talks about her..."

Oakley hums. "You think it'll stick."

"I do. And I'm glad," I put in quickly. "If she makes Wendy happy, of course I am. But when the hell did my little girl grow up, Oak? She's twenty-eight now, living on her own and paying her bills, and pretty soon she might be having kids of her own. I'm gonna be a goddamn grandpa."

Oakley's muffled laughter has me swatting his side.

"Stop. This is serious."

"Of course," he says, trying to keep his voice even. "Very serious, these hypothetical grandkids."

"You're sassing me."

"What? Nooo. How about this? I'll pick out a crib while you—"

Oakley squawks when I dig my fingers into his ribs.

"Mercy," he shouts, his twisting subsiding when I quit my torture. He heaves out a breath. "It'll be okay, Law. Whatever comes down the road."

"I know. I just worry."

"Mhm." He squeezes me in his arms, a soft sigh leaving his lungs. "Should we get ready?"

"Hold on. What about your sword?"

He snorts. "Happy to sheathe it."

I shake my head, turning my face into his neck and placing a kiss there. "Fuck my fist?"

His groan is low. "And you?"

"Maybe later," I tell him, slipping my hand down beneath his boxer briefs, curling around the morning wood that springs further to life at my touch. "Show me how good I make you feel, Oak?"

"Fuck, princess," the man rasps, rolling his hips into my grip as I twist and stroke. "You make me feel like no one ever has."

I run my lips over his neck, pressing kisses, breathing him in. "Yeah? And how's that?"

"Safe. Loved. Wanted."

"Always," I tell him earnestly. Because I understand what he means.

It's not just about sex. Intimacy is far more than that. Wanting a person can mean so much more than that.

And the way I want Oakley?

It's unlike anything I've ever experienced. It's unique to him. To me and him.

I slip my lips to Oakley's ear, my hand pumping him as he swells in my grip. "C'mon, cowboy. Make a mess of your husband."

That does it. Oakley spills over my fist, his groan a familiar song, the feel of his cock emptying as mesmerizing to me as it always is, whether it's him spilling into my hand or my ass. I wring him lightly until he falls lax, his breathing slowing. I run my fingers along his softening cock until Oakley presses a kiss to my hair.

"Now we really need to shower," he murmurs, his arm still around me tight.

I nod. "Time to meet the girlfriend."

We eat a quick breakfast before we go, Oakley latching the back door so Bell can't wander in. Even in her senior age, the Miniature Galloway cow gets into her fair share of trouble.

The drive to Wendy's takes about an hour, although we don't go straight to her house. We're meeting just outside the city. Even so, Wendy's apartment isn't far from Darling, all things considered. It's easy for her to come visit on the weekends or for us to do the same. Every once in a while, all four of us get together, my ex included. Although the times Oakley and I are in the same vicinity as Laura are rare these days. True to his word, Oakley has never forgiven her, and I haven't asked him to.

She didn't attend our wedding. She wasn't invited.

Part of me would have loved for Wendy to have returned to Darling after her college graduation, but it's not what she wanted. And I can respect that her choices, her life, are her own.

My stress starts to melt away the closer we get to our destination. Oakley seems to notice, a bemused smile on his face when I glance his way.

"I'm doing better," I tell him.

"I can see that. Ready to meet the grandkids then?"

He has the slap to his chest coming. He really does.

The skydiving facility is out in the middle of nowhere. Elyse, Wendy's girlfriend, is an instructor here. I find a spot to park, and Oakley and I seek them out.

We find the pair standing outside the building, clearly waiting for us. This is the first time we're meeting Elyse in person, but Wendy has shown me pictures. She's a striking woman, her jet-black hair pulled back in a thick braid, amber-colored eyes warm, if not a little nervous.

Wendy splits away to greet us, giving me a tight hug. "Hey, Dad," she says, emotion heavy in her voice, even though she tries to hide it.

"It's all right," I tell her quietly, rubbing her shoulder. "We're gonna love her."

She lets loose a breath, nodding before stepping back. She hugs Oakley next, Elyse waiting with a patient smile on her face. As soon as Wendy is free, she steps back to give introductions.

"Dad, Oak, this is Elyse, my girlfriend. Elyse, these are my dads."

I hold out my hand as Oakley bends at the waist beside me. Wendy's eyes go wide, and even Elyse looks alarmed, even as she shakes my hand.

"It's a pleasure, Elyse," I tell the woman. "I'm really glad to meet you."

"You, too," she replies. "Is, uh, he all right?"

"Oakley's fine," I assure her, the man nearly wheezing. "He's just having a moment."

"Nice to meet you," Oakley manages hoarsely, straightening enough to offer his hand for Elyse to shake. "Ah, God."

"Oak?" Wendy asks.

"Fine," he says, waving a hand through the air. "Holy shit, Lawson."

I rub his back soothingly. "I know."

As Oakley comes to terms with his hypothetical grandkids, I assure the girls everything is all right. We head inside soon enough, and Elyse sets us up in a small room where an instructional video plays. Oakley and I filled out all the necessary waivers ahead of time.

"Are you scared?" he asks me.

I take a second to truly think it over. "No."

Oakley huffs a laugh. "Your brothers think this is dangerous."

"So is driving a vehicle," I point out, the truth of that something we all remember, long ago as it was. "Are you worried?"

"No," Oakley says quickly. "Just a little anxious. I've never jumped out of a plane before."

"You'll have a parachute. And a guide. All you have to do is...fall."

"That's the part that makes me anxious."

I slip my hand around to the back of Oakley's neck, kissing him while we're still alone. It's soft and simple, but his shoulders come down some. "You don't have to do it," I tell him.

"Are you kidding? Like I'd let you have all the fun on your own." Oakley stands, holding out his hand. I grab on, and he tugs me to my feet. "Ready to fly?"

My chest squeezes tight. "With you? Always."

It takes some time to get outfitted in the proper gear. Oakley, Wendy, and I are each matched with a tandem guide. We're hooked in pairs before the plane leaves the ground, Wendy being strapped to Elyse. Oakley holds my hand as the engine roars, the small plane lifting into the air.

It feels surreal, flying up into the clouds. The ground stretches far and wide, a mixture of landscape that looks like a tiny toy replica from so high above. It's loud, so no one speaks. But a tug on my hand has me looking Oakley's way.

Clear goggles cover his eyes, a small, crooked smile on his face. I know that smile intimately. Excitement. Adventure. Love. I know every nuance of the blue-and-brown-painted eyes staring back at me. I know the sound of Oakley's, "I love you," even if I can't hear it.

I mouth the words back, shifting my grip so it's our pinkies clasped tight.

Oakley Beaumont always was the boy I flew through the clouds with, since the time we were young. Back when a kiss was a token, when pixie dust was so common it filled the very air, slanting through sunbeams and falling on the snow.

I haven't stopped believing, I suppose. Believing I can fly. Believing that magic exists.

Because what else can you call love if not magic?

It's there every day my heart beats alongside my husband's.

And now, as we fall once again?

Oh, how we fly.

The End

About the Author

Information about Emmy Sanders and her complete list of works can be found on her website. Subscribe to her newsletter, join her Facebook reader group, Emmy's Enclave, and connect via email or social media:

www.emmysanders.com

Find online:
www.facebook.com/emmysandersmm
www.instagram.com/emmysandersmm

www.ingramcontent.com/pod-product-compliance
Lightning Source LLC
Chambersburg PA
CBHW071356300726
48976CB00006B/1897